PLAYING
WITH
FIRE

PLAYING
WITH
FIRE

NEW YORK TIMES BESTSELLING AUTHOR
LEXI RYAN

DEDICATION

For Aunt Diane, who recognized a young girl's hunger for
words and fed it with poetry, nurtured it with empty journals.

CHAPTER ONE

Nix

"W<small>ANT TO GRAB A DRINK WITH ME?</small>" Krystal asks, sounding particularly perky, even over the phone. "Maybe we'll go to The Wire and let the college boys flirt with us. Or if you like 'em local, we can go to Brady's and wiggle our asses while we shoot pool."

I park the car in the driveway, climb out, and take the steps up to my front porch. "I can't. Max is coming over to figure out why my garage door won't close."

"*Max* is coming over?" she asks, suspicion lacing her words. "Max *Hallowell*?"

I roll my eyes at my gossip-loving friend. "Is coming over to fix my *garage door.*"

"Is that what the kids are calling it these days?"

"You're hopeless," I mutter. "There wasn't even a drop of innuendo in that sentence."

"I've seen pornos with setups more innocent than that."

Sighing, I unlock my door and step into the house. It's hard to believe this is my life now—a great job, a gorgeous home, and friends who tease me about potential hookups. It's not a life I ever expected to have, but I'd fight like hell to keep it. "Trust me, if it were something more, I'd be in the shower shaving right now."

"You should shave anyway. Just in case."

I snort. "Goodbye, Krys. Have fun tonight."

"You too," she sings.

Shaking my head, I end the call and toss my keys and phone into the basket by the door. I catch a reflection in the mirror, and I spin around, my heart pounding wildly.

Just your imagination. Just your imagination.

"Hello?" I call, walking into the dining room on unsteady legs. It couldn't have been him. "Hello?"

I want to run from the house screaming, but *no.* This is *my* house and *my* life. I won't let him scare me away from it. "He isn't even *here*, crazy woman," I mumble.

I tour the house slowly, but my heart is pounding as if I'm sprinting through it. When I'm convinced I'm the only one here, I head outside. I need fresh air. I need to remind myself where I am.

I'm not sixteen.

I'm not in Camelot.

I grip the porch rail and drag in ragged breaths. I

really thought I saw him, and that means one of two things.

Either I'm imagining an enemy who isn't there and feeling threatened in my own home—in other words, becoming my mother—or Patrick McCane has found me.

Max

I feel like a pimple-faced kid about to ask a girl to the prom. Frankly, this isn't so different. I came here to help a friend, yes. But I also came hoping to get a date. It's been a few years since I've asked anyone out. I'm so rusty that I almost expect my voice to squeak when I propose we keep each other company for dinner.

I park my car on the street in front of Phoenix Reid's house and shut off the ignition, but I don't get out right away. I sit here a minute just looking at her.

She's standing on her front porch, staring off into space, her hands wrapped tight around the railing. Her black skirt and button-up gray shirt are just visible beneath her white exam jacket. There's nothing about the outfit that says "sexy." Scratch that—there's nothing about the outfit that is *trying* to be sexy. And maybe that's why it is.

To say Nix hadn't caught my eye before would be a lie. When she rolled into town and started hanging with the Thompson sisters, I definitely noticed her. It was hard not to. She was so stiff and awkward those early months, and to watch her get comfortable here was to see a flower blossom. For some reason that transformation always intrigued me, but I never thought of her as anything more than a friend.

Until today.

Until she looped her stethoscope behind my daughter's neck and grinned. She gave a little speech about how Claire could be a doctor too. She promised to give Claire her very own stethoscope when she graduated from medical school. It's probably a bit she does for all her pediatric patients, but this wasn't just any patient. This was my daughter, who idolizes the cartoon character Doc McStuffins and has a mother whose inconsistent presence in her life has her confused about who she is and what her future will look like. For *my* daughter, they weren't just nice words. They were the best words Nix could have said.

So here I am. I arranged for my mom to watch Claire so I could come over and help Nix with a garage door problem I could probably talk her through on the phone. I don't exactly have a plan, but I'm thinking I'll fix her door and casually invite her to grab dinner with me after. Maybe I can talk her into going somewhere with a good wine list, and I can watch her cheeks flush with the warmth of the alcohol and the pleasure of good food. *Fuck,* that sounds good.

She turns and spots me sitting in my car then waves tentatively, so I climb out and walk up her drive. "Hey."

"Hey," I call back. "Is everything okay? You looked a little distracted when I pulled up."

She meets me in the driveway and shrugs. "I'm fine. I had an unexpected visitor, but he's gone now."

"What did he need?"

She swallows, her eyes darting to avoid mine. "Nothing. Just wanted to remind me he's thinking about me."

Suddenly my plans to ask her out seem presumptuous. "I didn't know you were seeing anyone." My voice drips with disappointment but she doesn't seem to notice.

"I'm not. This wasn't someone I wanted to see."

I frown. "Need me to talk to him? Get him to leave you alone?"

"No, no. Nothing like that." She attempts a smile, but it's not very convincing. "Anyway, thank you so much for coming."

"My pleasure."

Her cheeks turn pink and she ducks her head. "I really could have called someone, though. Where's Claire?"

"I dropped her off at my mom's. It's spaghetti night, and Mom makes the best sauce." I turn to the house. "Beautiful place and a great neighborhood. My mom lives a couple of blocks down. You like living here?"

"Yeah, I do. I feel a little foolish buying such a big house when it's just me, but when it came on the market I couldn't resist."

It's a gorgeous Cape Cod in historic New Hope. The houses here were the first built when New Hope was founded, and with their proximity to campus and downtown, the area remains a favorite with wealthier locals. Like Nix's, most of the houses have been kept updated.

"It's a good investment. This the door that's giving you trouble?" I head toward the open garage bay.

"Yeah. It just won't go down and stay down. I'm kind of weird about security, so . . ." She swallows. "I hate that it's not working right."

Sinking to my haunches next to the garage door's laser eyes, I nod. "I had this problem on my door not so long ago. If these laser eyes aren't lined up just right they think there's something blocking the door, so it goes back up as a safety precaution."

"Oh." She tugs her lower lip between her teeth and nods. "That makes sense."

I make the adjustments then step back. "Try it now."

She goes to her car, grabs her purse from the passenger seat, and pulls a small garage door remote from inside it before stepping inside the garage with me. When she presses the button, the door slides down easily, and then it's just the two of us in the dimly lit garage, and my excuse for being here is all used up.

"Thank you, Max," she says. She takes two steps toward me, stops, and interlaces her fingers in front of her. "I feel bad that you came over here just for that."

"Don't. I'm happy to help and didn't have any other plans. And anyway, I wanted to thank you for what you said to Claire at the office. It might not seem like it matters what you tell a three-year-old—"

"It does matter. Kids hear more than people think,

and if we're constantly telling them they're pretty or funny, they can start to think that's *all* they are." She tucks her hands in her pockets. "Sorry. I mean, you're welcome. She's such a smart little girl."

"She is. Just yesterday she was telling *me* how babies are made."

Her eyes go wide. "Seriously?"

"Yep. She told me all about how mommies go to the store and buy a special seed and swallow it so a baby grows in their bellies."

She bursts into laughter. She looks good laughing. It lights up her face.

Cautiously, I close the distance between us and look down at her. Nix is tall, but I still have a few inches on her, and when I'm this close she has to crane her neck to look at me. She fidgets, shifting as if she's not sure if she should back up or stay put. It hits me for the first time that I don't really know anything about her. Sure, I know her career and her best friends, her life as it is now, but I don't know anything about what came before. "Where are you from, Nix? Where's your family?"

"Why?" Something changes, and her face goes from soft and friendly to cold and distant.

"Because I'd like to know more about you."

She shakes her head. "I'm pretty sure you don't, Max."

Maybe it's the pain I see on her face that makes me do it. Or maybe it's because I see loneliness in her eyes that I understand all too well and I want to wash it away. Or maybe it's simpler than that. Maybe I need this in the most basic, primal sense.

Whatever the reason, I lower my head and press my lips to hers. She doesn't pull away. She doesn't even seem surprised.

She inches closer and moans against my mouth. That sound unravels any sense left in my brain, and instead of breaking the kiss and asking her to dinner—a logical next step with a woman who's more an acquaintance than a friend—I slant my mouth over hers and thread my fingers into her hair.

Her hair falls in heavy swaths around my hand. The clip that was holding it off her neck loses its hold and clinks as it hits the garage floor. Her hands go to my shirt, taking fistfuls of it until I have to break the kiss because she's yanking it off over my head. Then her hands are on my bare chest, sweeping across my stomach and over my pecs, dipping into the waistband of my jeans and—*Jesus Christ*—skimming the head of my cock through my briefs.

I groan into her mouth and give all my concentration to keeping my body still and not thrusting into her touch. I don't want her thinking I'm pathetic and sex-deprived. Even if it's true.

Following her lead, I drop my hands from her hair to free her of her jacket. By the time I have it halfway down her arms, she's unbuttoning my pants and shoving them down my hips, along with my boxer briefs.

Christ.

Everything seems to happen at once. One second, I'm slipping her jacket off her arms, and the next she's pulling us to the floor. Our mouths barely part and we kiss the whole way down before she leads me to settle on top of her, her skirt bunched around her hips, my cock nestled right against the thin strip of cotton between her legs.

There's something about the way she kisses that makes me want to give her anything she needs. Anything she wants. It's almost a desperate kiss—as if she's been waiting a lifetime for *my* mouth and I'm the only one who can bring her pleasure. It's not just the way she rubs her tongue against mine or the fact that she's already so wet I can feel it through her panties. It's more than the little moans she can't seem to hold back and the way she rubs her hands over my body. It's all of that and more, and even while a voice in my mind tells me this is crazy, there's no way I could put the brakes on this.

I slide my hand between our bodies and stroke her through the saturated fabric. Her whole body shudders, and I want to make her shudder more, to feel her muscles tighten around me as I slide my fingers inside her.

I have to pull my mouth from hers so I can think straight.

"Nix," I say. Her lips are swollen and her eyes are hazy. I stroke her again, just so I can watch the pleasure move across her face. "Should we stop?"

It will hurt like hell if she says yes, but someone needs to ask the question. I'd rather deal with my own blue balls than her regret.

"Please," she whispers.

"Please . . ." I swallow. "Please stop or please touch you?"

She lifts her hips off the ground and rubs against my hand. "Touch me."

Groaning, I yank her panties to the side. Her flesh is slick and smooth. My fingers slide over her clit and her head rolls to the side as her hips lift, leading my fingers to her center. I sink one inside. She's so damn tight. All I can think about is getting inside her and feeling her squeeze my dick.

Slow down, asshole.

"Do you have a condom?" she asks.

Oh, damn. Oh, fuck, fuck, damn.

"I have one," she says quickly. She wiggles out from under me and grabs her purse. The next thing I know, she's ripping a condom from its package and I'm on my knees, watching her roll it on me.

She steps out of her panties, then we're on the floor again, Nix under me, her legs wrapped around me. Something somewhere in the back of my mind warns that this is all happening too fast, but her hands cup my ass, urging me inside, and I can't deny her.

I dip my head and press a kiss to the crook of her neck as I drive into her.

"Yes," she breathes. Her fingers curl and her nails bite into my hips, as if she's afraid I'll get away if she doesn't hold me close. But I'm not going anywhere.

At first, I let her set the pace, matching my strokes to hers, but soon I'm drowning in the sound of her moans and the heat of her sex squeezing my cock, and I lose my control.

I drive hard and deep and fast and she's right there with me, her head back, her back arched, her legs locked behind me.

Suddenly, the pleasure's too much. It's been way too fucking long and she feels way too fucking good. I come hard and fast in an intense explosion of light and pleasure that leaves me panting into the crook of her neck. So that just happened.

Ho. Lee. Shit.

She strokes my hair as I catch my breath. "Thank you," she murmurs. "You probably think I'm some crazy nympho who jumps men in her garage, but thanks for not letting that scare you off."

I rise onto my elbows so I can see her and make sure she's kidding. Only there's no humor on her face. She's serious. "Why are you thanking me?"

She bites her lip and cuts her eyes away from me. "Because that was . . . nice. Not that I expect it to happen again. We're adults. I know it was a fluke and now we can move on."

What the hell? "Nix, look at me." I don't speak again until she obeys. "You're killing me. It's bad enough that I got off so fast I didn't tend to you, but now you're *thanking* me?"

"Yeah."

"For a job I didn't finish?"

She blushes. "It's not a problem. I'm . . . content."

For fuck's sake. I lower my mouth to hers and kiss her before she can say anything else. I let the kiss go long and deep—the kind with roaming hands and muffled moans. When I pull back, her eyes are hazy again. *Damn straight.* "I can do better than *content*, sweetheart."

CHAPTER TWO

Max

"YOU CAN GO." Nix pushes onto her elbows, and I'm forced to roll off her. "I'm totally cool with skipping the awkward part of"—she waves her hand between our bodies—"this."

Standing, I pull up my pants just so they don't fall to my ankles, and I go to the trashcan by the door to deal with the condom.

When I turn back to her, she's off the floor, sliding her panties back up her legs. She smooths her skirt down with one hand and grabs her jacket off the floor with her other. The whole scene is so ridiculous that I

13

laugh without meaning to.

"What?"

Stepping forward, I cup her face in my hands and rest my forehead on hers. She sighs, and her shoulders drop, as if the tension is no longer there to hold them up.

"I will leave now," I say softly, "if that's what you *want* me to do. But if you're only saying that because you think that's what I want to hear, I'd rather stay."

"You would?" Honest to God, the woman looks shocked when she says it. "Why? For what?"

I can't help it. Another chuckle rumbles in my chest. "A few ideas come to mind, Doc."

"Like . . .?"

I stroke her bottom lip with my thumb. "Like seeing your bedroom."

"You want to see the house?"

My gaze slides down her body and over the tight curves never exposed to my eyes and barely explored by my hands. In our frantic rush toward the finish line, we never even got naked. A mistake I intend to remedy as soon as possible. "I want to see your *bed*," I clarify. "Preferably with you in it. Preferably naked. Preferably while giving you a *reason* to thank me that I don't find completely ego-crushing."

"You don't have to—"

I don't have words for an argument, so I cut her off with my mouth, and again she kisses me like she *needs* me. Like I'm some sort of god. So I kiss her until she's breathless and holding me close again, because I like doing that to her, and when I pull away, I fucking *love* the heat in her eyes.

Her tongue darts out to taste the lip I just kissed. "Yeah, so my bedroom is this way."

She leads me into the house, through a mudroom area and into the kitchen, where she grabs a bottle of whiskey off the counter and a couple of glasses from the cabinet.

I follow her past the dining room and into a large bedroom at the back of the house, and she goes straight to the dresser, sets down the glasses, fills them each halfway with whiskey, and hands one to me.

"Cheers." I take a sip, watching as she downs half of hers in two swallows. I cock a brow. "Nervous?"

She nods. "Yeah." She tips the glass back and drains it.

"Slow down, gorgeous. I have plans for you that require you being sober."

"And naked?" she asks.

I shrug. "No pressure, but I would *enjoy* naked."

She takes a deep breath then exhales. "Hoo-boy."

I take another sip of my whiskey and wait. I just fucked her on the floor of her garage, but she's being skittish about me seeing her naked. Interesting.

"Okay, so, I can't do naked. I mean, I want to. I *really* want to. But I have some body issues and I'm not really comfortable with . . ." She turns toward the wall. "I'm sorry."

"Hey." I turn her face so she's looking at me. "I didn't mean to push you."

"You didn't. No. I . . . ." She shakes her head and bites her lip as if to keep herself from saying more.

Slowly, she lifts onto her toes and locks her hands behind my neck. Then she kisses me.

I don't understand what it is that she wants or what she's afraid of, but I do understand this—our connection, our kiss, and how damn good it feels to hold someone again.

Nix

God. This is a dream. No. It's a nightmare-dream. One of those dreams that starts out horrifying—seeing Patrick's reflection inside my house—and somehow miraculously transitions into something *good.* Something fantastic—Max kissing me and touching me, and letting me turn off my brain when I need to the most.

Max kisses his way down my jaw and to my neck, and I shudder under him. Krystal was right. I should have shaved, but I'm not going to let a little leg stubble stop me from making the most of my night with Max.

"Are you hungry?" he asks against my neck. "I'll take you to dinner."

My brain takes longer than it should to piece those words together into meaningful sentences. "Dinner?"

"Mmm," he replies. His hand skims up my side and cups my breast, and I want to scream in frustration at all the layers between his thumb and my nipple. "Food, wine, talking."

I shake my head. "Talking?" Did I misunderstand his naked-in-the-bed speech? I want to slide my hand between our bodies to see if he's hard again, but that seems implausible, and hoping he might be capable of the implausible seems rude. Instead, I press my hand against his bare chest and trail my fingertips from his sternum to the V-opening of his unbuttoned jeans.

The feel of him under my fingers and the sound he makes when I touch him work together to make a combustible cocktail of dangerous need.

How am I supposed to keep my head about me when he's standing here with his eight-pack abs and broad shoulders?

But that's just it, isn't it? I don't want to keep my head. In fact, I'd like my brain to be as far removed from this experience as possible. He groans into my hair, then opens his mouth and nibbles along the juncture of my neck and shoulder. The sensation is more sharp than painful, but it sends electric currents of pleasure through me in a way I never could have imagined.

"Dinner," he murmurs. When I lean into his kiss and don't reply, he says, "Or we could keep doing this."

"This," I say. *Please, this.*

Slowly, he backs me toward the bed and lowers me onto it. His eyes are hot and hungry, and he positions himself over me, a knee on each side of my hips.

I don't need to touch him to know he's hard again. For me? God, this can't be real.

"No getting naked, right?" he asks.

I lick my lips. *Only if I can borrow someone else's torso.* "Right."

His eyes trail over me and he shakes his head. "I will never understand why women feel like they need to hide their bodies." He traces the hollow of my collarbone then dips his fingers down into my shirt, exploring the tops of my breasts. "You're gorgeous."

"Take off my skirt," I whisper. I reach behind myself and unzip it.

Max stands at the end of the bed and tugs it off my hips, his eyes all over my exposed legs and the most intimate part of me, currently covered by a pair of cotton panties with smiling yellow sunshines.

Sitting up, I unbutton my shirt and peel it off but leave my thin tank and bra.

He lowers me back against the bed and kisses my mouth, my neck, my collarbone, then down until he's opening his mouth against my covered breast.

His hand explores my thigh, my hip, the cotton band at the top of my panties. When his fingertips slip under my tank top, I press my hand over his, stopping it before it can move any higher.

"Okay." He removes his hand and lifts his head to study me, the question in his eyes.

Please don't ask.

But instead of a question about what I'm hiding under my shirt, he brushes his knuckles between my thighs and whispers, "What about these?"

I hook my thumbs into each side of my panties and tug them down, earning a grin from Max and his assistance dropping them to the floor.

He pauses a moment, his gaze skimming over every inch of me, and my brain threatens to kick back on. It wants to analyze what I thought I saw earlier, dissect every millisecond, and question how I reacted. Should I have assumed Patrick was really here? Why would he come and then play shadow games? And if he was in my house, what did he want? So many questions threatening to send me into an anxious fit.

But then Max parts my thighs and lowers his mouth to press between my legs. Then everything but the pleasure fizzles away.

Max

Nix and I definitely have the post-coital awkwardness down to a tee.

After I kissed her *everywhere*, we had sex again, this time slower and a little less crazed. Or at least *I* was a little less crazed. Nix fucks like she's running from something, like she's using sex to hide. I'm not complaining, but I am curious.

I am naked, but she's lying next to me in that damn tank top, staring at the ceiling and worrying her bottom lip between her teeth.

Her phone buzzes from the other room. "I need to go check that." She climbs out of bed, and I stay behind, enjoying the view of her bare ass. I don't get the body image issues. My ex didn't want to take her shirt off for a long time because she was embarrassed about her weight, but Nix is trim and toned, and it's not like she was exactly self-conscious about the rest of her body.

When she returns, she has my shirt from the garage and tosses it to me.

"Who was that?" I ask, blatantly ignoring the shirt and her hint that it's time for me to leave.

"A text from Liz. Nothing important." She sits on the edge of the bed and bites her lip. "Can we agree not to tell our friends about this?"

I roll to my side and prop myself up on my elbow. "You mean I can't show Will the video?"

Her eyes widen and her jaw almost unhinges.

"Oh, should I have told you about setting up the cameras?"

She smacks me on the chest, and I laugh as I grab her hand and bring it to my lips.

"I don't make a habit of telling my friends the details of my sex life." I kiss her knuckles but don't release her hand.

She stares at her hand in mine. "Good."

"At risk of you crushing my ego again, can I ask if there's a reason you're so worried about them knowing?"

"I don't want them to get ideas. You know the girls. They'll think this is something more than it is."

And what is it? I have too much pride to ask that question. Hell, I don't even know what I want it to be. I came over here looking for company at dinner, not a booty call. Not that I'm complaining. So I change the subject. "How do you feel about pizza?"

"Strongly." She smiles. She hasn't done enough of that tonight, and I like seeing it.

"Then how about I order one? Loaded?"

"Everything but the little fish."

"My kind of girl." I grab my phone and pull up the web browser to order online, and when I look back to her, she's staring at me. "What's wrong?"

"I'm sorry. You wanted to go to dinner, and I just thought you . . ." She shakes her head and wrinkles her nose. "You're hungry. I'm sorry."

Chuckling, I roll out of bed and tug on my jeans. "Nix, as a medical professional, I would have guessed you'd know more about men."

"What do you mean?" She finds her panties on the floor, then pulls her hair into a tie. Too bad. I liked seeing the mess my hands made of it.

"I mean on a guy's hierarchy of needs, sex comes first. Always. Then pizza."

When she grabs a pair of jeans from her closet, I take them from her hands and drop my gaze to her legs. "If you don't mind, I'd rather enjoy the view awhile longer."

She blushes. "Can I at least put on a shirt?"

She's already wearing a shirt, but I don't say that. "Here," I say, taking mine from the bed. "Wear mine."

"Why?"

Good question. I'm not sure I want to explain that I want to see her in it, that I fucking *love* the idea of leaving it here and letting her sleep in it. Of her waking up tomorrow and thinking of me, my mouth between her legs. Fuck. It's been too long since I've done this. "There's something infinitely sexy about you walking around in my shirt," I finally answer, because even if the truth makes me sound too eager, I'm not interested in playing games.

Her pink cheeks make me want to kiss her again. Damn. I like this side of Nix. I want to see that embarrassment turn to arousal, but it's getting late and I don't want to give her more of a reason to think this was just some random hookup.

We head to the kitchen, and when she opens her fridge, I'm surprised to see it stocked with beer instead of wine. "Good taste," I murmur as I scan her selection of microbrews. I grab an IPA for myself and turn to her. "Wouldn't have guessed you to be a beer connoisseur. Who turned you on to that?"

"Kent," she says. Then she pales, as if she realizes she revealed more than she planned. "An old, um, boyfriend."

There's a story there. But the bigger question is why I suddenly want to hear it so badly. Until tonight, I never thought about how much I don't know about her. We have mutual friends, and as far as I can tell she spends the majority of her social hours going out with the Thompson sisters, but the drama is always theirs. No one ever talks about what's going on with Nix. Is that because she lives a quiet life or a private one?

"Is Kent still around?" I ask.

"Nope. I'll set the table."

Private. But why?

She gathers paper plates and napkins and heads to the dining room, and the doorbell rings.

"I'll get it," I call, pulling cash from my wallet. But when I open the door, I'm not looking at the pizza guy. It's Liz Thompson. "You are not the pizza delivery guy."

She scans my bare chest and unbuttoned jeans. "No. I'm not." She cranes her neck to see over my shoulder to the dining room, where Nix is setting the table in my T-shirt, then she gives me an arched eyebrow. "So, you and Nix?"

So much for not telling our friends.

"Um. I think I'd rather let her answer that?" I turn to Nix, who's still oblivious to our company. "Lizzy's here."

The silverware clatters from Nix's hands and onto the table. "You didn't text back," Nix says.

Liz's eyes play ping-pong between us. "Something you two want to tell me?"

"Do you want to answer that or do you want me to?" I ask Nix.

"Just . . ." She starts toward us, then stops. "I need to get dressed." She wags her finger at me as if it's somehow my fault Liz showed up unannounced. "Don't say a word." Then she jogs back to the bedroom.

Liz clears her throat. "She's gonna come out here and try to convince me that you two get together and hang out half naked in a completely platonic way, isn't she?"

Probably, but I've been instructed not to speak, so I just shrug.

"How long has this been going on?"

I lift my palms then point my thumb toward the bedroom. If Nix doesn't want me to talk, I'm happy to let her answer the questions.

When Nix reappears, she's put on a pair of shorts. She scowls at me. "Go get dressed," she says.

"You're wearing my shirt."

She flinches, and Liz laughs. "Nix, it's not a big deal."

But clearly to her it is. Definitely a private person.

A red, beaten-up Escort pulls into the drive, and a teenager with a mop of black hair climbs out with a pizza box.

"*There's* the pizza," I say, leaving the girls to go pay for the food.

When I head back in, they're gone, but I can hear them talking in a room off the foyer that I assume is an office. Oh, to be a fly on the wall in that conversation. But I give them a minute and get the pizza set out on the table.

When I go to the office to get them, Nix is holding Liz, and Liz is sniffling against her chest. The sight makes something in my chest shift, and my crush on this sweet, caring, slightly mysterious, and very private doctor inches up another notch.

* * *

Nix

So that *didn't go as planned.*

Max Hallowell shoves his hands in his pockets and gives me a tentative smile. Tonight was nothing like I expected. One, I never would have guessed he was interested. Two, I had no idea I was such an easy lay.

Come for the friendly favor, stay for the sex.

I try to return his smile, but I'm too nervous. I'm too afraid he'll say what happened tonight was a mistake. Even if that's true—and, if I'm being honest, it totally is—it might kill me to hear him say the words.

His gaze drifts to the top of the stairs, where Liz is tucked in for the night. If she hadn't shown up, would he want to stay over? Would he have taken me back to my bed? Whispered more of those sinfully naughty words in my ear?

A shiver of pleasure runs through me, but I do my best to tamp it down. That line of thought is useless and doesn't change anything. Liz is upstairs, sleeping off her heartache, and Max is headed for the door. Could-have-beens are irrelevant, a waste of energy.

"Walk me out?" he asks.

I lick my lips and nod. Here it comes. *It's not you; it's me.* Or: *I hope we can still be friends.* Or maybe it'll be: *We just got carried away . . . twice.*

I shut the door behind us so I can avoid his eyes, and remind myself that I don't *want* this to be any more than a one-time thing. Even if Max's history with my friend Hanna didn't complicate everything, there's the fact that I'm an emotional train wreck with a full freight

25

of baggage, and I'm in no way a candidate for a long-term romantic relationship.

"So, tonight was . . ." He steps forward and the porch light reaches his eyes. Blue and a little smoky. With those eyes and that carefully sculpted body, could anyone blame me for being a floozy tonight? Add in how screwed in the head I was from what I did or didn't see in the mirror, and I should get some sort of prize for not meeting him at the door naked and begging him to fuck my brains out. Better brainless than crazy.

He takes one of my hands in his and squeezes. "You're not the kind of woman who plays games. Am I right?"

"I don't have the energy for games." *Here it comes.*

His lips quirk in a half-smile. "That's refreshing." His other hand goes to my face, cupping it softly, making me feel small and delicate and protected.

I want to close my eyes. I want to lean into his touch. But those things would make me vulnerable, so I do neither. "Thanks for your help with Liz. She's going through a hard time."

"You're welcome."

"Listen, about tonight . . ." The rest of the sentence stalls out on my tongue as his eyes drift to my lips. My stomach does an acrobatic flip-flop, and before I can say more, he lowers his head and sweeps his lips over mine. The kiss starts sweet and innocent, but one stroke of his thumb along my jaw and a slide of his tongue between my lips and that sweetness simmers into something more intoxicating. I arch my back to give his mouth a better angle on mine, and my hands find his hair. This man can *kiss*, and since this will mostly likely be the last time I get to experience it, I sink in deep and soak in the pleasure.

When he pulls his mouth away, he touches his forehead to mine. He slides his hand to wrap around the back of my neck. "Sorry to cut you off," he murmurs. "I needed to kiss you again quickly in case you were going to tell me I couldn't. You were saying?"

What was I saying? The words I planned to say have fled, and now my mind is cluttered with all the ones I shouldn't speak.

Kiss me again.

Stay the night.

And the absolute scariest: *Thank you for giving me the best night of my life.* Because what we just had shouldn't be the best night of *anyone's* life. To admit it was mine is to admit how pathetic I am.

Pulling away, he groans softly, as if he's reluctant to stop touching me. It's that kind of response that makes me want to say all the things I shouldn't.

"I'd like to call you," he says. "Maybe take you out somewhere nicer than your garage floor—not that I didn't have a perfectly good time during our visit there." His grin starts crooked and widens, transforming his face from devastatingly handsome to *cute*. I'm immune to devastatingly handsome. The first guy I loved was devastatingly handsome, and I've learned to protect myself from that. It's the cuteness that lowers my defenses.

"Maybe. That might be nice." *Shit.* Wrong answer. I should be definitively ending this. I blame my friends. I was ready to forgo romance forever, but they keep falling in love with great guys and making me second-guess my decision to become one of those cat ladies.

"*Maybe*, huh?" He sighs. "I thought you didn't play games."

"I don't." I swallow. "But your kiss made it too hard to say no."

He cocks his head, as if trying to figure me out. "So if I kissed you again . . .?"

I laugh despite myself. "Good night, Max."

"Good night, Doc."

Doc. Oh, hell, that's cute. He's cute. He makes me feel . . .

Yeah, need to pull the brakes on that little thought train right now.

When he reaches his car, he turns and skims his gaze over me one more time, his focus lingering on my thighs in my cutoffs. "We'll talk soon."

All sex appeal and *yum,* he climbs into his car and drives away, and I stand there in my little puddle of lust until his taillights fade into the distance.

It's only when he's gone and I'm alone in the soft glow of my porch light that I feel it—that sensation of being watched.

"Hello?" I call out into the night. The hair on my arms stands on end, and all the warm gushiness Max stirred in my belly goes cold. "Who's there?"

And I know it's not real. I know it's only memory rearing its head and reminding me why I can't have the things Max just made me want. I know my head's screwed up right now and my senses are playing tricks

28

on me, but suddenly . . .
    Suddenly, I smell smoke.

CHAPTER THREE

Nix
Three months later . . .

TEMPTATION HAS FOUND ME and moved himself and his fine ass into the house next door.

Marmalade weaves through my legs as I stare open-mouthed at the man unloading the moving van.

Well, shit.

From the second I saw the trucks pulling in this morning, I was apprehensive. It's not that I want the house next to me to sit vacant. But change always worries me. Since I moved to New Hope and my life got so damn *good*, I've been waiting for the other shoe to drop.

My mild apprehension at wondering about my new

neighbor turned to something else altogether when I saw the dark head poke out from the front of the house.

Three months ago, Maximilian Hallowell sexed me up so expertly I saw stars. Three months and a half-dozen declined invitations later, and he's moving into the house next door.

Fuckshitdamn.

Max directs one of his friends into his garage, then turns to look at me. His gaze starts at my feet and inches up slowly, and when he brings his eyes to mine, my stomach goes into full-out skydive free-fall—*down down down down*—never seeming to hit my feet.

Fuckfuckshitshitdamndamn.

Keeping his eyes on me, he opens the back of the truck. The metal clangs as it rolls up into the roof, and when I start back into my house, he actually winks at me. *Winks.*

I trip over my cat.

He sees it—of course he does—and grins. Never mind that we slept together three months ago. Never mind that every time I look at him I think of the way he slowly lowered his head to kiss me that first time. Never mind that I can't climb into my bed without remembering what he did to me there, turning me from insomniac to *hot and bothered* insomniac.

"Hey, neighbor," he calls.

"*You're* the one who bought the house?" It comes out much bitchier than I intended. He's free to buy any house he wants. He belongs in New Hope more than I do.

He nods and heads over to stand with me on my

31

porch. Close, but not as close as he was last time we stood here together. "It's a great neighborhood," he says. "It's near my mom's, and Claire loves the backyard."

"You don't owe me an explanation." But my tone implied I wanted one, didn't it? I take a breath and force my shoulders to relax. "Sorry, Max. I had a long night. You're seeing the dark side of my insomnia. Welcome to the neighborhood."

"Thank you." He studies me for a beat then drops his gaze to my calico cat, who has abandoned my legs to rub against his. "I didn't know you had a cat."

"I got her a few months ago." *You know, after you made me forget I'd sworn off love and romance. After you made me want things.*

He crouches to rub her between her ears, and Marmalade purrs so loudly the porch practically vibrates. As far as I can tell, Max has that effect on all females.

He cranes his neck to study me. Ever since that night we slept together—twice—he looks at me differently. It's as if his blue eyes can see all the pieces of me I don't show anyone. It's a ridiculous thought, of course, but it's there like an electric buzz, warning me every time his gaze is pointed in my direction.

"I'm having a little housewarming cookout tomorrow night," he says. "I'd love to see you there."

"I already have . . ." I already have plans with *Liz*, a.k.a. Miss Matchmaker. She's the only one who knows about what happened between me and Max, and she's been doing her best to push us back together ever since.

I'd bet a hundred dollars that tomorrow's "casual party" she's asked me to attend with her is *Max's* housewarming. "Crap," I mutter.

"What's wrong? Out of excuses to avoid me?"

"I'm not *avoiding* you."

He stands and arches a brow but says nothing.

I shove my hands into my pockets. "Sure. I'll stop by. I'd love to see the house."

"I don't bite, Nix." Without another word, he heads back to the trucks and starts unloading boxes alongside his friends.

I should do something neighborly, like bake him a casserole or something. Jesus, I've made a mess of this, and all because I don't want to have feelings for him but I do anyway.

Marmalade hops onto the porch rail and howls in Max's direction.

I scratch her between the ears. "I know how you feel, honey. But we don't need him. Life is good with just us girls."

Hissing, she hops down and saunters back into the house, only stopping once to turn and glare at me.

Max

William smirks and shifts his eyes to Nix's front porch. "And how'd *that* go?"

I glare at him. "I'm sorry I told you."

His lip twitches. "Why? Because you don't want anyone to know you're getting rejected every time you talk to her?"

I grab the rocking chair out of the truck and hoist it over my head with more effort than necessary. I need to lift something much heavier if I'm going to work out the frustration that conversation with Nix just inspired. The frustration *every* conversation with her inspires.

Will laughs behind me. *Fucker.*

I head toward the house and into my daughter's room, and as soon as I enter the pink-walled space, my aggravation fades away.

So what? I had a thing for Nix and it turned out to be unrequited. Big deal. What matters is right here in this house, where I'm making a life for my daughter. What matters is making Claire feel like her family is complete, even without all the traditional pieces.

"Hey," Will says from the doorway. He props the mattress to Claire's toddler bed against the wall and crosses his arms. "Sorry. I'm just razzing you."

"No apology necessary." Sighing, I position the rocking chair in the corner and sink into it. "I don't care anymore. I'm over her."

Will's face says *bullshit,* but he's smart enough to hold his tongue. I'm not sure if I'm trying to convince him or myself, but I need to hear the words out loud. "When Hanna left me, I decided I was going to focus on Claire. It was a good plan then, and it's a good plan now."

Will looks skeptical.

"What?"

"And that's why you bought the house next to the cute doctor?"

"Shut up," I mutter. "It's a good neighborhood, and I got this place for a hell of a deal."

"Mm-hmm."

"It's been three months, and she's had an excuse every time I've asked her out. I can take a hint."

"Good. Then you'll come out on a double date with me and Cally? She got a sitter for tonight and specifically requested you join us. Apparently, she has someone picked out for you who happens to have the night off."

I bite back a groan. God save me from meddling females determined to play matchmaker. "Dare I ask who?"

Will shrugs. "I didn't ask. I'm not gonna lie; I didn't think you'd be interested."

Claire's bedroom window overlooks the backyard, and from here I can see Nix gardening where our property meets. Her hair's in a ponytail, and when she wipes a stray lock from her face, she leaves a smudge of dirt on her cheek. She's dressed in a tank top—a modest one, not one of those flimsy things most girls wear—and cutoffs that show inch after inch of reason to believe there's a God and He is *good*.

Yeah. *Totally over her.* I haven't thought about the sounds she makes when I touch her or how it felt to slide into her in going on six minutes.

Pathetic piece of shit is what I am.

"So can I tell her you'll go?" Will asks. "Because

this lovesick thing you've got going on is kind of a downer."

No kidding. "Actually, I can't."

When I tear my eyes off Nix and look at Will, his eyes are wide. "Because you're going to tell the doctor how you feel?"

"No." I push to my feet and wipe my hands on my jeans. Only another four hundred or so trips to the moving vans, and we should be done. "Because I already have a date," I say on my way out the door.

"You do?" Will asks, matching my strides out to the van.

"Yep."

"And it's not with Nix?"

"Nope." I pick up a box and shove it into his hands.

"And are you going to tell me who your mystery woman is?"

I grab a couple of boxes for myself, and spin back toward the house. "Nope."

Nix

I would have driven my car to the hospital this afternoon if I'd suspected how my day might unfold. Instead, I thought I'd be heading home by dinner, and I left the car behind. An eleven p.m. walk through the dark streets of New Hope wasn't what I had in mind.

A few months ago, a stroll alone in the dark didn't scare me. For one, this is New Hope, and though every place has its moments, this town is about as safe as it gets. For two, walking helps me decompress after a long, stressful day.

But things have changed. Or I've changed. I'm not sure which.

I should have called Krystal for a ride. She would have happily picked me up and joined me for a drink or two—single chicks unite and all that—but I didn't feel like company. I was afraid that if I went for a drink with Krystal, I'd admit that I'm rattled by Max moving in next door and then I'd have to explain *why* that rattles me.

A twig snaps behind me, and I jump and then shake my head. Okay, clearly just thinking about whether or not it's safe to walk alone is enough to spook me. I don't see anyone behind me, but I pick up my pace.

An old, cautious tingle creeps up my spine, standing the hair at the back of my neck on end and making something spasm in my belly. The sound probably came from an animal. Or the breeze snapping a dead twig from a tree.

I can see the first streetlight ahead, and I lengthen my strides to reach it faster. There's a gasp, then footsteps, but I spin around and no one's there.

My heart pounds wildly against my ribcage, and the smell of smoke swirls wickedly in my nose, nearly tripping my gag reflex.

This has been happening more and more lately. I felt safe in New Hope. I believed I was safe. Then three months ago, I saw Patrick's reflection in my own home—like a specter from another life—and that sense of security was yanked away. Ever since, every time I'm alone the hair has prickled on the back of my neck like I'm being watched. I hear sounds in my house when I shouldn't, and feel like I'm being followed when I'm walking alone.

"It's your imagination, Phoenix," I mutter, but the sound of my voice is eerie in the otherwise silent night, and I wish I hadn't said anything at all.

When I reach the sidewalk and streetlights, I breathe easier, but I keep my pace quick and my strides long until I reach my house.

"Everything okay?"

I jump at the sound of the voice and spin around to see Max standing on his front porch. Since he spent his day unloading moving trucks, I'm surprised to see him dressed in a shirt and tie. Max owns a health club and does personal training, and his body is everything you'd expect to go with that package. Some women might find him too muscular, but I always appreciated a well-built man, and muscle looks even better on Max than most—and even better again when he's dressed this way. He's loosened his tie and unfastened the top button, and his sleeves are rolled to his elbows, revealing his thick forearms.

Yum.

"What are you doing out here?" I'm suddenly very self-conscious in my plain-Jane white blouse and black slacks, even though this is pretty much the kind of thing I work in every day.

"I could ask you the same thing." He picks up a beer and takes a long pull from it. He extends his bottle. "Want a beer?"

Desperately. "No, thank you."

"You usually walk alone this late at night?"

"I got stuck at the hospital longer than I expected." I climb onto my porch and prop my hip on the rail. "What's your excuse?"

"I had a date."

He had a date. I swallow the irrational hurt that surges up with that information. "Oh. Well, I hope you had a nice time. Good night, Max."

I rush inside before he can say more and go straight to my bedroom to shuck off my work clothes and pull on my pajamas. The gray cotton sleep pants and black tank certainly aren't going to bring anyone to their knees with lust, but I live alone, so I don't need to dress to impress.

I grab a beer from the fridge and a cigar from my stash and head out to the deck, feeling the need to remind myself that living alone is a *good* thing. I know smoking cigars is nasty, but I don't do it very often, and it's less about the smoking and more about what it symbolizes—independence, making my own decisions.

My cell rings, and I answer it before the late hour crosses my mind. "Hello?"

Breathing.

"Who is this?"

More breathing. Something crackles in the background. *Is that fire?*

"Stop calling me." I jab at my screen to end the call,

but my hands are shaking. That's the third call like that I've gotten in as many weeks. The number is always blocked, and I always think I can hear fire in the background.

I don't want to sit outside anymore. A cold stone sinks to the bottom of my gut, and I want to go in, lock all the doors, arm the security system, and hide under the blankets. But I'm living on my own terms now, and whatever this is—my old life creeping into my new one, or a bad case of paranoia—I won't let anyone make my decisions but me.

So I bring the cigar to my lips and light it with shaking hands, and when Max comes onto his back patio to gather the empty bottle of wine, two glasses, and whatever other date paraphernalia he left out there, I pretend I don't see him.

CHAPTER FOUR

Nix

THE ROPES CUT INTO MY WRISTS as I tug at them. He's tied me to the altar at the front of the church. "Let me go."

"Shh. Trust me. I'm only thinking of what's best for you."

"Please." I can't breathe around my tears, and I squeeze my eyes shut to try to stop them. "I don't belong here."

"You're my phoenix. I need you. Without you, I'm as good as the ash under the flame."

When I open my eyes again, Max is kneeling in front of me, his hands bloody and raw. The heat of the fire makes my skin feel tight, and the flames lick at the pews and crawl closer to my bare feet.

"Max," I whimper. "Please get out of here."

"Not without you." He fights my restraints with bloody fingers, but they won't release.

"You have to leave." It's hard to speak because it's hard to breathe. There's too much smoke in my lungs and too little hope in my heart. I know how this story ends.

"Why?" he asks.

"Because this is all my fault."

His face changes from desperation to accusation, and when he turns his head to take in our surroundings, we're in his house, and Claire is crying from beyond the fire. "What did you do?"

I want to explain, but it's too late. There's too much smoke.

I wake up coughing on smoke that isn't there and cowering from ghosts I'll never escape. I sit up and click on the light until I can catch my breath.

The clock reads three a.m. It was nearly one before I fell asleep, but I'd rather be exhausted all day than risk falling into that nightmare again, so I climb out of bed and pad toward the shower. I let the water rain on me until my skin is pruned and the memory of the smoke has lifted from my lungs.

After my long shower, I make myself coffee and breakfast, but my stomach isn't interested in either, so I sit at my kitchen table, take deep breaths, and wish I had anti-anxiety meds. I haven't had a prescription since medical school. After Kent left me, I had regular panic attacks, and one of my professors insisted I use pharmaceutical help to get me through. But then I moved to New Hope a few years ago and tapered off the meds because my life was changing and the anxiety fading away.

When the clock on my wall hits six, I pick up my phone and dial.

"Hello?"

I squeeze my eyes shut at the sound of my mother's voice. The only thing more bittersweet is the smell of her perfume. I miss her. And there's no one in this world—not Patrick, not Kent, not Max—who could hurt me as much as she does. No one who *has* hurt me as much as she has.

"Mom," I squeak. I sound like a little girl. I feel like one too. "It's Phoenix."

"I don't know a Phoenix," she snaps. "How'd you get this number? Don't call here again."

I slip my hand under my shirt and run my fingers over the thick rings of scar tissue covering my ribs. "Don't hang up. I need to ask you something."

"I don't speak to servants of the devil."

The rough tissue burns with her words. *Breathe. Just breathe.* "Did you tell Patrick where I'm living?" It's not that he'd have to be a sleuth to figure it out in the age of Google, but there has to be some reason he's contacting me now. *If* he's contacting me now.

She's silent for a beat too many, but just when I think she's not going to answer, she says, "No." Then, in the softest voice she's used the whole conversation, she says, "He still hasn't come home. I don't think they'd let him, no thanks to you."

"Do you know where he is?"

"On the outside. What does it matter *where*? Even if he had come home, I wouldn't tell him where to find you. You're no good for him, and I won't let him burn trying to save you."

Her words knock against deadened nerves. You can only be sliced open so many times before the feeling fades. "Are you okay? Do you need anything?"

"Salvation, child. That's all I need, and that's all I've needed since the day you were born and brought your hellfire into my life." She hangs up before I can respond.

"I love you, Mom," I whisper into dead air. "Take care of yourself."

Patrick still hasn't returned to Camelot. If that's true, that means he isn't coming to take me back there, so why would he be here at all? What does he get out of following me for months and spying on me in my own home?

But the only idea more terrifying to me than Patrick being back is that I've manifested this fear from nothing. The only thing more terrifying than being stalked by a madman is the possibility that I'm not being stalked at all and that I'm as paranoid as my mother.

* * *

"Take it *off*," Krystal Thompson says as she stares

out my front window. "Mm-mm-*mm*."

I look up from my pot of macaroni and cheese and into my dining room. There, at the front window, my best friends gather, shamelessly spying on the guys across the street.

My best friends. The words hang suspended in my mind and make me smile.

I don't know what I expected to find when I moved to New Hope, but I never would have dreamed that I could be the kind of girl who had girlfriends. Or at least not ones like these. The kind who joke so easily and laugh at themselves, ogle hot men, and talk openly about sex. The kind who look out for each other and will ditch their hot men for a girls' night *just because*.

Our special little group is comprised of Cally Fisher, the Thompson sisters—Krystal, Hanna, Lizzy, and Maggie—and me.

"One of these things is not like the other," I sing in a whisper.

Krystal's the only single one in the group, aside from me. Cally, Maggie, Hanna, and Liz have snatched up some of the sexiest—and most delicious—men I've ever seen. And they all seem like great guys too. Even Sam, whom I wasn't fond of there for a while, turned out to be pretty great.

I'd be an ugly shade of green with envy if a) I didn't think every girl in this crew deserves happiness more than I ever will, and b) I hadn't sworn off men during med school.

Been there, done that, scraped my heart off the ground, and don't intend to let anyone put it there again.

"That's right," Maggie murmurs as she twirls a red curl around her finger. "Scrub that hood."

I don't need to join them to know what—or rather, *whom*—they're looking at. "I swear they wait until they see you ladies here before they wash those trucks."

"Would be a waste for them to take off their shirts if no one was watching," Cally says. "If they need an audience to get their work done, I consider it our civic duty to stare."

"Mm-hmm." Krystal nods her agreement but doesn't take her eyes off the view. "I don't care what you say, Nix. You bought this house for the eye candy."

"She'll deny it," Maggie says, "but it's gotta be true."

That's not exactly the case, but they're not wrong either. The home's proximity to the New Hope Fire Station was a definite selling point for me. I hadn't considered the views that came with it until after I moved in and the weather heated up—hadn't considered it, but *definitely* don't mind. Regardless, it gets the girls over here more often. Maggie lives with her rocker husband in a beautiful estate on the river, and yet my house has the best scenery. And now that I'll need something to keep my mind off my sexy neighbor, I'm more grateful than ever for the hottie firefighters across the street.

I scoop the cheesy noodles into a glass dish, cover it with plastic wrap, and put it on the kitchen counter beside all the other pieces of our potluck assortment— pastries from Hanna's bakery, booze from Lizzy's stash, and a couple casseroles from Cally and Krystal. "Okay. I'm ready whenever you are." I stare at their backs. "Ladies?"

Nothing.

It's as if they can't hear me. Or don't want to.

On my dramatic sigh, Liz breaks away from the group and comes into the kitchen, her engagement ring flashing in the evening sun. "Let them look. We're in no rush."

I shrug and glance at the clock. If we leave now, we'll only be a few minutes late.

"It's a barbeque," she says, reading my mind. "The starting time is more of a suggestion than anything."

I swallow. "I just . . . don't want to be rude. Won't your guys be expecting you?"

"They'll wait. It helps them appreciate us." She grins then lowers her voice. "So, what do you think it will be like? Living so close to . . .?" She tilts her head in the direction of Max's house.

I look over her shoulder to make sure the other girls aren't listening, but they're still glued to the window, tittering like schoolgirls. Can't blame them. "It'll be fine, just like living next to anyone else."

"Things aren't awkward since . . . you know . . ."

So awkward that if awkward were a finite resource, I would be a rich woman. But only on my part.

Max doesn't seem at all bothered by the fact that one night we hooked up and it was hot and amazing and the memory makes my toes curl. When he called me and asked me out a couple of days after, I told him it was a one-time thing and I didn't want more than friendship, and he took me at my word. Or maybe he was grateful for the excuse not to make more of it than what it was. Maybe he'd been scratching an itch and I'd been convenient. Sure, he's casually invited me to join him for a movie or dinner here and there, but he probably feels like he owes me. Guys can be like that. Especially the good ones.

"It's fine," I mumble.

She arches a brow. "So no repeat performances of *that night*?"

And those, apparently, are the magic words needed to break the spell. The rest of the girls spin toward us with wide eyes.

Hanna pounces first. "You and *Max*? When did this happen, and why didn't you tell me?"

"Um . . ."

"I'm sorry," Liz whispers, but I'm not sure if she's apologizing to me or her sister.

"It was a few months ago, and it's nothing," I say, but the vultures are descending and now my kitchen island is surrounded by women hungry for drama. There hasn't been much since Liz and Sam worked things out at the beginning of the summer. Krystal's entertained us with tales from her dating escapades but, all in all, there's been a shortage of meaty gossip. I wasn't looking to fill that shortage with my own love life. I turn to Hanna. "I promise. It was one night. There's nothing between us."

She narrows her eyes and shifts them to Liz, then to me and back to Liz. "Why does it sound like she's apologizing to me for sleeping with Max?"

Liz flips her blond curls. "Because in Nix's mind, Max is yours forever and always."

Hanna frowns at me and folds her arms. "You know I married the other guy, right? Because I *thought* you were at the wedding, but maybe that was somebody else."

"I know." I throw up my hands. "It's not that I think he's *yours* . . ." Not exactly. But kind of. "It's just that, well, it's weird, isn't it? He used to be in love with my friend—sleeping with you, engaged to you. It would be *weird* for me to be with him now. Who does that?"

Cally, Maggie, and Krystal all exchange looks before bursting into laughter.

"What?" I ask. "What am I missing?"

Maggie bites back a grin and clears her throat. "Well, Krystal and I were each with William Bailey before Cally came back to town."

Now it's my eyes that go wide. "You two slept with Cally's husband?"

"I never slept with him," Krystal says. "I was going through a born-again phase. But . . ."

"We were both engaged to him," Maggie says. "I mean, at different times of course."

Krystal winces. "I'm the bitch who scooped him up after Maggie played runaway bride." She turns to her sister. "I'm still sorry about that."

Maggie shrugs. "It worked out. If I hadn't come back for your wedding, I wouldn't have met Asher."

I look to Cally. "You knew about this?"

She nods and looks completely unconcerned. "Yeah. It's not like we sit around and compare Will's bedroom techniques or anything."

"But only because it would piss off Asher." Maggie grins at Cally and whispers, "We all know your boy's got skills."

"Oh my God," I whisper. They're all so *cool* about it.

"And Max had a crush on Liz for years before he and I started dating," Hanna says. "Never mind *Meredith's* history with our men."

The girls all scowl at the mention of their common enemy.

Krystal smiles. "There is no reason Hanna's history with Max should keep you from dating him. It's just the past. It makes us who we are."

Yes, but I doubt any of them have a past like mine. This is New Hope, after all. Small town, USA, where they sell live bait at the gas station, and everyone knows everyone's business.

"Wait, you said *three months* ago?" Hanna asks. She turns to Liz. "You kept this from me for *three months*."

Liz lifts her palms then ticks her reasons off on her fingers. "One, I promised I wouldn't tell—I didn't even tell *Sam*. Two, I was sure one of you would catch on soon enough by the way Max looked at her after."

"What do you mean, the way he *looked* at me?" Something buzzes in my belly, less like butterflies and more like the vibration of hundreds of buzzing bumblebees. And bees scare the crap out of me.

Liz rolls her eyes. "Come on, you're going to pretend you didn't notice? Max wears his heart on his sleeve, and every time you two are in the same room, the way he feels about you is all over his face."

"I think you're seeing what you want to see," I protest, but the bees take their vibration up a notch. *Why, why, why* do I so badly want her to be right? Why do I love the idea of Max looking at me like some lovesick teenage boy?

"I was seeing what was there," Liz says. "And then he bought the house next door to you. Plenty of other houses, but he bought that one. Hmm."

"He bought the house because it's convenient to his business, close to his mom, and has a great backyard for Claire to play in."

"Mm-hmm," Liz says.

"So you and Hallowell?" Maggie asks with a grin. "I could see that."

"No," I say. "*Not* me and Hallowell."

Maggie arches a brow. "Well, hell, we already know he's one of the good ones—"

"The best," Hanna says.

"It wasn't like that, you guys."

"Then what was it?" Maggie asks.

"It was . . ." *Panic that my old life was coming back to get me.* "Lust and loneliness."

Krystal snorts. "I'd say we need more than two words, but those are pretty on-point."

"Don't encourage her, Krys," Liz says. "Now that it's okay to talk about it, I'd like a *lot* more than two."

"Lust because . . . well, you've seen him. He's like two hundred pounds of sculpted muscle topped with blue eyes and the sweetest damn smile you've ever seen."

"Spoken like a woman smitten," Krystal says.

"But why loneliness?" Hanna asks. "Are you lonely?"

So lonely. But I say, "No. I just said *loneliness* because 'horny' is an ugly world, and I'm a sucker for alliteration."

My joke works, and the girls laugh. Thank goodness. I really don't want them hung up on that loneliness thing.

"So why not?" Maggie asks.

Because I can't get my heart broken again. But I don't say so. I don't want to admit—not even to my friends—that I'm already in deep enough with Max to know he *could* break my heart. How pathetic that after one night together I already know that's true.

"Ooh," Krystal says. "Is he bad in bed?"

Hanna snorts. "Hardly." When we all turn to her, she blushes and wrinkles her nose at me. "That's the *weirdness* you were referring to, isn't it?"

I clear my throat. "Pretty much."

She blushes and lowers her voice. "Don't tell Nate I said that." Then she shakes her head and grins. "Or maybe you should, and he can do that thing where he gets all jealous and determined to prove he gets me off like no one else. And he does, but I *do* enjoy it when he takes up that particular mission."

Krystal props her hands on her hips. "Wait a minute. It's still a legitimate question. Just because he was good in bed for Hanna doesn't mean that he was for Nix. Sex is . . ." She waves her hand as if she's looking for the word.

"Fun?" Maggie says.

"Underrated?" Liz puts in.

"Emotional?" Hanna suggests.

"Subjective," Krystal says. "God, when did my little sisters become such hussies?"

"I've always been a hussy," Maggie says.

Liz nods. "Yeah, me too."

"Back to the point at hand." Krystal turns her attention back to me. Then they're all staring again.

Cally cocks her head. "We've all shared. Now it's your turn. *Dish.* We want to know about Max's skills between the sheets. With *you.*"

But, technically speaking, we never made it between sheets. Nope. He just took me right there in the garage, the humid air making our skin slick with sweat. Then he took me to my bedroom, and when I lay on top of the quilt, he gave me that mischievous grin and parted my legs.

I squeeze my eyes shut and bite my lip.

Maggie hoots. "She's turned on."

My eyes fly open. "What?"

"Look at you!" she says. "You're turned on just thinking about Max. Your cheeks are pink. Admit it. He. Was. Good."

"I never said otherwise," I grumble.

The thing is, I didn't expect much from a guy like Max. I didn't think beautiful men could also be amazing lovers. I mean, sure, my friends have gorgeous men and constantly sing their sexual praises, but I thought the girls were just too inexperienced to know their beautiful men were truly just average lovers.

In my experience, no man is as good in bed as one who feels grateful to have you there, and there's an indirect correlation between a man's sexiness and how giving he is in bed. Meaning that pasty-faced computer nerd who's a little soft around the middle may just be the guy to rock your world.

But when it comes to any expectations I had about Max, oh *hell,* was I wrong.

The girls squeal in delight, and Hanna claps her hands. "I love this. I love this so much. Max deserves someone good, and so do you. You guys could be great together!"

I force a smile, but I'm not the kind of *someone good* she wants for Max. "Well, thanks for your opinion, but don't get your hopes up. Now, can we get out of here before he thinks I'm the world's rudest neighbor?"

Liz grins. "Yeah, we don't want to keep her from Max."

Krystal glances longingly toward the dining room, where they were spying on the firefighters across the street. "I guess."

CHAPTER
FIVE

Max

"How'd the date go?" Will asks.

I cover the grill with burgers and avoid his eyes. "Fine."

"Max had a date?" Sam asks.

"Yeah," Will says, "but he won't tell me who it was with."

"It doesn't matter. Nothing's going to come of it."

"Why not?"

I shrug. It's not that it wasn't a perfectly pleasant date. She's a friend of a friend who lives out west, and she called me, told me she was coming to town, and asked me to take her somewhere nice for dinner. When

I picked her up, she was dressed to kill in this black-and-white skirt that hid *nothing* and a top that exposed the strip of skin below her navel. She was gorgeous and sweet, and I brought her back here and we had wine on the patio and talked.

But every time that shirt would shift and I'd see that perfectly smooth skin of her stomach, I'd think about Nix and what she's hiding under her shirt.

"Listen," I tell my friends. "She's going to be here tonight, but play it cool, okay? We've only been on one date, and I'm not even sure I'm interested. I don't need you idiots making a big deal out of it."

"Hey there!" Janelle Crane steps out the back door and onto the patio and smiles at my friends. Then she saunters over to me and presses a kiss to my cheek. "Hey, sexy. You need anything?"

I feel the guys staring at me, but I refuse to look at them. Janelle Crane is an actress brought to New Hope when her brother, Nate, moved in with my ex-fiancée, Hanna Thompson. It's shit from the daytime soaps, I swear, but my drama aside, Janelle's sweet and sexy, and the guys are totally pissing themselves with envy because *she* was my date last night. "No, I'm good. Glad you could make it."

"Wouldn't miss it! Nate just got here with the twins. Mind if I go inside and play with my nieces?"

"Make yourself at home," I say.

The silence turns stereo as we watch her walk back into the house.

"Janelle Crane?" Sam asks when she's gone. He and Will are both staring at me as if I've grown a second, then third head. "You're trying to figure out *if you're interested* in Janelle *Gift To Men's Eyes Everywhere* Crane?"

"Keep it down," I growl.

"Is this about Hanna?" Sam asks, and I groan.

"It's not about Hanna," Will says, matter-of-fact.

Sam's eyes narrow, as if he's trying to get a read on me. "There's somebody else, isn't there? You fell for somebody else and you've kept it from us."

"Nobody can keep secrets in this town," Will says. But the corner of his mouth twitches with his grin. That *I know your secret* grin.

Bastard.

"Who is she?" Sam asks.

"There's nobody else." I turn to flip the burgers. "I'm just not sure I'm interested in a long-distance relationship."

"But it's *Janelle Crane*." Sam clutches his chest. "Come on, man. You owe this to us. Let us live vicariously."

I arch a brow. "So if you had an opportunity to go home with her tonight instead of Liz, you'd do it?"

"Fuck no," Sam says.

Then I look to Will. "And you'd risk what you have with Cally for a chance with a hot actress?"

"Hell no."

Sam laughs. "But you pretty much just admitted there's somebody else."

Fuck. I did. "There's not."

A chorus of female laughter pulls my attention away from the grill and over to the group of women entering my yard.

It's hot out tonight, and they're dressed for it, all of them in flip-flops, tanks, and short skirts or jean shorts. In other words, there's enough soft exposed skin in my backyard right now to give a teenage boy mental material for months. But my eyes are drawn to only one of them. And it's not Hanna. I would have given anything to be with Hanna just two years ago, but Sam is wrong in thinking I'm still hung up on her.

My gaze is drawn to Phoenix Reid, whose long legs are exposed in a pair of cutoffs.

"Lord have mercy," Sam whispers beside me.

"There's a sight for sore eyes," Will says, leaving us to go to his woman.

"The doctor?" Sam asks as I tear my eyes off Nix.

I look around, but we're alone for the moment. "What?"

"You and Nix? When did that happen?"

Fuck. I follow Sam's gaze across the yard to where Nix is laughing at something Krystal said. "It's nothing." God, I feel like I'm in high school again. This is ridiculous. "She's not interested. So it's nothing."

"But it was," Sam says. "It *was* something? Enough to make you hem and haw about dating Janelle Crane?"

"Drop it," I mutter.

He rocks back on his heels and his lips twitch. "Sure thing."

"Don't you need to go feel up your woman or something?"

"She's inside playing with her nieces. That woman loves those babies like they're her own."

"Yeah? And why don't you give her some of her own?" I've had enough of the third degree tonight. Might as well turn the tables.

But instead of squirming and dodging the question, Sam just smacks me on the back and says, "I plan to just as soon as she'll let me. Now go ask out your doctor." Smirking, he takes the spatula from my hand.

Instead of arguing, I head toward Nix, if for no other reason than to not have to listen to Sam's shit anymore.

Okay. There's another reason. Those legs. *Holy hell.*

My eyes lift to meet hers. She's standing by William and Cally, already watching me, worry etching her features. Before I get to her, she ducks her head and darts off in the opposite direction.

Nix

The food table is nearly empty and the air is filled with laughter. Any fears I had about Max approaching me again tonight have been put to rest. He's kept his distance—not that I can blame him after the way I practically ran away. Anyway, there are at least twenty people here, so it's not like he's avoiding me. He's been spending his whole night playing host—grabbing beer and making sure there's enough food to go around. Up until he went inside to tuck her into bed about fifteen minutes ago, he had Claire to contend with as well.

I'm relieved we haven't been cornered into an awkward conversation. Or I should be.

Clouds slide across the moon and the ground shakes with a clap of thunder that isn't so much heard but felt.

My eyes go to the sky just as it opens, and sharp needles of rain slice into my skin.

"Everybody get in the house," Max calls from the door.

The table is littered with beer bottles, martini glasses, and tumblers. I'm not so worried about the beer bottles weathering the storm, but the wind is picking up, and I don't want it destroying Max's nice glasses, so I gather what I can into my arms and take them into the house.

Everyone is gathered in Max's kitchen, laughing, joking, and dripping wet. The rain isn't going to slow this party down.

I head straight to the counter. A second later, Max is behind me, his arms also full of glasses.

"I'm in your way," I say by way of an apology.

He slips his gaze from my face to my damp tank top and back up. "Not at all. Thanks for helping."

"Here." I take the glasses from his arms and set them on the counter one at a time. I feel really shitty for avoiding him earlier. I moved here determined to live life on my terms, but the truth is I'm letting my demons rule my decisions. If I'm ever going to give a guy a chance, I couldn't do better than Max—nor could any woman who enjoys that whole tall, dark, and charming thing. It's just that it feels like my past is creeping back in on my life. And I'm scared.

When did I become a coward?

"Thanks," he murmurs. He steps away from me, his face unreadable, then disappears into the living room on the other side of his throng of guests.

Safe to say I screwed that up.

Krystal left early, and my other friends are wrapped up with their men, so I'm not sure what to do with myself. I could leave, but I feel like I need to talk to Max before I go—if for no other reason than to thank him for inviting me.

But maybe more? Maybe I'll tell him I hope he'll ask me out again sometime.

The thought terrifies and exhilarates me all at once.

After filling the sink with hot, soapy water, I set to work washing the dishes, busying myself as people slowly make their way to the door. When just about everyone is gone, I spot Max on the other side of his kitchen, in the hallway opposite the remaining guests.

Showtime.

I turn off the water but stop when a gorgeous brunette joins him, tucking herself between his hard chest and the wall. I blink because that's Janelle Crane, and there's something proprietary about the way she's touching Max.

I force myself to pick up a glass and get back to the task at hand.

"So are you going to ask me out again?" she asks. "Because I'm running out of excuses to stay in town."

The glass slips from my hand and falls with a crash into the sink, but Max and Janelle are too engrossed in their conversation for the sound to disrupt them. Even so, I bow my head and hide the horror I know is all over my face.

No way can I hide how I feel about Janelle asking Max out. I just can't. That's like trying to keep a blank face when someone slugs you in the gut. Yet my eyes won't mind their own business, and I find myself watching their exchange anyway.

"Be my date for Asher's bonfire next weekend." She rises onto her toes and presses her mouth to his in a kiss that's neither chaste nor passionate. "Please?"

"Sure," Max says. "I'll pick you up at your brother's?"

I tell myself not to think about it, and fish through the sudsy water for the drain so I can clean up the broken glass. "Shit!" I draw my hand to my chest and hold it tight, wrapping my opposite hand around my bleeding fingers.

This time Max hears and walks toward me. "Are you okay?"

No. Fuck no. I'm not.

I nod and escape to the bathroom, where I sink to the toilet seat and close my eyes.

Time to face facts. I've been lying to myself, convinced I didn't want anything with Max. Just when I admit maybe that's not true, Janelle steps in and takes what I was too much of a coward to.

Max might have been willing to give me a chance after our night together, but there's no way in hell I can compete with sex symbol actress Janelle Crane.

The bathroom door creaks open then shut and I tell

myself to breathe.

"Jesus, Nix."

I open my eyes and see Max, his broad shoulders filling the doorway, his blue eyes narrowed in on my chest. Not that I have much of one but—no, not my chest. He's staring at the growing circle of blood on my white T-shirt.

He turns into a model of efficiency, running the tap and collecting first-aid supplies. Taking my hand, he leads me over to the bathroom sink and holds it under the water. The bathroom is small and my back is pressed to his chest as he stands behind me and tends to my wound.

This man smells amazing. Like clean, hot-blooded male. If sex appeal had a scent that could be bottled and sold, the cologne companies would need to study Max.

God, I'm pathetic.

"I don't think you need stitches," he says softly into my hair.

"That's my line."

He grunts. "Right. Here, turn around." He steps back as much as he can and spins me so I'm facing his broad chest. "How's that feel?" he asks.

"What?" Oh. My hand. "It's not as bad as it looks."

He grunts softly in disbelief and sinks onto the toilet seat. "Come here. Let me wrap it up."

I step between his legs as he wraps gauze around my hand. I wonder if he and Janelle will get married, if she'll move to New Hope and help raise Claire. They'd make a beautiful family.

His expert fingers have me bandaged too soon, and

then he's frowning at me. "Are you okay?"

"I'm fine. Really."

Then he smiles. *Really* smiles. And my tense and worried insides melt into a puddle of want. *That. Smile.* "Thanks for your help tonight, but you don't need to do my dishes."

I open my mouth to tell him I can finish them, that I don't mind, but then I remember my hand is wrapped in gauze. "Thanks for inviting me."

"You're welcome. Always."

I wish I weren't too proud to pretend to faint in his arms. It might be worth sacrificing a large chunk of my pride to feel Max hold me.

Unable to think up any excuse to linger, I step away and out of the bathroom, say my goodbyes, head home, and change out of my bloodstained shirt.

The rain has stopped, so I take a beer to my back porch, dump a puddle of water off a chair, and sit. My ass will be wet, but I don't care. It's still drizzling, so I'll just be damp all over.

"Hey. You want some company?" At the edge of Max's yard, Hanna's heading toward me, a glass of water in her hand.

I have a sinking feeling she's here to talk to me about Max. I hope I'm wrong.

"Come on over," I say. "The water's fine."

She smiles and wipes the water off the chair next to mine before sitting. She's so gorgeous. Long, dark hair and curves she carries with pride. And she's an amazing person—sweet and caring, and unfalteringly optimistic. It's no wonder Max fell for her.

"He's a good guy," she says.

"I know that." I turn my hand in my lap and stare at the bandage. Max is the kind of guy who stitches you when you're cut, picks you up when you're down, and gives you company when you're at your loneliest.

"I don't know what's holding you back," Hanna says, "but if it's me, I'll tell you now to cut that crap out. I have enough guilt where Max is concerned. I'm not going to be the reason he can't find some happiness with someone as awesome as you."

"It's not really about you, Hanna." I swallow hard. "I don't know how you guys do it. You've been hurt and you put yourself back out there."

"I didn't mean to," she says. "My thing with Nate was supposed to be a fling." She rolls her glass in her hands then looks up at me. "Why don't you give yourself permission to have a fling and see what happens?"

"Because he's dating your sister-in-law."

"Max and Janelle?"

I nod but don't look at her. I don't need to look to know there's pity on her face. I can't compete with Janelle. And, hey, maybe that's good. Maybe I dodged a bullet.

No. I didn't dodge anything. I kept my heart for myself so love couldn't hurt me, and tonight I realized that was like putting distance between me and the man holding the sniper rifle.

We sit in silence, staring at the storm clouds, and I wrap my hands around my beer when they really want to go to my lonely, aching heart.

CHAPTER
SIX

Nix

H<small>E'S FOUND ME.</small>

"Holy shit, Nix!" Krystal screeches from the driver's seat, and jerks the car to a stop. "What is *that*?"

"Fire," I murmur. Fire in my front yard. Fire where there should be none. The fire always finds me.

She parks the car by the sidewalk instead of pulling into the drive and hops out. We spent the night at Brady's, helping Liz pin down the final details for her wedding. A night of laughter, friends, and fun ruined by fire.

The flames dance in the moonless night and cast ghoulish shadows on the front of my house. I force myself to get out.

It's nothing. It's nothing. Just some kids screwing around in your yard.

"Dr. Reid?" a deep voice calls from across the street. "Are you okay?"

"Does she seem okay?" Krystal asks sharply. "Her *yard* is on fire! Get one of those fire trucks over here!"

I faintly register the sounds of footfalls coming closer.

"Did you start it?" the man asks. I hear the frown in his voice, but I don't look to his face to see it.

I can't take my eyes off it. I'm mesmerized by its return to my world. It's like I'm gazing into the eyes of the man who tried to kill me.

"Of course she didn't start it," Krystal says. "We've been out all night. How could she have set the fire? And *why?*"

I shake my head, and I'm only faintly aware of the man's movements, the squeak of the hose spigot as it turns on. I'm entranced by the fire until the flames are dosed with water, and then there's nothing left but smoke and piles of charred twigs.

"What's going on?" Max's voice is the one that snaps me from the spell. He's standing by the sidewalk, frowning at the shape burned into the ground.

"Nix's lawn was on fire," Krystal says. "The fire department is *right across the street* and they didn't even notice."

"It was the size of a campfire," the firefighter says, winding up my hose. "I assumed she was roasting marshmallows or something out here."

A shiver crawls up my spine and sends icy prickles

shooting through my limbs.

"Who builds a campfire in her front yard? Isn't that against the law in city limits?"

"Step off, okay?" the man says. "No one was hurt."

Finally, I turn to the stranger in my yard. He's tall, broad-shouldered, and sexy as hell. New Hope is the Mecca for sexy men, apparently. I probably wouldn't notice in my shock, but I've seen him out washing the fire trucks before.

"That's no campfire," Max says, stepping closer. "What's that supposed to be?" He points to the charred sticks, like a triangle with one side that extends beyond both corners. "Is that supposed to be an ax?"

"Thurisaz." The word springs from my lips as if shoved from a high ledge, as if it could no longer fit into the chaos in my mind.

"*Thor is what?*" Krystal says.

Max says, "Who the fuck builds a fire on someone's lawn? Is that some kind of threat? I'm calling the police."

"Yes," Krystal says. "Please call the police. This is freaky."

I feel as if I'm drowning in memory and need to kick my way to the surface for air—the rune stone cool in my palm, Patrick's voice in my ear. *"Best not to start a battle . . ."*

"No police." I shake my head. "That's not necessary."

The firefighter steps forward. "I have to file a report, ma'am. This is vandalism to your property at the very least."

Ma'am. So strange to be addressed with such a mature word when I suddenly feel sixteen again.

Max is on the phone. Krystal and the firefighter are talking about something, but I can't hear them over the voice in my head. It's a voice from my past and one I hope to never hear again.

"Best not to start a battle, but if you do, you'd better finish it."

Max

The asshole dispatch sent from the New Hope PD scratches down a few more notes for his report and nods, but it's obvious he's not going to do shit about this. I wish my friend Cade had been on duty. He would have taken my concerns seriously, but this kid punk didn't think someone lighting a fire the size of a grown man was a big deal.

Nix is lost in her own head. She answered the officer's questions, but barely.

"Is she okay?" I ask Krystal.

Nix sits down on the porch steps and stares into space. "I'm fine," she says. Not that I believe that for a minute. "You guys go home. It's no big deal."

Krystal's face draws into a frown and she looks at me. "I don't want to leave her."

I know she has to be at Hanna's bakery early to

open, so I wave her off. "I've got this. Go home."

She takes a deep breath then exhales slowly. "Okay. But call me if she needs anything."

"You're rather optimistic if you think she'd let either one of us know that she needed something."

"Good point," Krystal mutters. She joins Nix on the porch steps and whispers something in her ear as she hugs her. Nix hugs her back and nods.

When Krystal pulls away, I take a seat beside Nix on the steps. She's staring at the charred piles of sticks in her yard.

"What does it mean?" I ask.

She shrugs. "Probably nothing. It's probably just kids screwing around."

"Not the fire, Nix, the symbol. You said something when you first saw it. And, frankly, you looked like you'd seen a ghost."

"I'm . . ." Nix clears her throat. "I'm afraid of fire."

"A Phoenix who's afraid of fire?"

"Rebirth hurts more than you'd imagine." She lifts her eyes to mine, but her face is guarded. "I said something? What did I say?"

"Thor-something?"

She rubs her bare arms. "Oh, that. That's nothing. I used to . . . I knew someone who liked runes. It kind of looked like one of those."

"Kent?" I ask. It's the only name I have from the past she doesn't talk about, but when I say it, her face pales.

"What?"

"Was your boyfriend Kent the one who liked runes?

You mentioned Kent a few months ago."

"No," she says carefully. "Kent was a doctor."

As if that explains anything at all. Fuck, this is frustrating. "If I ask you a question, do you promise to answer truthfully?"

She just looks at me, and I know she'll not make any such promise.

I sigh and ask anyway. "Do you think someone's trying to hurt you?"

She shakes her head. "If they were trying to hurt me, why set the fire to my yard? Why not my house? And why when I'm not home?"

I suppose she has a point, but I still don't like it. The thing is, if she hadn't reacted the way she did, I'd probably think it was kids too. But the fire panicked her. I saw it in her face. "Would you stay at my place tonight?" I ask, and when her eyes go wide, I add, "In the guest bedroom. Just so I know you're safe."

"I'm safe." She pushes to her feet and rolls back her shoulders, looking less like someone who feels comfortable alone in her house and more like someone preparing for a fight. "I have a security system that's tied into the smoke detectors, so even if I *did* think this was something of concern, I wouldn't be worried about sleeping under my own roof."

"I'd feel better if you were sleeping under mine." I can already tell this is an argument I'm going to lose, and I stand too.

"Good night, Max," she says. "Thanks for worrying about me, but I'm going to be fine."

You're a terrible liar, I think, but I know she's had a

hard enough night, and I don't know that either one of us is up for me calling her on her lies. "Good night, Nix."

CHAPTER SEVEN

Max

"SOUNDS LIKE HIGH SCHOOL KIDS," Will says.

The river rushes beside us as we approach the final stretch of our run. I kick up the pace a few notches as downtown New Hope grows closer. "I don't think so."

"Remember all the times we'd steal beer from Sam's parents' fridge? We'd find a place to make a campfire and drink it while we tried to impress whatever girl was on our arm that week." He smiles at the memory, but I shake my head because he's missing the fucking point.

"If it were in her backyard, I *might* buy it, but this was in the middle of her front yard. And the sticks were laid in this weird shape that was nothing like a campfire." Never mind this feeling in my gut that tells me there's more to it.

"So what do you think it was?"

"I don't know. But I have a feeling Nix knows more than she's saying." *If only she'd let me in.* Will looks skeptical as hell. "What's that face for?"

"You're so into her."

"I'm not."

"Do I need to remind you that you do this?"

"Do what?"

He wipes the sweat from his forehead with the back of his arm, and we turn off the river path and toward the sidewalk that leads to my health club. "Swoop in? Save the girl?"

"I don't—" I stop running and stare straight ahead, and Will stops too.

"Speak of the devil," he mutters.

Half a block ahead of us, Nix is passing Will's art gallery and headed our way. She's dressed for the office in her typical slacks and button-up shirt, and she's looking at us, but I have a feeling she doesn't see us. Her face is drawn, as if exhaustion hangs on every cell. My first thought is how much I'd like to take her home and tuck her into bed.

I don't want to *save* her, not exactly. But damn, someone needs to watch after her.

"Good morning, Nix," Will calls before I can find my tongue.

She shakes her head and blinks, as if registering our presence for the first time. "Hi."

"How are you this morning?" I ask. "No more problems last night?"

"No, it was fine." She frowns. "I'm sorry I didn't want to stay with you. I just knew it wasn't a big deal."

At that, Will arches a brow. His expression says he can read me like a fucking book.

"Can I talk to you alone for a minute?" I ask Nix. Will doesn't need any more ammunition than he already has.

Nix looks to Will and then back to me. "Me?"

"I could use your medical advice about something," I lie.

"I told you to go to the clinic for that discharge, man," Will says, barely choking back his laughter at his own joke. "One little shot will clear it right up."

I punch him in the arm, and he stumbles sideways and rubs his bicep, but it doesn't wipe the smirk off his face.

"Um, sure," Nix says. She leads the way away from Will and into Hanna's bakery.

I follow, and when the doors close behind us, she drags me to the corner. An older couple sits at a table on the opposite side of the bakery and a few women stand in line at the register. Thank goodness it's not as crowded in here this morning as it usually is, but I'd still rather have this conversation in private.

"Should I be tested?" Nix asks in a whisper.

It takes a minute for her meaning to click, but when it does, I release a horrified laugh. "Nix, Will was razzing me. He's just being a dick to be funny." *And to prove to me that I have a thing for you.* She ducks her head, and I cock mine for a better view of her blush. "Seriously."

"So, no discharge?"

"Fuck no. And if you're thinking about *discharge* next time I get you alone, I swear Bailey's going to pay for it."

That wipes the blush right off her face. In fact, she's gone damn near pale. "Next time you get me alone?"

Well, fuck. I'm making a mess of this already. I got one night with Nix. Hell, not even a full night. I got part of a night, and then Liz showed up and dissolved into tears because Sam was being a fucking idiot.

I got *part* of a night, and I thought it was pretty spectacular. And I'd thought *she* thought it was pretty spectacular too. For a minute, I'd thought maybe *we* could be spectacular together. Until she avoided me every day thereafter.

"Max, listen, I know we've never, um, we've never talked about it directly . . ." She surveys the counter, probably to make sure none of her friends are listening in on this conversation. Hanna's not around—she's probably in the back—and Krystal is busy with a customer. "I guess it's time we do. That night was . . ." She shifts from one foot to the other and then drums her fingers on her thighs. The movement takes my eyes down to her long, long legs and reminds me, as if I needed a reminder, how much I want a chance at a *full* night with Dr. Phoenix Reid. The kind that starts with wine and good food and moves on to slow seduction and doesn't end until we're sipping coffee and warming the water for our morning shower.

William's wrong. I don't want to save her. I want something much more satisfying.

I shove my hands into my pockets. "Is there going to be a next time, Nix?"

She lifts her head and locks her eyes on mine. The morning light slants in the bakery windows, highlighting the sharp angles of her cheekbones and making her big eyes captivating.

Captivating. Fuck. A few nights ago, I was drinking wine in the moonlight with an honest-to-God Hollywood starlet, and I didn't once think of her as *captivating.* What's happening to me?

"Any chance we could forget that night ever happened?" she asks.

For a moment, I'm so tangled in my thoughts that I think she's talking about my date with Janelle, then I realize she's talking about *our* night together. "You want to forget the night at your house happened?"

She nods. "Yes."

"You mean, so we can hang out together without me imagining your legs wrapped around my waist?"

Her lips part. *Hot.* Then she licks them. *Hotter.* "Yeah," she whispers, her voice catching. "Something like that."

"I'd rather not forget it, if it's all the same to you." I step forward—close enough that I could kiss her, though I won't. Close enough that I could bury my nose in her hair and take a hit off her scent, but I won't. I love the way she smells. She uses this soap that smells like crisp linens. Not sweet or flowery, just clean. "As memories go, it's a favorite of mine."

Her eyes widen. "It is?"

And there it is, that contradictory bit of her. On the

one hand, sometimes she seems more mature than the rest of us and unfazed by the petty bullshit we let rule so much of our lives. She's confident in who she is and what she's about. On the other hand, any time I've given her a compliment on anything other than her skills as a doctor, it takes her by surprise.

I drop my gaze to her lips. "Yeah. It is."

She backs up a few steps and her body tenses.

"Are you all right?" I ask. "For a few months now, it's seemed like you've been on edge. I've been worried about you."

Nix

He's been worried about me. That explains so much. "You don't need to date me just to take care of me. I can take care of myself."

He laughs. Actually *laughs*. I don't see anything funny about any of this.

"Huh." He rocks back on his heels and crosses his arms over his sweaty T-shirt. You'd *think* such a motion would assist me in taking my eyes off his broad chest. Instead, it makes the muscles in his arms bulge, and it's as if a magnetic force is drawing my eyes to him.

Dear God. After Patrick, didn't I swear I'd never fall

for a man this beautiful?

"I thought you were smarter than that," he says, and that gets my attention.

"Uh . . . what?"

He cocks a brow. "I thought you were smarter than that."

"Yeah, I heard the words the first time. Still don't know what they're supposed to mean. Just because a woman won't sleep with you doesn't mean she's not smart." I throw the words up like a shield, but when Max flinches I know they strike like a knife.

"Jesus, Nix."

"I'm sorry." It's my turn to flinch. I suck at this. What does Lizzy say when something is difficult? It *sucks hairy goat testicles.* Pretty much. "I shouldn't have said that. That was bitchy."

"Yeah, it was." He rocks back on his heels and rolls his shoulders.

"I *am* sorry. It's just that I don't need you pretending to like me just to lift my spirits."

He studies me for five wild beats of my heart, his expression unreadable. "I'm mature enough to handle it when a woman isn't interested. Don't sweat it. But for the record, I don't ask women out to lift their spirits. Did that once before, and it didn't end well. I think I've learned my lesson." When I only stare at him, completely unsure what that's supposed to mean, he sighs, shakes his head, and backs toward the door. "Have a good day, Nix. Give me a call if someone tries to set any more of your shit on fire."

"Good morning," Krystal says when the door swings

shut behind Max.

I turn to her and grimace. "How much of that did you hear?"

"Only the last bit about the fire, sadly. Did I miss anything good?"

I glance out the door after Max, who's joined Will on the sidewalk. All broad-shouldered and sweaty, those two are giving every college girl walking by unrealistic expectations.

"He's just checking on me." And maybe that's not true, but I'm going to need to turn that conversation with Max over in my head a few times before I know what to make of it.

"And how are you?" Krystal asks as I head to the counter. I know she's worried about me, which is fair, considering the way I zoned out last night. "Okay this morning?"

I haven't been anything close to *okay* in a lot of years, but at least there's a good chance I'm not crazy.

God, I'm being dramatic, but that's the best I've got.

When I saw that symbol burning in my yard last night, my first thought was of Patrick McCane, my first boyfriend, my first love, and my biggest mistake. My first thought was the terror that he'd found me. It wasn't until I made myself go to bed that the next thought really clicked into place. *Maybe I'm not crazy.*

That's the irony of that burning Thurisaz. It was a threat, and I have no doubt it was intended to be sinister, yet it gave me hope. Maybe there's an explanation for all of this—seeing Patrick's reflection, feeling like I was being followed, believing the phone calls weren't random.

Of course I'm not going to tell Krystal all of that, not in the middle of Hanna's bustling bakery, not ever. I say, "I'm fine, but a little tired. Could I have a double shot of espresso with cream and one of Hanna's chocolate croissants?"

"For here? I could take a break and sit with you."

I shake my head. "To go, please. I need to get to the hospital."

"Got it. Coming right up." She hits some buttons on the espresso machine and grabs a bag for my pastry. Instead of handing it to me across the counter, she calls into the kitchen that she's leaving for a few minutes, and then comes around the counter to meet me. "I'll walk you to work."

We walk in silence toward the hospital for a while, and I'm grateful. I insisted on staying alone at my house last night, but not a minute of the night passed when I didn't regret that decision. The fire did what I'm sure it was intended to do—freak me way-the-hell out.

When she finally speaks, I expect her to ask about the fire at my house again, but she doesn't. "Are you coming to the bonfire at Asher's this weekend?"

I cut my eyes to her, but she seems serious. "I think I've had all the fire I can handle for a while."

"This is the good kind of fire," she says, smiling. "With beer and hot dogs and *friends*. Not the crazy shit that happened on your lawn."

I shrug. I want to say no, but the desire not to let my fears control me makes me say, "Sure. I can come."

"And will you be bringing a date?" She tries to keep

the question light, but since I wasn't born yesterday, I know she's digging for information.

"If you're asking if I'll be attending on Max's arm, then the answer is no. I'm pretty sure he's going with Janelle Crane."

"Oh." Her eyes widen and she looks horrified on my behalf. See? Even my friend doesn't think I can compete with the likes of Janelle. Not that I want to. "Want to tell me the real reason nothing ever came of you and Max?"

"What?"

She crosses her arms and narrows her eyes at me. "I talked to Will when he was in the bakery the other day. I asked him what he knew about you and Max, and he admitted that Max has carried a torch for you for *months*. He said you were going to let Max take you out but then you suddenly changed your mind."

My steps slow. I'm trying to imagine Max caring enough about dating me to talk to his friends about it.

Krystal puts her hand on my arm, stopping me before she pulls me to the edge of the sidewalk. "Tell me the truth, please. Something's going on. What is it?"

"I got spooked," I blurt.

"What do you mean? Did he do something to freak you out? Drop to a knee and propose marriage?" She quirks a brow. "Or maybe he just called you beautiful, and you thought he might mean it and ran."

"No—wait. What? Called me beautiful? What's that supposed to mean?"

Krystal rolls her eyes. "It means you're totally uncomfortable with the idea of being sexy. Sure, you dabble in it from time to time, but mostly you wear unflattering shirts buttoned to the top, hide your body, and keep your hair tied back in a knot. *You* have a problem with being pretty."

I shake my head. We'll come back to that later. *Or never.* "Well, no. He didn't call me beautiful. I just . . ." The bumblebees are back in my stomach. The blade-winged bastards stir at the idea of saying it out loud, but suddenly I want to. I need to. Maybe it's just sleep deprivation talking, but this is my new life—here in New Hope with my new friends who have become more like family than those who share my blood. Maybe I don't have to carry all of this alone anymore. Maybe I can share some of my fears, even if explaining everything and exposing my past is out of the question.

"You just what?" Krystal asks.

"I smelled smoke," I whisper, and the bumblebees spasm, their sharp wings slicing up the inside of my stomach.

"What does that mean?" Krystal's voice has gone softer. She must see the fear on my face.

"Liz ended up showing up that night and staying over, but after Max left I could smell smoke." I wait for her face to change and for her to look at me like I'm crazy. Like I'm my mom. But she doesn't.

She says, "Tell me what you mean, Nix."

"At first, I thought it was just my memory playing tricks on me. Me and fire . . ." I shake my head. "But the longer I was in the house, the more sure I was that the smell was real. I couldn't find a fire or any evidence that there had been one. But I smelled it." I bite my lip hard then force a smile, my desire to unload my burden tempered by the fear of anyone I care about knowing the truth. "I convinced myself it was all in my head, but any thoughts of pursuing a relationship with Max burned up in that fire I could never find."

Krystal studies me for a beat. "You want to tell me what's up with the fire thing?"

I shake my head. "I don't want to talk about it. It's . . . my old life." *And you'll never look at me the same way if I tell you.*

"You smelled smoke after sleeping with Max, and then he moves in next door to you, and someone lights some symbol on fire in your yard. You're obviously scared as shit of it, and *somebody* knows that. This isn't just a prank, Nix. This is straight-up harassment. I'm not saying you have to tell *me*, but you need to tell someone the truth. The whole story."

CHAPTER EIGHT

Max

THE CONVERSATION WITH NIX left me feeling antsy, so I convinced Will to run another mile with me. We pushed hard, nearly sprinting the whole thing, and when I step into the club I'm drenched in sweat, and the muscles in my legs are twitching with fatigue.

"Look at you!" someone calls as I head to the shower.

I turn to see Meredith, my daughter's mother, weaving her way through the weight room. Her long blond hair shifts softly over her breasts as she rushes toward me and takes my hands.

"Hey, Mer." Grabbing a towel off the rack, I glance

at the clock. I have twenty minutes before my next training session, and my chances of a shower are looking slim.

Meredith dropping back into town unannounced isn't a surprise to me. She works for a Parisian company that makes fancy hair products, and she travels around France doing hair shows for them. Or something. I don't really know the details or care to. But the job keeps her away from Claire more often than she's around her. Meredith comes and goes as she pleases—but she doesn't typically drop by the club uninvited. Unless she wants a favor.

"Where's Claire?" she asks, scanning the gym, as if I'd bring my daughter here to play while I work all day.

"At preschool."

She nods and waves her hand to indicate my sweat-soaked appearance. "Obviously you're not with a client right now. Can you spare a minute? It won't take long."

"Yeah, sure."

"Good." With a flirtatious smile, she steps forward and loops her arms behind my neck. She rises onto her toes and presses her mouth to mine. I can tell she wants the kiss to become more, but I don't lift my hands to touch her or open my mouth for hers. Once, I couldn't keep my hands off her. She wanted Will, and I wanted her, and every once in a while she threw me a bone. Claire was the result of one of those times. Maybe if things were different, Meredith and I could have made it work. Maybe if Meredith didn't hide that I'm Claire's father, or maybe if she didn't try to destroy my first healthy relationship, she and I would be raising Claire together now.

She takes her lips from mine and falls back to her heels.

I don't owe her any explanation for not returning her kiss, but she's been a friend too long, and I hate seeing the pain on her face. "Mer—"

"You still haven't forgiven me," she says, as if that's the only reason a man wouldn't want to make out with her. "Are you still in love with her?"

I frown. "Who said I was *in love*?" How on earth did she find out about me and Nix?

She cocks her head. "It was kind of implied when you were going to marry her."

Oh. Here I am thinking of Nix and Meredith is still asking about ancient history. "Hanna and I broke up almost two years ago. She's happily married now, has another man's babies."

"I didn't ask when you broke up or the state of her marriage. I asked if you're still in love with her."

I swallow, and my mind immediately conjures the only brunette who's been in my thoughts lately. "I can confidently say I'm over Hanna."

Meredith studies me, a wrinkle in her brow. "Well, good."

"And I've forgiven you. I just don't feel that way about you anymore."

"Okay. Understood." She drops her arms and steps back, putting some space between us. I'd have to be dead to miss the hurt in her eyes.

"What was it you needed to talk about?"

"Oh yeah." She shakes her head and her expression

shifts from wounded to carefully masked. "Would you do me a favor and pack Claire's bags? Let her know we're going to be taking a trip soon? We'll be heading out Sunday night."

I sigh. It would be nice if she asked if I had plans, but when Meredith comes home she expects the entire town to stop its normal orbit and rotate around her. "Sure. How many nights should I pack for?"

"Three weeks," she says.

"No," I reply. "That's ridiculous. You can have her through the following weekend, but—"

"No, Max. I'm taking my daughter to Paris with me when I leave next week. Please pack enough for three weeks."

"What the fuck, Meredith? She's a *child,* not some toy you can borrow as you please."

"She's *my* child."

"This is her home."

Meredith sighs heavily. "I don't understand why you're acting so shocked," she says. "We've talked about this for months."

We've talked about the possibility of Claire joining her in Paris some time, but the conversation was always in the abstract. Truth be told, I never thought Meredith would want the bother of having her daughter with her. "You could have warned me it was coming so soon," I say, trying my best to keep my patience. "She has school."

"I'll pay you back for the time she misses."

"It's not about the money."

"I think she'll be okay if she misses a few days of

preschool. I promise to practice the alphabet with her every day."

"I don't like this."

She gives me a sad smile. "That's because you're an awesome father. I'm grateful that she has you, Max, but I want my daughter to be with me for this trip."

"I'm just pointing out that it might not be what you imagine. She's not some teenager you can drag around to your favorite cafes, and she's not old enough to appreciate the attractions." Never mind that she's used to living with me. Spending a few days with her mother every few months hasn't exactly established the kind of connection Claire needs to leave me for three whole weeks.

"I know you think I'm a terrible mom," Meredith says, "but this is important to me."

I shake my head. "I don't think you're a terrible mother." *I think you're an absent one.*

"Please. I think this would be good for Claire. She needs a relationship with me. I know I haven't been good about making that happen, but I'm trying here."

Fuck. She's right. I hate it, but she's right. And I could fight her about how sudden it is and insist she take Claire on a later trip, but what's the point? Letting her go for three weeks is going to kill me if it happens now or this winter. "Let me know if she's having a hard time, okay? I'll jump on a plane and come to get her early."

"Okay." She rubs my shoulder and gives a half-smile. "I promise. I wish you understood that I've grown up a lot in the last few years. I'll be okay with her."

"You're not the one I'm worried about, Mer."

Nix

"Do you know the way to Camelot, to Camelot, to Camelot? Do you know the way to Camelot, to Camelot my dear?"

The old song runs through my head like a record on repeat, so the minute I step into my house I turn on the stereo, cranking an Ani DiFranco CD at top volume. Then, in the spirit of facing my fears head on, I sit down at my computer, pull up the web browser, and type in the name I've spent the last thirteen years trying to scrub from my brain.

Patrick McCane.

The first six results are all social media profiles, and none of the pictures look like the man I'm searching for. I click through a few more pages of results and find some athletes and a lawyer by that name, but none appear to be the guy I believe burned a symbol from my past into my front yard.

I was sixteen when I met Patrick. I was a bit of a dorky teen, more interested in books than boys, and more apt to daydream about college and grad school than parties and romance. Back then, I thought I wanted to get my PhD in physics and be a college professor. My mother was rarely stable and never rational, and as a means of self-preservation, I loved science and math and everything that could be quantified. The library was my church, and logic was my gospel.

One day I was at the public library and I ran into Patrick—literally. I had my nose stuck in *A Brief History of Time* by Stephen Hawking and was pacing the stacks while I read and *bam!* I ran smack into a rock-hard chest.

I'd never understood girls who lost their brains when cute boys were close, but when I looked up at Patrick it was like someone opened the drain on my brain, and all I'd ever known spilled right out into a puddle at my feet. He was . . . *everything*. Tall, with a runner's lean form and ropy muscles in his arms. His face was striking—all strong features and hard angles, like something you'd see in a magazine. Then he smiled and said, "Good book."

"It is." I stepped back to respect his personal bubble, even though I wanted to be close, where I could smell his soap and feel his heat.

He extended a hand. It was a good hand. Big. Strong. Not too rough and not too soft. "My name's Patrick."

On the verge of that precipice over which you become nothing but a giggling, tittering girl, I made myself take it and shake it hard. "My name is Phoenix."

"Phoenix? Like the bird that's reborn from the ash?" His grip was firm. Confident. Long enough that I felt as if he liked touching me, but not so long that it seemed creepy.

"That's the one."

"Wow. What a name. It must kick ass to have a name like that."

Not really, given my mom's reasons for choosing it, but I didn't say so.

Over the next few weeks, I fell. Hard. Partially because he was the most gorgeous guy I'd ever seen, and partially because of the way my stomach seemed to bloom with life every time he looked at me, but mostly because he could talk books and philosophy the way no guy I'd met ever could. Unfortunately, my mom and little sister fell in love with him as quickly as I did—and maybe more so—and as soon as they were in his snare, all our lives were inextricably tangled with his, and I found my whole family dragged into Patrick's world.

The months that followed may have been easier if my brain had stayed in a pool at my feet, but bit by bit my mind returned to me. By the time my mom had decided to move us to Camelot, I wasn't sure about Patrick anymore, and by the time I caught my mom secretly planning the wedding ceremony for her sixteen-year-old daughter, I wasn't just skeptical, I was terrified.

Thirteen years later, and my months at Camelot feel almost more like a dream than a memory. In fact, my time in New Hope made it easy to pretend my past wasn't my own. As if my memories were just something I saw in a terrible movie once, but I'd turned off the film and was free to carry on with my normal life.

I go back to the search bar and decide to try a different angle. I can't search "Camelot" and expect any relevant results. I try "Camelot commune" and get information about a new senior housing program in Boston. The results for "Camelot Indiana" don't prove any more useful.

With shaking hands and a sick feeling in my gut, I try "Camelot cult."

The results have something about some hotel in England that's believed to be connected to Scientology, but there's no Scientology connection to the Camelot that I'm looking for, and the rest of the results are too far afield to be relevant.

I close my computer and bite my lip. I could call my mother again, but I wouldn't expect answers any different than last time.

The problem is, I don't know where to look for answers because I don't understand what's happening. I left Camelot thirteen years ago and worked my ass off to build the life I have. Why is he after me now? I hardly believe that he couldn't find me before, not in the age of computers.

For the first few years after, I never fully lived my life. I was waiting for Patrick to come back for me— waiting for him to finish the job he started in that church. But he never did, and by the time I enrolled in medical school, I was beginning to believe I could live a normal life.

I was wrong about that. Normal people don't have to hide their past. Normal people haven't done the things I have.

In the years after, I've learned that I'll never escape my past. You can't escape what's part of you. But I believed I escaped Patrick.

"I will never let you go. You're my phoenix. I need you. Without you, I'm as good as the ash under the flame."

The symbol burned into my front yard isn't just a reality check, it's reality *whiplash*. Every time I stand on my porch, I'll see the reminder of everything I thought I'd left behind.

If he's back, it's because he wants to punish me for what I did. But why now? And what lengths will I have to go to escape him this time?

CHAPTER NINE

Nix

JANELLE CRANE PULLS MAX HALLOWELL CLOSE. Her hands are in his hair, her tongue down his throat. They're tucked away from the party a bit, beyond the crowd and into the tree line, where they can grope like horny teenagers without an audience.

On my other side, surrounded by what appears to be half the town of New Hope, flames of a massive bonfire dance across the river's edge, crackling and sizzling as they lick the starry night sky.

I don't know which is worse. Or why I'm here. I mean, I could have guessed that "bonfire" meant "big-ass fire," but I thought I could handle it.

I was fucking wrong.

Even far enough away that the flames no longer warm my skin, I can still hear the mini-inferno hissing at me, like a snake that's found its prey. I can't go back there. I don't have the stomach for fire tonight. But I can't stay here either. I can't take my eyes off them. Janelle Crane, a legit Hollywood actress with the perfect skin, body, and hair. How can I compete with that?

You didn't want to, a voice in my head reminds me. *He could have been yours, but you blew him off.*

The voice bears a striking resemblance to that of my good friend Lizzy Thompson. For a moment, I let myself imagine what might have happened if I hadn't smelled smoke after Max left my house that night. Would I be the one with him in the forest tonight?

Max trails kisses down Janelle's neck, and I force myself to turn around and march back toward the crowd and my friends. The upside? The image of those two kissing makes it easier to move closer to the fire.

"There you are!" Liz calls from the crowd. She extricates herself from her fiancé's embrace and rushes over to me. "Krystal and I have been looking for you. You disappeared!"

"I'm not feeling great." Not a lie, conveniently. "I'm thinking of heading home early."

Liz frowns and lowers her voice to a whisper. "You aren't pregnant, are you?"

I roll my eyes. "No. I'm sorry to disappoint you, but I'm not carrying Max's love child."

"He's a good dad," she says, as if this is enough

reason to hope for an accidental pregnancy.

"It's just been a long day."

Maybe if this excuse were given to another friend, it would have worked. But because she's Liz and her sexual Spidey Sense is off the charts, she immediately looks toward the tree line in the direction I came from and cocks her head. At the most, all you can see from here is their silhouettes—a shadowy blob of faint movement in the darkness.

"Hmm," Liz says. Then she starts walking in that direction, her long strides covering ground at an impressive clip. She's a woman on a mission.

I start to follow—intent on stopping her—and then stop when she calls his name.

"Max!" she calls. *Oh, shit. Please don't make a scene.* "Oh, oops! Sorry." She doesn't sound sorry. "Yeah, your baby mama is looking for you."

"Her name is Meredith," Max mutters. "And when did she get here?"

Liz shrugs. "Not my circus, not my bearded lady."

I can't make out Max's reply. He's probably warning Liz not to be bitchy about Meredith, but I can't be sure. It's a low, distant rumble that reminds me of his body over mine, his sexy words in my ear.

Pleasure squeezes hot and tight at the memory, starting at my gut and splintering out like a sunburst. It shimmers up my spine and dips down to regions farther south. Because, yeah, the memory is *that* good.

Meredith and Max have a child together, and their relationship is . . . well, I know from our mutual friends that Max calls it complicated. I call it good material for daytime soaps. Their little girl lives with Max during her mother's long stretches in Paris, but Meredith likes to complicate his life the weeks when she's home. Either this is going to be one of those weeks, or Liz is full of it and making shit up just to separate him and Janelle.

Liz saunters back to me, her lips twisted into a smirk of satisfaction. She folds her arms and shoots a dirty look in Max's general direction.

He's returned to the party to find Meredith. I have a better view of him in the firelight. His dark hair is mussed, his fitted polo tight across his shoulders and half untucked at the waist.

"Janelle fucking Crane," Liz mutters. "*Ugh.* This is all your fault, you know."

I prop my hands on my hips. "*My* fault?"

"Oh yeah. You with your 'I just don't want a relationship' and your 'he's a nice guy but it's a bad idea.' You blew him off, and now when you come to your senses and realize he's the best thing that ever happened to you, you're going to have to compete with a Hollywood starlet."

"Want to talk a little louder, Liz?" I grumble. "I don't think the whole party heard you."

"I'm just saying . . ." She swings her gaze around to mine and lowers her voice. "Nix, you should see your face right now. You don't get to be hurt. You waived that right."

"I know."

"It's been three months," she says.

"I know."

"You totally blew him off."

"I know."

Her eyes soften. "I don't understand you."

I know, I think, but I don't say it this time because a screech rings out from close to the fire. The crowd shifts as a flaming log lands outside the ring. I watch it burn where it shouldn't. Its flames immediately die down, but not before it marks the grass, leaving a scar.

Fire is like that. Powerfully dangerous, even as it dies.

"Don't make a bigger deal of this than it is," I finally say. "It's fine. I'm glad he found somebody."

"You're a shitty liar."

Max

Meredith isn't anywhere to be found, and when I give up, I find Janelle by the fire. She slips an arm around my waist and leans her head against my chest. She smells good and her body feels nice under my hands. She's going to expect to go home with me tonight. The teenage boy in me is disgusted by how uninterested I am in that possibility, and *fuck* I've been trying but it's not working. I brought her here as my date, asked about the movie she's working on next week, even let her drag me into the woods to make out like a couple of horny teenagers. I should be so into this woman, and I *want* to be. I want to forget about my feelings for Nix and the way her lips feel under mine. I want Janelle's kiss and body to be what I'm thinking about when I'm alone in bed with my aching cock.

I'm trying but it's not working.

I scan the crowd for Nix and can't find her. Did she go home? She'd better not be walking alone. For me, tonight's fire is a reminder of the look on her face when she watched that symbol burn in her yard. I bet this is the last place she wants to be.

Janelle presses her hand to my chest. "Where's your mind tonight?"

"All over the place," I answer honestly.

"For instance?"

"Claire's mother is going to take her to Paris for three weeks."

"That could be a fun break for you."

I shake my head. "I don't need a *break* from my daughter." The words come out harsher than I intend, and she flinches. "I'm sorry. That sounded bad. I'm having some trouble adjusting to the idea."

She shakes her head. "You don't need to apologize. I'm a selfish idiot, and I guess I was thinking it might be fun to hang out more. You could fly out to LA and spend time with me on set."

Hang out more? Fly to LA? Shit. "You're not an idiot."

She looks up at me with sad eyes. "Then why have I been getting the feeling all night that you're about to break up with me?"

Break up? I didn't think we had anything to break.

When I look away, she draws in a sharp breath. "It's okay, you know. I mean, sometimes it's more like we're brother and sister than potential lovers."

Guilt eats at me as I meet her eyes. "I'm sorry. You're great, Janelle, but you deserve a guy who's going to put all his energy into sweeping you off your feet. Not some fool who's only in possession of half his heart."

"Yeah, yeah, and someday I'll find him, right?" She sighs then squeezes my arm. "You're a good guy. I hope you can recover that other half of your heart from whoever stole it."

I watch her leave, and when she disappears into the house, I stare at the fire and try to figure out what the hell just motivated me to dump Janelle Crane.

Liz saunters up beside me before I can sink too deep into that thought. "Happy reunion with Meredith?" she asks, the sneer in her voice.

I can't blame any of them for hating Meredith. She earned it. And yet I wish they wouldn't, because no matter the mistakes she's made, she's Claire's mom and she'll always be part of my life. "Couldn't find her."

"Huh," Liz says. "She must've left."

"Or she was never here at all, and you were just trying to get me away from my date."

"So, you and Janelle?" she asks, unfazed by my accusation.

"I'm not talking about this with you, Liz. It doesn't take a genius to know you're angling to see me with Nix."

She presses a hand to her chest and gasps, all bouncy

curls and righteous indignation. "I'm marrying your best friend. Maybe I just *care* about you finding *true love*."

"Right." I sigh and decide a change of subject is in order. "How are the wedding plans coming?"

Fifteen minutes later, Liz has completely forgotten that she wants to grill me about Janelle, and I know more details about her upcoming wedding than I ever needed to. I let her finish describing the flowers before I join Will and Sam, who are guarding the beer coolers.

"Where's Janelle?" Sam asks.

I shrug. "I think she left."

Will sighs heavily. "You broke up with her, didn't you?"

"Why does everyone think a couple of dates constitutes a relationship?"

"It was *Janelle Crane*." Sam rubs his forehead. "I don't *understand* you."

"He's got it bad for the doctor," Will says.

I grab a beer from the cooler and growl, "Shut up. I have bigger things to worry about than grade-school crushes right now. My daughter's going to be in fucking France for three weeks, and I'm supposed to be okay with it."

William has the courtesy to look abashed. "Sorry. Are you going to be all right?"

"Not exactly," I mutter, and Will nods. He has a little girl too, about a year younger than Claire, so he understands that Meredith is ripping my heart out by taking her away from me, even temporarily.

"So seduce your doctor," Sam says. "I can think of

worse ways for you to distract yourself until Claire comes home."

I scowl at him. Why does everyone think my daughter's absence is nothing but an opportunity to relive my bachelor days?

"Who are you seducing?" Cade Watts asks as he joins our circle. "Because I've talked to half the beauties here tonight, and I'm beginning to think I couldn't find a single woman in this town if my life depended on it."

"Cade," I call in greeting. "Are you having a good time?"

Cade's new to town. He moved here for a position on the New Hope PD and has worked out at my gym from the beginning, and I invited him along tonight so he could meet some more locals.

"Maybe our friends know someone for you," I suggest, nodding toward the spot a dozen yards away where Liz, Hanna, Cally, Krystal, and Nix stand laughing in a group.

Cade follows my gaze and grins.

Sam cuts his eyes to Cade, then me, then back to our new friend. "Eyes off my woman," he growls.

"Ditto," Will says.

I grunt. Will and Sam can be as possessive as they want, but their women are not the kind men are going to keep their eyes off. "Good luck with that, boys."

"That's a lot of beautiful in one group of women, so you're going to need to be more specific about which ones are claimed," Cade says. "I call dibs on the curvy one. Because *damn.*"

There's no need for the guys to announce which women are theirs. Lizzy and Cally join us and walk straight into the arms of their men.

Lizzy wraps her arms around Sam and he presses a kiss to her head, and Cally kisses William on the mouth before rising on her toes to whisper something in his ear.

Krystal and Nix hang back, stopping to talk to some other party guests, but Hanna follows closely behind the other two.

She's as beautiful as ever, her curves on display in a little black dress and her hair falling in waves around her shoulders, and I'm just glad I can finally look at her without that ever-present ache in my chest.

Cade clears his throat and gives Hanna the once-over. "Care to introduce me to your friend?"

My lips twitch. He's going to be disappointed when she takes her hand out of her pocket and he sees her wedding band. "Hanna, this is Cade, NHPD's newest recruit. Cade, this is Hanna. Hanna is married."

"It's nice to meet you," Hanna says, completely oblivious to the fact that I just ruined Cade's whole week.

Cade winces, uninterested in hiding his disappointment. "Are you *happily* married or just married, because . . ."

Someone clears his throat and then Nate Crane is there, wrapping his arms around his wife and pulling her back to his front.

"Mine," Nate growls. He presses a kiss to Hanna's neck.

"Cade, this is Hanna's husband, Nate Crane. You might be familiar with his music?"

"Holy shit, man," Cade says. "Your last album rocked my world."

"Thanks," Nate mutters. "And the answer is *happily. Really fucking happily.*"

Cade cocks his head in confusion.

Hanna smacks Nate's hands, but he keeps them tight around her waist. "He's saying that I'm happily married," she explains to Cade. Then, craning her neck to look up at her husband, she says, "He wasn't serious. Relax."

And that's Hanna in a nutshell. A man meets her and is so attracted to her he offers to commit adultery, and she assumes he was just being nice.

"Sorry." Cade rocks back on his heels and tucks his thumbs in his pockets. "I haven't had much luck meeting single women since I moved here."

"Oh!" Hanna hops up and down. "Krystal is single."

"And Nix," Nate says, following Hanna's gaze to the two single women in question.

"Um." Hanna turns back to me, and I see it in her eyes. She knows.

I'm not sure what to make of that. Nix swore me to secrecy after our night together, and I know Hanna was on the top of her list of people she didn't want finding out.

"Yeah, Nix too," she says softly, but she's still looking at me and the question is in her eyes: *Is* Nix single? Do *I* want Nix to be single?

I don't have an answer to that. I like Nix. A lot. But

it's not like I haven't made that clear, and she's not interested. That should be the end of it. So says the guy who just ended a romance with Janelle Crane before it began.

"Nix," Liz calls. "Come over here and meet Sam's friend, Cade."

Nix wanders over, and Cade's eyes go straight to her long legs. She extends a hand. "Nice to meet you," she says as he takes her hand in his. "I'm Phoenix Reid."

"She's a doctor," Liz says. "Nix, Cade is a police officer."

Sam looks at me then whispers something to Liz, who shrugs and mutters, "Too bad."

"It's nice to meet you, Cade," Nix says. "I'd love to chat, but I was about to head home."

"You know," Liz says, "I'd like to stay a little longer. Why don't you have Cade walk you?" Her gaze lands on me, as if to say, *Make your move.*

"I can go alone," Nix says. "It's no big deal."

"Let me walk you," Cade replies. "It's dark, and no city is as safe as people think it is. I insist."

Nix gives Cade a smile I can only hope is forced. "Okay. Let me thank our hosts and I'll be ready to go."

"Great," Cade says.

The group disperses, leaving me alone with Cade for the moment. "Listen, about Nix . . ." I shift my gaze to where she's standing by the door and shake my head. I have no right to stake my claim, but fuck that.

Cade follows my gaze and lifts his chin. "Yours. Understood."

* * *

Nix

"You really didn't have to do this," I tell Cade as we leave the party.

"It's a beautiful night," Cade says. "I never mind a chance for some fresh air."

I'm not sure what to think about Lizzy's sudden shift in matchmaking efforts, but it's obvious that's what this is about. Maybe she realized Max and Janelle are good for each other. Who knows? Truth be told, I didn't want to walk home alone, and I would have felt bad asking one of the girls to go with me before the party was over.

"What do you think of New Hope?" I ask.

"It's different," he says. "An adjustment, I guess."

"Where are you from?"

"LA. I was a homicide detective out there before I took this position."

I frown. Big-city homicide detective to small-town Indiana cop. "Why the change?"

His lips press into a thin line. "What about you?" he asks instead of answering. "Where are you from?"

"A lot of places," I answer. I can dodge a question as well as the next guy. "I grew up in the Midwest, then when I finished my residency, I decided to come back this way."

We work our way toward my house, silent for a while, and when I slow in front of my drive, Cade puts his hand on my arm to stop me. "Wait. The house with the weird lawn fire was yours?"

"It's not a big deal. Just kids, probably." God, I'm so sick of lying, but I'm not ready to say, *Yeah, I'm pretty sure my psycho ex-boyfriend from thirteen years ago is stalking me.* "Good night, Cade."

When I start toward my driveway again, he pulls me back. "Do kids around here typically use kerosene and tied bundles of wood to burn symbols into yards?"

I pull from his grasp and cross my arms. "I don't know, but I'm not worried about it, so you don't need to be either."

Cade arches a brow. "Don't know many cops, do you? I'm escorting you to your door."

"Fine." I lead the way to the front door, unlock it with my keys, push it open, flick on the lights, and disarm the alarm. "See? All good."

He looks over my shoulder. "Want me to go in and check the place out first?"

Yes, I do. "No, Cade. I just want to go to bed."

He nods, his face grim, and I close the door behind him as he leaves.

As I watch him go, my phone buzzes with a text message.

Unknown Number: I never thought you'd cozy up to the police.

The strange message makes my stomach twist painfully, and my hands shake as I reply.

Nix: Who is this?

Unknown Number: A friend.

Nix: If you're a friend, you'll tell me your name.

Unknown Number: Do you really think he can protect you?

Nix: Who do you think I need protection from?

Unknown Number: Be careful who you trust. You never were very good at choosing your allies.

I put my hand to my mouth and squeeze my eyes shut.

"I will never let you go. You're my phoenix. I need you. Without you, I'm as good as the ash under the flame." I once took comfort in those words, but tonight they ring in my ears. Tonight, they haunt me.

Thirteen years ago . . .

My family has eaten dinner at the commune before, but this is our first night as one of them. Before we were outsiders, and even though we were made to feel welcome, it was clear we were seen that way—

outsiders no one should trust.

After dinner is over, I follow the lead of the other girls my age and help clear the table, wash the dishes, and put the leftovers into the big, commercial-grade refrigerator.

They watch me as I work, and I'm not sure if they're looking down on me because I'm new or if they're simply fascinated by someone from the outside. Maybe both.

I want to hate this place. I wasn't happy when Mom told me we were moving. But I don't. I can't. There's food on the table without me putting it there. There are clothes on my sister's back that *I* didn't have to make sure were clean. And the community here is like the big family I never had but always dreamed of.

Even feeling like an outsider, and even worrying about what it's going to be like to live with a lot of rules when I'm used to none, I'm cautiously optimistic.

We're wiping down the counters when Patrick comes into the kitchen, and all the eyes go to him. One thing that's been clear from the beginning is that all these girls have a thing for Patrick. Maybe because he's Vicar Jeremiah's oldest son, and therefore the next in line to lead Camelot. Or maybe because he's so gorgeous you just want to look at him.

Their obsession with Patrick makes me feel special. All these girls to choose from, and he picked me.

Their eyes are glued to our every move as he approaches and tucks a lock of hair behind my ear. "Go on a walk with me?"

"Um . . . okay."

I put my dishrag into the laundry bin and follow him outside. The commune sits on eighty wooded acres between Terre Haute and Lafayette. The church and the other common areas are in the center, with all the tiny homes set around them in two circles, one that sits inside the other. Behind the homes there are gardens, and behind that nothing but forest trails for hiking.

"What's wrong tonight?" he asks when we're alone on the trail. "You were so quiet at dinner."

"Nothing." I smile at him. I don't want to offend him by explaining all the ways his world seems weird to me. "I'm just not used to this life yet."

"But it's better, isn't it? Better than having to take care of your mom and sister alone?" He squeezes my hand. "I was worried about you."

The way he looks at me sends a rush from the bottom of my tummy through my toes. "I know you were."

The night is cool but not cold, and I relax into the sounds of the wind in the trees and the crunch of woodchips under my feet.

I'm not sure if this is against the rules—a boy and a girl on the trail alone together—but I am sure that it would be frowned upon at the very least. That's all the more reason I like that we're doing it.

All the rules of this place are starting to creep up on me, like a thick blanket being pulled over my mouth and nose little by little until no air can make its way in. There's a security in rules I never had when it was just Amy, Mom, and me, but I still don't know that I understand them all, and part of me wants the rules *and* the freedom to break them.

"You're going to love it." He rubs the back of my hand with his thumb as we walk along the trail, and the moment is so nice and so normal that my worries fall away.

A log cabin appears at the curve of the trail. "What's that?" I ask.

"It was there before my dad bought this property, so now it's the honeymoon cottage."

"The honeymoon cottage?"

"Yeah." He grins. "I mean, newlyweds don't necessarily want their neighbors close enough to hear everything, you know." He winks at me, showing me the Patrick I fell for—the one who's a little mischievous, a little rebellious.

"Hmm. Is anyone in there now?"

"Nope."

I smile and rush to the door, pushing it open when I find it unlocked. Evening light filters in through the windows of the rustic cabin, giving me enough light to make out the small fireplace and the four-poster king-size bed. "It's kind of romantic."

He follows me in, shuts the door behind himself, and leans against it. "You like it?"

"I like it," I murmur, leaning against the bedpost. I bite my lip, something buzzing in my belly and sinking lower. I'm not sure if I like the cabin or if I like the idea of what happens here. "Will you bring *all* your wives here when you're vicar?"

Patrick straightens and stalks toward me slowly, something in his eyes I don't recognize. Maybe this is what the books are talking about when they talk about the "heat" in the hero's eyes? "Does it bother you that my father has so many wives?"

I shrug. "It's different, but they all made the choice on their own, so who am I to judge?" What bothers me is the idea of Patrick someday wanting me to be one of his. Not that I'm ready to think about marriage or anything like it yet. But when I do marry, I won't want to share my husband. I know that much about myself.

"I can't change anything now," he says, as if he knows my thoughts. "It's not my place. But things will change when I'm vicar, Phoenix."

When I'm vicar. I don't want a future as vicar to be in his plans. I wish he would leave this place with me, go to college, get a job, and have a normal life.

"There's only one woman I want as my wife." He tucks a lock of hair behind my ear, and the buzzing in my stomach sinks lower—a lot lower—as his eyes dip to my mouth. "I can't stop thinking about kissing you."

We haven't done more than kiss and a little outside-the-clothes-and-above-the-waist touching. My mom wasn't the type to have such talks with her daughter, but I've read enough that I know about more. And I've definitely *wanted* more. Though I've been afraid to ask.

His mouth drops to mine, and his tongue sweeps across my lips. I open, and tilt my head to give him better access, and the kiss turns hard and deep in an instant. His hand slides into my hair and he presses his body against mine.

High on the idea of what we're doing and where we are, and feeling bolder than usual, I slip my hand between our bodies and rub my palm down the length of his erection.

He gasps and tears his mouth from mine, his eyes squeezed shut. "Don't, Phoenix."

"Am I hurting you?" I start to pull my hand away, but he grabs my wrist and presses it back against him.

"You're killing me," he murmurs, guiding my hand up and down the length of him so I'm stroking him through his pants. "We shouldn't."

"It's okay." God, what a thrill. *I* did this to him. He's breaking the rules—or at the very least pushing their boundaries—because of how he feels about *me*.

"They'll judge us." His breathing is heavy, his body pressing into my touch.

I'm not sure who "they" are. All I know is my body is tight with need and want and feelings I don't understand but desperately want to explore, so I repeat, "It's okay."

He shoves me back onto the bed and lies on top of me, kissing me hard. Before I can get my bearings, he's unzipping my shorts and yanking them down my hips. I moan with equal parts lust and surprise.

Then—*oh, shit*. I cry out because it hurts. He's thrusting his hips and grunting on top of me, and I have to bite my lip so I don't cry, because I didn't mean for it to go here, and definitely not so quickly. But it's my fault, isn't it? I'm the one who goaded him on when he wanted to stop. I'm the one who insisted.

I squeeze my eyes shut and tell myself not to cry.

The hurt subsides, but then it's over. Patrick jumps off me—his eyes wide, his jeans and boxers around his thighs.

"What did you do?" he whispers. "What did you *do*?" He yanks up his pants and drags a hand through his hair. "What have you done to me?"

I climb off the bed and pull up my shorts. My breath catches at the blood on the mattress—bright red and blossoming on the bedspread like a flower in a Monet painting. "Patrick," I whisper.

He punches the wall, and the plaster crunches as his fist breaks through it. "What have you done?"

"It's okay," I say instinctively. His anger terrifies me. I've only seen him like this when he was angry with his father, but it's never been directed at me. "Please don't be mad."

He spins on me, his eyes dancing with anger that scares me. "Your mother was right," he whispers. "You're dangerous. The devil's fire runs through your veins."

CHAPTER TEN

Max

IT WAS ALL I COULD DO not to follow Cade and Nix to make sure he didn't make a move on her, but I stayed at the bonfire for another fifteen minutes after they left before I walked home.

I want to sit on my porch with a beer and look at the stars, but I smell like smoke from the fire, so I take a quick shower and tug on my sleep pants before grabbing a couple of bottles of beer and heading out front.

"Have another one of those?" someone asks as I take a seat.

I look up to see Nix climbing the steps to my porch.

"Sure." I twist the top off both bottles and hand one to her.

She takes a long pull from the bottle and looks out into the night. "Is Claire in bed?"

"She wanted to stay with her nana one more time before she leaves for Paris."

She spins to face me. "Your mom's going to Paris?"

"No." My heart tugs painfully just talking about it. "My *daughter* is going to Paris. Her mom wants her for a few weeks."

"I'm sorry, Max. That sucks."

"It'll be okay." I shrug, then lean forward in my chair and prop my elbows on my knees. "Her mom hasn't been around much the last couple of years, and I've gotten used to having Claire to myself. Hell, take this house. It's all about her. I chose this house for its proximity to her grandmother. For the backyard, where I'm going to build a kickass tree house. For the basement that I'll convert to a rec room before she's old enough to have friends over. My every reason for buying this place centered around my daughter."

"Not for the crazy doctor chick next door?"

I grin, and my gaze drops to her legs. I can't help it. "I sure as hell don't mind the view."

"I never thought you bought this house because of me, you know," Nix says, "just for the record. But I guess I didn't realize how close you are to your daughter either."

"She's my world. I don't have a wife or a girlfriend. I have my gym and I have Claire. Hell, when Hanna broke it off, I wasn't even interested in dating for a long while. I figured maybe I didn't get the typical family—the wife and the two-point-four kids—and I decided that was all right with me because I got Claire."

She gives me a tentative smile. "You won't lose her just because she spends a few weeks in Paris."

"It's not that I don't want her to have a relationship with her mother. And it's not even about the three weeks." I sigh and take another long pull from my beer before I admit the truth. "I'm so fucking scared Meredith is going to realize what she's been missing and take her away from me."

Nix sinks into the chair next to mine and rolls her beer between her hands.

"What are you thinking?" I ask.

The corner of her mouth twitches up into a sad smile. "I was thinking how lucky Claire is to have a dad like you—you'd fight for what was best for her. Not all little girls have dads who are so concerned about their wellbeing. Not all dads are willing to raise their daughters alone."

"I'm guessing yours didn't."

She tugs her lip between her teeth and sighs. "My father died in a fire the night I was born. Thirty years ago next month."

"Jesus. That sucks. I'm sorry." Then it clicks. "Is that why your mom named you Phoenix? Because of that fire?"

"Something like that."

It's not much as far as opening up goes, but it's more than she's ever shared before.

She tilts her bottle back, polishing off her beer. "I

don't suppose your offer stands? Maybe that fire freaked me out more than I thought, because I really don't want to stay alone in my house tonight."

That surprises me even more than her sharing information about her family. "You're welcome to stay here. Anytime." I touch my fingers to her cheek and nudge her to look at me. "And I hope I don't need to say this, but I will just in case. You're welcome to stay here anytime and without any expectations. Okay?"

She nods, and those emerald-green eyes drop to my lips. Then she shocks me by giggling.

"What?"

She shakes her head and bites her lip, but more giggles slip through.

"*What?*"

"I was just . . ." More giggling. And *damn*, but I like that sound. "I was just thinking . . ." She laughs again and then takes a deep breath as if to calm herself. "Did Hanna ever tell you about the conversation I had with her before she left the hospital? You know, after the accident? When you were still engaged?"

My frown is inspired more by that little trip down memory lane than by confusion, but I say, "No. I don't think so. What conversation?"

She giggles again, then throws her hand over her mouth and clears her throat. "Okay. Um. Promise you won't be mad?"

I arch a brow. "I'm not sure that's ever a wise promise when you have no idea what the person is going to tell you."

"Fair enough." She bites back a smile.

"Nix?"

"I'm sorry. It's just so ridiculous now that I know you. I thought . . . well, I was worried that maybe *you* were the one who pushed her down the stairs."

"Say what?"

"I'm so sorry! And if it helps, Hanna never believed it was a possibility, but to me you seemed . . ."

"Like an abusive asshole trying to kill the woman he loved?" Suddenly I'm glad I didn't promise anything, because *Jesus Christ*. "My God, Nix, I—"

She leaps out of her chair and throws a hand over my mouth. "You seemed too good to be true. *To me.* Which says way more about me than it says about you. *I'm* the screwed-up one who didn't believe guys could be both insanely sweet and . . ." Her gaze slips down my body and back up.

Wrapping my fingers around her wrist, I remove her hand from my mouth. Her pulse jumps under my fingertips. "Insanely sweet and *what*?"

"Are you fishing for compliments, Max Hallowell?"

"I'm trying to feel better about the fact that you thought I was like my asshole father."

All the humor drains from her face. "Your father . . ."

"Was a fucking worthless piece-of-shit asshole." I soften that news with an attempt at a smile. "Now tell me. You didn't believe guys could be insanely sweet and what?"

She licks her lips. I wonder if she has any clue how crazy it makes me when she does that. If she's trying to tempt me into kissing her when she's more or less told me to fuck off, romantically speaking.

"I don't think it's any secret that I'm attracted to you." Air puffs from her lips in a humorless chuckle. "Hell, who isn't? But I've been with attractive men before, and I believed they were representative of the whole—pretty on the outside, ugly on the inside. Don't you see? That's why I think it's so funny now. You're not just a pretty face, and you're not just a good guy, Max. You're . . . great." She tugs her lower lip between her teeth, and I want to bite it next. "Are you mad?"

"That depends," I murmur.

"On what?"

"Are you just now figuring out that I'm not the man you thought I was?"

She shakes her head. "No, that was pretty clear a long, long time ago." She looks at her wrist, still wrapped up in my fingers, and then sinks into my lap. That's when her change of demeanor—her honesty and uncharacteristic openness—clicks for me.

"You're drunk." Her beer is empty, sure, but Nix is a social drinker. One beer shouldn't put her over the edge like this, and yet every other sign points to intoxication.

She leans her cheek against my chest, and I feel her nod more than see it. "A little. Right before I saw your light on, I had a shot of whiskey. Or maybe three. It just took a minute for it to hit me. I needed—what do they call it? Liquid courage?"

I can't resist, and my fingers find their way into her hair. "Tell me what you need liquid courage for, Doc." She tilts her head back so she's looking at me, her eyes soft and dreamy. *And drunk*, I remind myself.

"Can I tell you something, Max Hallowell?"

I nod, not trusting myself to speak when she looks at me like that.

"I think you're . . ." She drags her bottom lip through her teeth and sighs. "You're more than an amazing father. You're an amazing man, and at risk of sounding like I'm trying to get in your pants . . ." She giggles again, but softly. "I just want you to know that I think any woman who ends up as your wife and making your remaining one-point-four children should thank her lucky stars."

"Then why do you keep pushing me away?"

She stands, completely ignoring my question. "I'm gonna go grab my clothes and come back here to take total advantage of that nice-guy thing you have going on." She reaches the stairs before stopping, and at the look on her face as she turns toward her house, something squeezes hard in my chest.

"Do you want me to go over there with you?"

She nods. "I know it's pathetic, but yeah, I do."

Nix

"Listen," I tell Max when we get back to his house, "if this is weird, I don't have to stay with you." I don't want to go anywhere else. I want to stay here, at his place. With the guy who waited by my bedroom door for me to pack a bag because he knew I wouldn't want to be alone. But I'm beginning to feel foolish for my presumption that he wouldn't mind me staying. "I could bunk with Krystal or something."

"You're staying here. The guest bedroom is down the hall, clean sheets on the bed and everything."

"Thank you." I bite my lip and go in the direction he indicated. The truth is, I don't want to stay with any of my friends. I'm too afraid of what's happening. I know it's selfish, but I feel *safe* when Max is around. Safe and good. And if Patrick is going to ruin my life, I want to gobble up the last little bit of its goodness before it's gone.

After brushing my teeth and changing into my PJs—a black ribbed tank and blue cotton shorts—I crawl into bed, draw up the covers, and cling to my pillow. I can't bring myself to turn off the light. Even though I try to go numb, the tears fill my throat.

I don't cry anymore, but my throat goes thick in my weaker moments. I've gotten very weak since I came to New Hope. This place had fooled me into believing I didn't need to be strong anymore.

The door clicks as someone opens it, startling me. I look up to see Max standing in the doorway. He's dressed for bed—or *undressed* for bed may be a better way to put it—in navy athletic shorts that hang low on his hips, and nothing else.

"What's wrong?" I ask.

He stalks toward the bed and starts throwing my pillows to the floor while I stare at him. When I'm left with nothing but the pillow beneath my head and the pillow at the head of the empty spot next to me, he turns off the light then pulls back the covers and climbs in behind me.

Before I can question him, he wraps his arm around my waist and spoons me against the heat of his chest.

"Good night, Nix," he whispers.

That's the kind of guy Max is. He makes space for me when I need a place to stay, and then he climbs into bed with me when he knows I'm too afraid to be alone.

We lie in the dark in silence for a long time, but I know he's not any closer to sleeping than I am.

"Have you always been like this?" I ask him.

"Like what?" The words are spoken against my neck in a puff of heat that has me squeezing my eyes shut and my legs together.

"Maximilian Hallowell," I say slowly, enjoying every syllable as it rolls off my tongue. "Such an appropriately knightly name. Are you always riding to the rescue of the nearest damsel in distress, Maximilian Hallowell?"

His body shakes against my back with his silent chuckle. "Sweetheart, you're no damsel."

"I'm a little bit too much of a tomboy to qualify, huh?"

He grunts, and the arm around my waist tightens. "The night I moved in, I saw you on your back patio smoking a cigar and playing video poker. There's no 'little bit' to your tomboy."

"You can't tell anyone about that." I smile despite myself. I should be embarrassed that he saw, but I like the idea of Max caring enough to watch me. "I'm a *doctor.*"

"Doctors can't be tomboys?"

"Doctors shouldn't smoke cigars."

"Your secret's safe with me." He presses his lips against my neck, and I melt into him. "I can be trusted with secrets, Nix. If you need someone to hold some of yours, I'm good for it."

I close my eyes and focus on my breathing. People say things like that. *You don't have to hide who you are with me.* Or *You can tell me the truth.* But then they see the real you or find out your secrets, and everything changes. "Thank you for saying so."

"I'm not looking to rescue anyone," he says softly. "But if you're the one who needs saving, I'm happy to invest in a stallion and learn how to ride."

Just like that, the tears surge, warning me I could spend the whole night feeling suffocated with them trapped in my throat. But Max is here and I feel safe in his arms, so they simmer back down and I can breathe.

I close my eyes, and I sleep.

CHAPTER ELEVEN

Nix

HE'S HARD.

When I woke up, I was convinced it was all part of a dream. I fell asleep with his arm around me, but the morning greets me with chirping birds, and his fingertips brushing the underside of my breasts through my tank, and his very hard, very *impressive* cock nestled against my ass.

Dear God, please give me the strength not to move.

Because I want to. Yes, sweet baby Jesus, I want to wriggle against him and invite him to touch me. I want to guide his hand farther north and feel his rough fingertips toying with my nipples.

I bite my lip and keep myself as still as possible. This isn't about me. This is just how guys wake up. I'm a doctor. I'm familiar with the physiology. And the hand resting under my breasts? I'm sure that was just an instinctive reaction to sleeping with a woman. He's probably dreaming. He probably thinks I'm Janelle, and he's . . .

Oh, shit. Janelle.

I scramble out of bed, but the sheet snags my foot and I stumble forward. I have to catch myself with my hands so I don't face-plant on the floor. Wriggling my foot, I try to extract myself without pulling all the blankets off the bed, and when it comes free, I fall to a heap on the floor with a loud *oomph.*

I'm not sure there's a woman in the world with less grace than me. The question is, did Max see that?

Slowly, I make myself turn back to the bed. *Please still be sleeping.*

He's not. Of course he's not. And he's not simply awake, either. Max has moved to the edge of the bed to watch my early morning sheet escape, and, judging by his twitching lips, he found it very entertaining.

"So, do you always panic when you wake up in bed with a man, or am I special?"

"You're special, all right," I mutter.

Oh hell, that smile. If there were a way to telepathically alert him to the fact that he can just climb down here and do me now, I would totally do it.

Except for Janelle. Right. *Janelle.* How convenient that I forgot all about her until this morning. And I sat *in his lap* last night.

"How'd you sleep?" he asks.

"Great. Fine. I mean, okay, I guess." *Better than I have in weeks. But let's not think too hard on the reason behind that.* I smile stupidly. I'm not sure what to do now. I could stand and go get ready for work. Yes, that would be good. But I don't want to move as long as he's looking at me. Unless he's going to join me in the shower. In that case . . .

Janelle. Sexy actress. His girlfriend. Or . . . kind of girlfriend. Whatever. It doesn't matter. Even if they're not exclusive, *that* is the kind of woman Max needs. Not me with my metric ton of baggage and the creeper ex-boyfriend.

"Are you going to get back in bed?" he asks.

Is that an invitation? I swallow then force myself to breathe. Oxygen deprivation must be doing things to my brain.

And *oh, damn.* He runs his gaze over my legs in a way so apparent even *I* can't miss it, and my already hot cheeks crank up to inferno. There's no way this amount of blood can rush to my face without melting off a couple of layers of skin. "I'm done sleeping."

His voice is all sexy and husky when he says, "Yeah, Doc. So am I."

"But Janelle," I blurt.

He sits up, groans, and drags a lazy hand through his hair. "What?"

"Janelle. Janelle *Crane.* Sexy actress. Ring any bells?"

"Do I want to know why you're bringing another woman into this conversation?"

128

"Because you had her tongue down your throat at the bonfire last night," I say, and he flinches.

"I wasn't aware we had an audience."

"You're *with* her."

He studies me carefully, as if he's trying to figure me out, which is fair, since I'm sending him *all* the mixed signals lately. "Janelle and I were never *together*. Not officially."

"But you were dating."

"*Dated*," he says. "As in twice—two dates. But we're not now."

"Why not?"

His eyes soften when he says, "Because I'm interested in someone else." His gaze slowly moves down my body, as if to make certain I know he means me.

"Me? When Janelle Crane of *Roommates* fame wants to screw you silly? Janelle Crane, wet dream of men everywhere? She wants you but you want *me* instead? Do you have issues?"

He sighs and leans his head back against the headboard. "Did you ever wonder why I got a sitter that night? I could have walked you through the garage door repair on the phone. The eyes are an easy fix, and I knew it when you described the problem."

I throw up my hands in frustration. "I didn't mean for you to go out of your way."

The deep rumble of his chuckle grabs my attention, and I look at him. Grinning fully now, his eyes crinkling in the corners, he climbs out of bed. "I got a sitter, Nix. I could have brought Claire."

I scramble to stand in front of him, and he offers a hand to help me up. "I wouldn't have minded," I murmur, but no matter how much I want to deny what he's saying, it's sinking in.

"I didn't have to come, but I wanted to. I didn't need to get a sitter, but I wanted to." He steps forward, his fingertips brushing the sensitive inside of my palm before he twines his fingers with mine. "Maybe *you* slept with *me* because I was convenient, but convenience had nothing to do with me kissing you that night. I like you, Nix. Honest to God, you're the cutest damn thing. Your mental block about how I feel about you notwithstanding, you're also really fucking smart. I like smart. And I like cute." His gaze drops down past my face, neck, breasts, and nearly to the floor before it makes slow work of its return path to mine. "And I fucking *love* your legs. I can't stop thinking about those legs."

I swallow. Hard. He's serious. For whatever reason, he's attracted to me in a crazy serious kind of way. And, yeah, this should have been clear about the time he was suiting up with latex in my garage, but hookups happen between normal people, right? He *likes* me.

My heart squeezes hard at that revelation, and that's what scares me—the way my heart thinks it's been invited to this party.

"I need to take a shower," I say stupidly.

His eyes burn hot on mine. "Want company?"

"Yes," I whisper. "But we can't have everything we want, and Max, I can't have you. You have a little girl who needs a family, and you have a heart that deserves

130

forever. I'm not built for forever, and I don't know the first thing about family. Not the good kind."

His nostrils flare as he draws in a sharp breath. "What happened to you? What are you hiding from?"

I open my mouth to answer then close it. Because there's honesty, and then there's stripping bare and pointing out all the scars on your soul. Suddenly I'm cold, and goose bumps cover my arms and legs.

"Have a good day," I say. "I'll find somewhere else to stay tonight so I'm not in your way."

"Nix—"

"Don't." I hold up a hand.

"Don't what?" he asks.

"Don't make me want something I can't have."

Max

As sexually frustrated as my time with Nix leaves me, I'm on track to reach epic levels of fitness by Christmas.

I drop down from the pull-up bar and put my hands on my thighs as I crouch to catch my breath.

Cade jumps up, grabbing the bar for his set.

"Do you have any leads on the fire at Nix's house?" I ask. After I ranted to him about the officer who took the report, Cade promised me he'd follow up on it himself.

"Some," he grunts mid pull-up.

"And?"

"And I can't talk about it."

I force myself to take a deep breath. Of course he can't talk to me about an ongoing investigation. What did I expect?

"She doing okay?" he asks.

I sit on a weight bench and lift my face to the ceiling. "I don't think so. Despite what she says to the contrary, she's pretty freaked out about it."

"Did she say why?"

I shake my head. "We all process stress differently. She's not exactly the type of woman who cries on your shoulder and tells you how she's feeling."

He arches a brow. "So I'm guessing you were happy to let Nix 'process' her stress in your bed?"

Will chooses that moment to join us. He grunts in response to Cade's question. "She'd have to be willing to get in his bed for that to happen."

Cade takes a few swallows of water, pulls the bottle away, and frowns at me. "I thought she was your girl."

Will grunts again.

"You have something to say, you can say it," I growl.

He holds his hands up. "Oh no, I'm not saying a word."

"She's not your girl?" Cade asks.

"Why are you so interested in my relationship status?" I ask.

Will bites back a grin as he jumps to grab the pull-up bar, and Cade says, "I'm more interested in *her* status than yours."

I scowl. "It's complicated."

"How would you feel about me asking her out?" Cade asks. Is this guy serious? "How would you feel about me kicking you in the nuts?"

Nix

It's just a house. It can't pull you back into the past, and it cannot control you. It's just a house.

I force my shaking hands to slide the key into the lock.

Cade called me today and told me they're concerned enough about the fire that they're going to have a patrol car drive by the house every hour or two the next couple of days. I appreciate the gesture, but if I believed police could protect me from the likes of Patrick, I wouldn't be the hot mess I've been since I saw his reflection in my mirror.

When I open the door, the alarm beeps at me in its steady high-pitched warning tone. I disable it with slow, steady movements, but I can't breathe until the door is locked behind me and the alarm system is re-enabled.

I listen for the four reassuring beeps that indicate the system is armed, then I slide down the wall and cradle my head in my hands, all my courage eaten up by walking in my own front door.

"Are you okay?"

The words make me jump, and I swing toward the voice so fast I knock my arm against the doorjamb. "Shit!"

A woman steps out of the dark living room and into the foyer, toying with her long braid of sandy blond hair.

"Mom?" The word slips from my lips before I can stop it, and she smiles. She's too young to be my mother, but she looks so much like her it makes my chest ache. "Amy," I say, correcting myself.

"Phoenix." She wrinkles her nose as she watches me rub the back of my arm. "Sorry. I didn't mean to scare you." She offers me her hand, and I stare at it as if she's trying to get me to engage in some strange foreign custom. "How have you been?"

I shove my hands into my pants pockets and ignore her hand. "How did you get in here?"

She gives a coy smile. "I have skills, remember?"

Right. How could I forget?

She lifts her palms. "No hug?"

I arch a brow and try to keep my cool, but my stomach is in knots. "I don't hug people who break into my home."

"I guess I deserve that." Her eyes are all over me, studying my face, then my hair, then my jacket and black skirt, even down to my shoes, as if she's cataloguing it all. She probably is. And she probably searched my house before I got home and helped herself to anything of value she could use.

But there's not a damn thing in this house I care

about as much as the girl in front of me.

I cross my arms and rub the goose bumps covering my flesh. "Why are you here?"

She turns away and studies her reflection in the mirror that hangs in my foyer. "I heard Mom on the phone with you, and I thought you might need help. I would have come sooner, but I couldn't get away. You were asking about Patrick?"

I nod. "Do you know where he is?"

"He's not a good man, Phoenix," she says softly.

"I know that."

"Then why do you want to find him?" She drops her voice lower, and I can barely hear. "If you choose to be with him, they'll never let you come back."

I squeeze my eyes shut, because my baby sister somehow still believes that the worst thing that could happen to me is to not be allowed back to the commune. "You're the only one who wants me back there, Amy. Even if I *did* want to go back, I wouldn't be welcome."

"They don't know you were planning to run away," she says. "Vicar Jeremiah thinks you left because of what Patrick did. He blames Patrick for all of it."

"Someone started a fire in my yard," I say. "It was in the shape of Thurisaz. You wouldn't know anything about that, would you?"

She frowns, and the skin between her brows puckers just like Mom's always did when I was proving to be a difficult child. "Phee Phee," she says, and it's been so many years since I heard that nickname that it tugs painfully at my heart. "Why didn't you tell me right away?"

Once, after Kent proposed, I tracked down Amy in Camelot. My full heart made me foolishly optimistic. I wanted my sister to know that I was happy—and I wanted her to be happy too. On the outside. With me. I promised her a college education, a home, anything she needed or wanted if she would leave Camelot and live with me. She declined.

She looks out my window, taking in the charred grass in my front yard. "It's not safe out here."

"Safer than it is *inside*."

"That's what *they* want you to believe. Can't you see that?"

You've been brainwashed—the ironic anthem of the brainwashed. "Tell me you're here because you've reconsidered my offer."

"No." The word is a knife plunged into my chest. "Camelot is my home. God is good to keep me there."

Plunge the knife. Twist the blade. My lungs don't want to work, but I force them to take enough air so I can speak. "Then you need to leave my house. Now."

"I know you still care. You wouldn't have decided to live so close to Camelot if you didn't."

"I'm here to be close if you needed me, not because I plan to come back. I want nothing to do with that place." I open the front door and point toward the street. "Get out now, or I'll call the cops."

She studies me for a beat, and it takes almost more will than I have to stand strong.

Once, Amy and I were as close as could be. The late-night whispers, the comfort of someone who sees your soul as it is and believes it's perfect. There were nights in my first months away that I thought it might be worth going back just so I could be with my sister.

Once, she was the one I trusted with all my secrets. Now she's simply the one who knows them.

"Okay then," she says. She steps onto the porch, and I start to shut the door, but she stops it with her hand before I can close it all the way. "I wish you'd come home."

"I am home."

"Is that so?" She scans me again, then the empty rooms behind me, and this time she doesn't bother keeping the disdain from her face. "Then where's your family?"

Thirteen years ago . . .

The birds are singing and the air thick with morning dew. I sit on the porch of our cabin and try to lose myself in an Anne Rice novel.

The porch steps creak and I see Patrick approaching in my peripheral vision, but I keep my nose buried in my book. I'm too embarrassed to look at him. Embarrassed and hurt and *pissed.* I may be inexperienced, but I know I didn't deserve to be treated like that, and I may be living here with these people and their twisted ideas of right and wrong, but I know that sex isn't dirty. Yet he made me feel like it was. Like *I* was.

I spent half my evening in the shower house, the spray never hot enough, only coming out when one of the girls threatened to tell Vicar Jeremiah that I was doing "something filthy" inside.

But the only thing I'd been doing was trying to wash off my heartbreak and scrub away the grime Patrick's words had left on my soul.

"I'm here to apologize. I'm so sorry," he whispers. I look up, despite myself, and he's standing next to my chair, his eyes on the ground, his shoulders slumped. Even beaten down and dejected, he's the most beautiful thing I've ever seen. "Do you hate me?"

"I should." I look around me, worried someone might overhear our conversation, but we're alone.

"I never meant . . ." He lifts his gaze to my face, and his eyes are brimming with agony. "I shouldn't have taken you out there. That was my fault. I know what my weaknesses are." He drops his gaze again. "I know *who* they are."

"I don't want to have this conversation." I close my book and stand, but he grabs my wrist before I can get away.

"Please listen to me."

"Why?"

"Because I need your forgiveness. I need you. But you don't understand this world. It's not like the outside. What I did . . . what *we* did . . . I could get exiled."

I close my mouth to trap the words I know he won't

want to hear. Exile would be the best thing that ever happened to Patrick. Maybe then he could have a normal life. But I can't expect him to understand that. I'm new here, and even I'm struggling with that truth. Because following it to its logical end would mean leaving my mother and sister.

"I didn't have the right." His voice has dropped from a whisper to something even softer, and I step closer just so I don't miss his words. "I'll be the next vicar, but I'm nothing until I am."

"You aren't *nothing.*"

"I'm a kid who lives in a community that has *rules.* You weren't mine to take."

"What is that supposed to mean? No one is going to 'take' me, Patrick. I don't care what the traditions are here. I'm only here to make sure my mom and sister are okay. I'm not going to allow someone to *take* me. I'm never going to become one of you!"

I've thought it before. It was the silent promise I made myself when I moved here. We'd come because my mom wanted to. We'd come for the security. But I wouldn't ever be one of them. I promised this to myself, but it's the first time I've said it out loud, and his face pales.

"You didn't *take* me," I say. "I *gave* myself to you. And maybe it was pretty shitty and didn't go as I planned, but at least it was my choice. That's how I plan to live my life. *My* life. *My* choices."

"Lower your voice," he whispers. Then he turns on his heel and rushes away from me.

I wrap my arms around myself and wish hard that I

could believe my own speech. It's all a lie. What happened was a violation I wouldn't have allowed if given the choice. But pain is easier to bear when repackaged into lies that make us sound strong. And nothing about yesterday makes me feel strong.

CHAPTER TWELVE

Nix

"LOOKS LIKE IT'S JUST US single girls tonight," Krystal says as she slides into the booth across from me at Brady's. She tilts her neck from side to side, stretching it. "Liz thought she was going to be able to join us, but their wedding DJ canceled, so she's spending her Sunday evening interviewing a potential replacement."

I take a sip from my beer and frown. "Why do you look so sad?"

Krystal's eyes go distant. "All my little sisters are getting married, and I don't even have any prospects." She shakes her head. "It's stupid. I know. It's not that I'm not happy for them. I am. I want the best for them.

But *shit,* Nix, I'm jealous. I thought I'd have a minivan and a baby or two by now."

"Yeah," I say. "I understand that."

"I was engaged and was *so close* to having that life, but it wasn't quite mine. You know what I mean?" She drags a fingertip through the condensation on her glass. "What about you? Have you ever had anything serious?"

"I was engaged once too," I admit. I don't typically share that, but for some reason, sharing seems to be my new drug of choice. It makes me feel connected to my friends. Less soul-shakingly alone.

"Really? When? Tell me about him. What happened?"

"Med school," I begin. "His name was Kent."

"Hi, ladies!" Krystal and I turn to see Janelle standing at the end of our booth. "I feel pathetic asking, but can I join you?"

Krystal and I exchange a look. *Awkward.*

"Sure," I say before Krystal can come up with some excuse to blow her off. "The more, the merrier."

"Thank you!" She grins. "You don't know how much I need this. Hanna's my only real friend around here, and she can't drink with me, since she's knocked up again. What are you girls talking about?"

"Breakups," Krystal says, eyes shifting to me, then back to Janelle. "You have any good ones?"

Janelle sinks into her seat. "Plenty, but right now I'm kind of mourning the loss of my fling with Max Hallowell."

Krystal arches a brow. "It didn't work out? I'm sorry

to hear that." Her words are at odds with the glee she can hardly keep off her face.

"I've never ever dated a guy who's both sweet and sexy," Janelle says. "My ex-husband? Hot as hell, but definitely not sweet. My ex-boyfriend? Also not sweet and not all that hot once you get to know him. And my . . ." She frowns. "You know, before Max, I don't think I ever dated a sweet guy. Or at least not one who's sweet once he gets me into bed."

"Max got you into bed?" Krystal asks.

Janelle sighs dramatically. "No. He didn't even get me to second base. What a waste!"

"I thought you told Max you felt *sisterly* toward him?" Krystal says. When I gape at her, she says, "What? Max told Sam, who told Liz, who told me. These things get around."

Janelle slumps. "I just said that so he wouldn't feel guilty. I didn't want him to feel bad. I think . . ." She looks around the bar then leans over the table. "I think he's seeing someone else."

Krystal chokes on her beer, and I scowl at her. Her eyes are watering and she's barely biting back her smile. "That's interesting. Do you have any idea who it might be?"

Janelle looks to me. "You're friends with him, aren't you? Do you have any idea?"

Krystal coughs to cover her laugh.

"Maybe there isn't anyone else," I say. "He's a good dad. Maybe he just wants to focus on Claire."

"But she's about to leave for three weeks. What better time to have a fling?" Janelle leans back in the booth and squeezes her eyes shut. "I suck at men, you guys."

"I'm sure you don't," I say. "You're beautiful and smart and talented. Max is an idiot if he doesn't want you." Krystal's heel connects with my shin, and I yelp and shift my gaze to her. "It's *true*."

"Maybe it's not because Janelle isn't awesome," Krystal says, "but because he has *feelings* for this other woman."

"That doesn't mean he wouldn't be better off with *Janelle*," I say between my teeth.

"You're sweet," Janelle says, "but Krystal's right. He's hung up on somebody else. He said I deserved someone who'd sweep me off my feet, not a guy who only had half his heart. At the time I thought he was saying that he still hasn't gotten over Hanna, but I've been thinking about it, and I don't think he was talking about Hanna. I've seen them together. He's moved on. He's not in love with her anymore. I wouldn't have made my move if I thought he was still hung up on her. Trust me. I've been interested for a long time."

"So what you're saying," Krystal says, "is that some other woman has half of Max's heart."

Janelle shrugs. "Apparently. The lucky bitch."

Krystal snort-laughs at that, but I ignore her because my eyes are glued to the group of men who just walked in the door. Sam, Will, Cade, and Max make their way into the bar.

My eyes want to stay on Max, but it's Cade who's locked his eyes on me, Cade who's making his way to our booth.

"*Hello,*" Janelle says. "Krystal, let's get out of here. I think Nix has company. Oh, look! Liz made it."

Then, before I can protest, the girls hop out of the booth and hustle toward the pool tables, where Liz is wrapping her arms around Sam and probably whispering something dirty in his ear.

Krystal winks at me from across the bar as Cade slides into the booth across from me.

He tilts his head to one side. "So why didn't you tell me that you and Hallowell aren't an item?"

"Um . . ." *What?*

His gaze flicks to the bar, where Max is sipping on a beer, still completely oblivious or ambivalent to my presence. The girls, however, have edged their way back toward the booth.

"I would have asked you out last night, but I was under the impression you were taken."

"I'm . . . not taken."

He grins. "Neither am I."

A few months ago, I would have killed for a fling with a guy like Cade. But now I'm all screwed up. "I'm not taken but not sure I'm looking either," I say. "But I think Janelle Crane is."

"The actress?" He shakes his head and shudders. "I'm sure she's sweet, but I can't fucking stand Hollywood types." The side of his mouth hitches up into a grin. "I prefer insanely intelligent, down-to-earth women."

My cheeks are blazing because he's totally flirting with me, and I don't flirt. It's not a skill I ever mastered. Hell, it's hardly a skill I ever attempted. So I do what any socially awkward woman would do when confronted with a sexy man coming on to her—I take the beer I've been nursing all night and down half of it.

He leans his back in the booth, watching me, and his shirt stretches across his chest, outlining his pecs.

Though I usually consider myself a strong woman, I have a bit of a weakness when it comes to man-muscle. I have to give him credit: Cade has quite a bit. Add to that the midnight-black hair and intense brown eyes, and he's really quite a package.

When I realize I'm staring and jerk my eyes back up to his, he's grinning. He totally caught me looking. How flipping embarrassing.

"Can I take you out some time, Nix?" His voice is all rumbly and low so no one else can hear. "I'd like a chance to get to know you without all the curious eyes on us." He cuts his eyes to our friends around the nearest pool tables, and I follow his gaze to see Sam and Liz watching us with unabashed interest.

I clear my throat. "I think . . . maybe . . ." *Now* Max is looking my way. Max, who likes *me* of all people and could do so much better. Maybe if I went out with Cade, Max would give Janelle the chance she deserves—the chance *he* deserves with someone like her. Maybe if I went out with Cade, I'd stop wanting something I've already decided I can't have. "That'd be nice, Cade."

"Yeah?"

"Yeah."

"I'm off-duty on Wednesday. Does that work for you? I'll pick you up at your place at, say, six?"

"Okay."

"I'll look forward to it." He grins, straightens, and climbs out of the booth. He takes a couple of steps, then reverses and dips his head to my ear. "Just so you know, you totally made my fucking night."

I watch him go, my cheeks burning with embarrassment, and when I tear my eyes off him I find that Liz and Sam are still staring at me. Sam's brows are lifted in surprise, but Liz looks almost disappointed.

Living in New Hope is like that. On the one hand, it's a tight-knit community, and there's always someone looking out for you. On the other hand, it's a *tight-knit community,* and there's always someone in your business. Can't have one without the other, I suppose. Privacy is pretty much a memory, and that would scare the shit out of me if I didn't already feel this town rooted into my soul.

So if getting Liz as a friend means I also have to suffer her disapproval when I don't pursue something with Max, so be it. I've suffered worse. I'm going out with Cade whether she likes it or not. I have my reasons.

Max

"Are you going to get over there and make your

move?" Sam asks. "Or are you just gonna sit back and watch Cade steal your woman?"

When I turn toward the booth where Nix is sitting, Cade's already headed our way, the grin on his face making it clear that he's planning on making his move on Nix. Or that he already made it. "Today is shit," I mutter.

Will claps me on the back. "If you want to drink faster, I can get you another beer. You've earned it."

I shake my head. I spent my morning with my little girl and then sent Claire with her mom. It's tempting to drown my sorrows, but I have no intention of getting drunk—not if there's any chance I might get to spend my night with Nix again. Taking a breath, I put down my beer and head over to my best chance of salvaging my day from hell. "Could you come outside with me for a minute? I need to show you something."

"Sure." She hops out of the booth, and I'm almost disappointed to see she's not wearing the Daisy Dukes she seems to favor in this miserable late summer heat.

When the parking lot gravel is crunching under our feet and we have nothing but the streetlamps for company, I pull the spare key from my pocket and put it in her hand.

"What's this?" she asks.

"It's the key to my front door. There's no reason you need to stay alone. Any time you're scared, I want you to know you're welcome."

She studies it for a beat before lifting her eyes to mine. "You don't have to do this."

I shrug. "I have the room. And I'm glad to have you.

You're welcome, even if you don't know until you go home that you don't want to stay there, and even if you want the bed to yourself this time. There's no reason for you to stay alone when you're scared." *And you can tell me what has you so freaked out so I can deal with it.* But I leave the last unspoken.

She studies me for a minute. "Oh, shit. Claire left today, didn't she? That's why you look like that."

I frown. "Look like what exactly?"

"Like someone just stole your organs for the black market and didn't bother leaving you with even *one* of your kidneys."

I have to laugh. "Yeah, that's probably the best description I've heard yet of how this feels."

She bites back a smile. "Thank you for the key. It means a lot to me, and just so we're clear, so do you."

I reach out and skim my thumb along her jaw, but she shakes her head and steps away from my touch.

"You're a great friend, Max, and I need as many of those as I can get right now."

"Understood," I say softly. But she makes a liar out of me as soon as I say the word, because she rises onto her toes and presses her lips to mine in a kiss that should be the definition of chaste but feels anything but. I don't understand at all.

PLAYING WITH FIRE

Nix

I used his key.

I got home from Brady's and checked on Marmalade, then put on my PJs, and decided there was no way I was sleeping alone tonight. So I used the key.

I slide into bed with him and he rolls toward me. "Nix?"

"Yeah," I whisper into the darkness.

He sits up and clicks on the bedside lamp. "Is everything okay?"

Oh, God, I'm ridiculous. Wasn't I the one who gave him the "we're just friends" speech? And now I'm making a surprise visit to his bed. *Awkward.*

I sit up next to him, my body twisted sideways, my shoulder leaning into the headboard. "You didn't want to let her leave. You think it's good for her to spend the time with her mom, and you don't want to stand in the way of that relationship, but having her taken so far from you for three weeks is killing you." I'm rambling, so I stop and take a breath, before trying a second time to explain why I climbed into his bed. I mentally processed this justification just moments before I opened his door. This is about more than selfishly wanting to sleep in his arms. "When I had a bad day, you made me feel better by sleeping next to me and reminding me I'm not alone. I wanted to return the favor. But I can leave if you'd rather have your privacy."

"So you're not here to console me with really great sex?"

I bite back a smile. "Afraid not."

"And you don't need me to console *you* with really great sex?"

"You don't struggle with confidence in that area, do you?"

His lips twitch. "Would you prefer I be some insecure man begging you to reassure me that your lack of interest isn't a reflection on my skills between the sheets?"

I feel my eyes go wide. "You think I don't want to have sex with you because I didn't *like* it?"

He chuckles. "No, I really didn't think that at all. You didn't leave much room for interpretation in the 'whether or not you liked it' department."

"Would you rather not know?" I smack him in the stomach with the back of my hand, and he lets out a light "oomph" as he chuckles.

"I didn't say that. I liked listening to you. Liked it a whole hell of a lot." He tucks a lock of hair behind my ear, and his smile slowly falls away. "But I'm not such a Neanderthal that I think a woman's choice of whether or not to sleep with a man is as simple as whether or not she thinks she'll enjoy it."

"That's good," I whisper.

"But I'm also not such a Neanderthal that fucking is the only way I can enjoy myself with a woman." His fingers slip from behind my ear and slowly down my neck. "I liked sleeping with you in my arms last night, and you're right, I had a shit-tastic day, and having you here makes it better." He swallows. "I was hoping you'd come."

I want to say that I'm glad and sink into the blankets to fall asleep, but his fingers are still doing magical things that have turned my neck into a highly erogenous zone, and I don't want to do anything that's going to make him stop.

His fingertips skim over the pulse point at my neck, and his eyes dip to study that spot. "Is it okay if I kiss you now?"

There are so many reasons that's a bad idea, but when I open my mouth to tell him that, I say, "Yeah," and then he's lowering his mouth to mine and his lips are so soft and gentle and warm that I'm glad my lips are little sluts who can't resist Max's special brand of sexy.

He sweeps his tongue across my mouth, and that hot, wet contact makes me moan. I tilt my head to the side and open my mouth under his, and he kisses me fully.

What I love about Max's kisses is that they're all different. With some guys, every kiss is the same, every move done by rote. But Max seems to have a kiss for every occasion. There were the frantic, gotta-have-you-now kisses of our first night together, then there were the tender kisses after, and this one is something else altogether. It's long and deep and intense without asking for anything at all. His mouth is on mine and his hand is on my neck, but even though we're in his bed together, that's it. He doesn't pull me down and roll on top of me. He doesn't try to cop a feel. He just kisses me until my mind is fuzzy and my lips are tingling.

When he pulls away, I'm breathing hard and ready for more. I'd take the frantic kiss now, or the playful one, even. Anything that keeps his lips on mine.

"I know you have a lot going on, Phoenix Reid, and I know you haven't shared half of it with me *or* your posse, but I'm here when you need someone. I hope you know you can trust me."

"Why do you think I'll need someone?" I ask.

"Everyone needs someone. Some of us are just better at lying to ourselves than others." Then he clicks off the light and sinks into bed. When I roll to my side, he wraps his arm around my waist and pulls my back against his front. "Is this okay?" he murmurs in my ear.

No. It's not okay. It makes me want things I've already decided I can't have. "It's okay with me. Is it okay with you?"

He groans and presses a quick kiss to my neck. "Let's go to sleep now. Before I forget what I said about not being a Neanderthal."

That makes me smile despite myself. I take his hand from my waist and guide it just under the hem of my shirt but below my scars so I have the heat of his skin against my belly. "Sweet dreams."

"With you in my arms?" He grunts. "You bet your ass."

CHAPTER THIRTEEN

Max

When I open my eyes, she's in my arms, all warmth and softness, her sweet smell filling my head, her breathing the slow and measured rhythm of sleep.

The clock reads six a.m. Not so long ago, I would have been at the club by now, would have opened the doors for the five o'clock crowd and been starting into a fifteen-hour day. Thank Christ things have changed since then. Now, I mostly manage the business side of the club and train a select few clients who've been with me from the beginning. Back then, I did it all—the business side, the training, the cleaning, the marketing, and the endless budgeting to bring it all together.

Things are different now. I have Claire. I have the house. And right now I have Nix in my arms.

We slept like this all night, in a position that was both intimate and innocent, but there was nothing innocent about my dreams. I dreamed of touching her, tasting her, getting her to let go of whatever fear it is that makes her pull away from me.

I'm not sure what we're doing here, but I know that slow is what she needs. Hell, maybe it's what I need too. Regardless, I'm willing to roll with it and see where it takes us.

She shifts in my arms, stretching in the dance of the well rested waking with nowhere to go.

"For an insomniac," I say, "you sleep like the dead."

She sighs heavily and shifts to face me. "How long did we sleep?" She looks at the clock then back to me. "Almost six hours? I rarely manage more than three in a stretch. You're magical."

My arms tighten around her. "Happy to help."

"You know, you could sell your services. Go around holding sleepless women so they can relax enough to rest."

"Hmm. I'll remember that if things don't work out at the gym." I want to drop a kiss to her lips—quick or slow, I'd take either—then roll onto her and kiss my way down her body. I settle for brushing her hair out of her face and looking into those emerald eyes.

"I forgot what this was like," she says.

"What's that? Sleeping?"

She laughs. "For starters."

I trail my fingertips down her neck, and her eyes

155

close softly, her dark lashes resting against her cheek.

"Being held all night. Waking up in the arms of someone you care about."

Someone you care about. I take that, wrap it tight, and put it away to examine later. "When was the last time you had that?"

"His name was Kent. We met in medical school."

I hold my breath, hoping she'll share more, desperate for a window into the soul of the woman who somehow grabbed a hold of mine.

"He was charming and self-assured. He made me laugh like I hadn't in years."

I hold her gaze, and the hand at her neck drifts lower, tracing the peaks and valleys of her collarbone. "Was he in med school too?"

"He was a trauma surgeon, about ten years older than me. Medical school destroys more romances than it creates, and I wasn't looking to get involved with anyone. It was all about the goal and having tunnel vision until I reached it. But Kent was . . ." She shrugs and seems to search for the words. "He wasn't something else on the to-do list. He was my reprieve. He didn't really have a family either—was raised by a single mother who'd passed away while he was in college. I fell hard and fast, and two years later we were engaged."

"And he was the one who held you while you slept," I say softly.

"You know, a lot of men can't stand to listen to a woman talk about how great another guy was."

I shrug and shift my weight onto my elbow so I can

continue my exploration down her body, between her breasts but over her tank top. "He couldn't be that great if he let you go."

A shadow passes over her face, and she turns her eyes from mine. "He was amazing. *I* was the problem."

"Nix . . ." I take her chin in my hand and gently tilt it until her eyes meet mine again. I want to understand everything she's not saying, but if eyes are windows to the soul, hers have blackout shades. She's giving away nothing. "Was Kent attractive? How'd you put it? Pretty on the outside, ugly on the inside?"

She shakes her head. "Not in conventional terms. He was beautiful because he was kind. But he wasn't beautiful in all the ways you are."

The rest of my questions dissolve on my tongue as she lifts a hand to my chest and runs it across my pecs and down until she's scraping her nails over my abs.

"Kent didn't leave me because he was a jerk," she whispers. "He left because *I'm* screwed up. And I still am. I'm smart enough to know that, but I don't know if I can resist this."

"This?"

"You and me. We're playing with fire here."

Her touch is killing me, so I do what I've wanted to do since I woke up with her in my arms. I kiss her.

The second my lips touch hers, she moans and slides her fingers under my waistband until they're brushing the tip of my cock. My whole body shudders as I fight the urge to push into her touch, to get her hand wrapped around me. She arches her back and opens her mouth under mine, and my tongue sweeps in to rub hers as she takes me in her grip.

Holy fuck, that's good.

I break the kiss and touch my forehead to hers, fighting for control. She's stroking me, her grip tight, as if she needs this as much as I do.

"What happens if we don't stop, Nix?"

Her hand stills and she squeezes her eyes shut. "I imagine we'd have sex again, and then I'd spend the rest of my day feeling guilty for letting my libido drag you into my mess of a life."

I swallow. Hard. And pull her hand from my shorts. I should get a fucking medal for overruling my cock on this. I press a kiss to the back of her hand. "Then let's not. Next time I'm inside you—and there will be a next time, Nix. With you and me it's inevitable—I won't have you feeling guilty after. Maybe sore, maybe exhausted, but not fucking guilty."

She draws in a ragged breath.

"And for the record," I whisper, "I'm already in your life and you didn't drag me here. I'm in it because I choose to be."

Nix
Thirteen years ago . . .

The click of my bedroom door closing yanks my attention from my book.

"You haven't been around much," Patrick says.

Since what happened in the honeymoon cabin, I've done the majority of my living in the pages of books and as little as possible in my own world. Luckily, no one seems to mind my reading habits as long as I do my chores, show up for worship every evening, and complete my requisite "supply runs"—a.k.a. burglaries. You see, the rich are worshipping a false god in their wealth, so says Vicar Jeremiah, and this justifies his disciples stealing what they need. Whatever. I did as much from time to time before moving here. Everyone has morals until they have an empty belly.

I frown as Patrick sits on the edge of my bed. "Should you be here?" Mom and Amy are across the camp learning quilting from one of the vicar's wives, so Patrick and I are literally alone behind closed doors, and I'm not sure that's a good idea.

"I've been praying about what happened in the honeymoon cottage. Every moment I'm awake, I set my mind to it. Praying. Asking for forgiveness. Promising God I'll do whatever it takes to repent."

I close my eyes. It's not like he's tarnishing a beautiful experience for me—it was more traumatic than beautiful—but it still hurts, and his remorse is only another reminder on top of the hundreds I get every day that I don't belong here.

"I asked Him for a sign," he says. He lifts his eyes to mine, and the pain in them makes my heart hurt for him. "Because every moment I'm not praying, I'm thinking about touching you again."

I fold my arms over my chest. "Patrick . . ."

"I asked God for a sign. I asked him to tell me which path I'm supposed to take, which way I'm supposed to go, and when I opened my eyes, the camp was covered in clouds, but a single beam of sunlight shone down onto your cabin." He shakes his head. "I thought you were Satan's temptation when all this time you've been God's gift. I should have known before. That's why He saved you from the fire. For me."

He holds my face in his hands, and I'm so horribly lonely that I welcome his lips touching mine. When he climbs on top of me, I spread my thighs to take him. He's gentler this time, and when he leaves, he's smiling instead of angry, but I'm just confused.

I still don't want to be here, and even if Patrick believes our intimacy is God's will, I know the others won't see it that way. What we're doing is dangerous, but in a life where I've been starved for attention, I'll take any scraps I can get. Even if they're tainted by guilt and fear.

CHAPTER FOURTEEN

Nix

I LIKE TO TELL MYSELF that staying at Max's house is as good for him as it is for me, that I'm doing my part to keep him company until Claire comes home. But the truth is, I'm terrified to sleep in my house alone. If Patrick got in once, he can get in again.

I don't understand, though. If he wants to hurt me, why hasn't he done it? If he wants revenge . . .

My stomach clenches. *Don't think about it.*

I have ulterior motives for going out with Cade on Wednesday. I need him to get me some answers, and I think he might be able to. I'm counting on it.

When I get to Max's house after work, Amy is

waiting for me on his front porch.

"What are you doing here?"

"Visiting."

I'm surprised she didn't let herself in—she could have, I don't doubt it—but I'm guessing she wants to stay off Max's radar. I'd prefer she did too.

I nod toward my house, and she follows me over, silent as I unlock the door and disable the alarm.

She follows me into the kitchen, her face a mask of uncertainty. I don't know what she's after, but I do know how much trouble she'd be in if they found out she was here. She'd disagree. She's always tried to convince me I'd be welcomed back to Camelot, and she might believe Vicar Jeremiah would forgive her visit to the outside if I were the reason.

"Are you hungry?" It's really a rhetorical question. I hate that I sent her away last time she was here. This time I'll feed her and listen, even if hearing her brainwashed speeches breaks my heart.

"I could eat."

I open the cabinet and start pulling out ingredients for pasta. She's skinnier than I remember, her face gaunt, her arms as thin as twigs, and I want to feed her but I also want something to busy my hands with while she talks.

"The vicar's preparing to choose a new wife," she says. "It might be me."

My stomach twists in disgust. "Oh." The idea of my little sister marrying that old man . . .

"I *hope* it's me. This is all I've wanted since I first visited Camelot." She toys with the stack of napkins on the table and her eyes flick to mine. "Do you ever think about what life would have been like if you hadn't run away?" I still at the question, but Amy goes on. "Maybe we would both be wives to the Chosen One."

I drop the box of spaghetti and watch it spill all over the floor.

I grab a dustpan, stoop to sweep it up, and dump it into the trashcan before turning to look at her. "Why are you visiting me like this? What do you really want?"

"What's it like? Living on the outside?"

Normal, I want to say, but Amy's probably forgotten what normal is. She was ten when we moved to Camelot. "What part?"

"You were engaged to that doctor and planning a big wedding. What was that like?"

"Someone told him what happened at Camelot, and he called it off and left me. It sucked." I drop my shoulders. I'm being defensive. "Why do you want to know about life on the outside?"

She stares at me a long time, then shrugs. "I want to know what's so great that it's worth abandoning your family."

I rush around the counter to wrap her in my arms because I hear the pain in her words. That was why I stayed in Camelot as long as I did. I never wanted to leave my sister. "When I left," I say, smoothing her hair, "I wanted to take you with me. I would have if there had been any way."

"I don't understand why you want me to leave so badly. It's not like you're happy. I might understand if you *liked* your life."

I drop my arms and step back. "I love my life."

She arches a brow. "If you say so, but I think I'd take sharing my husband over sixty-hour work weeks and living alone in a big house."

"It's not the polygamy that bothers me, Amy."

"And it's not that you live alone that bothers me," she says. "Have you ever even stopped to ask yourself if this life makes you happy? Because to me it looks like you're so busy running from your old life you've never bothered to consider if this is the one you want."

Max

Thurisaz.

I stare at the picture of the rune on my computer screen and frown. Stuck doing paperwork at the club, I thought I'd go all Sherlock Holmes with what's happening with Phoenix. But either I suck at this or I don't have enough clues.

Although I know way more about runes now than I did before my Internet research twenty minutes ago, I still don't understand. Thurisaz is the name of the rune symbol that was burning in her yard last week, and unless there's more that she's not telling me, it's the reason she's still staying at my house five days later.

I read several websites and they all explained that the symbol is like a thorn. Many people believe it to be something sharp, grim, or evil, but it is a positive symbol in the sense that it's about combining wisdom with the need to use brute force. It's also a fertility rune or can reference technology, or some such shit.

I'm no closer to figuring out what she was afraid of than I was before my little online investigation. None of that seems particularly threatening, but Nix feels threatened. Aside from those first two nights, we've slept in separate beds. I keep waiting for the night she goes to her own house, and the fact that she stays at mine even while trying to keep distance between us tells me that she's terrified of something.

A knock sounds at my door.

"Come in."

The door cracks and Hanna Thompson pokes her head in. "I was hoping we could talk."

"Sure."

She closes the door behind her and sinks into the chair on the opposite side of my desk.

Not so long ago, Hanna showing up to talk to me in my office would have screwed me up for days. Her closing the door would have made it weeks. There would have been part of me that prayed she was there to reconcile. Even after she chose Nate, even after she had his twins and put on his ring, I carried around hope that she might come back to me.

Or I *thought* it was hope. But hope should be light and airy. It should lift you up and make your burdens lighter. What I carried for months after Hanna left me wasn't like that. It was heavy and burdensome. It wore me down and made everything harder.

I'm fucking grateful that's passed.

Nix played a part in that. I mean, I was getting there and I would have been okay, but that day in her garage was a huge milestone for me. She wasn't just the first woman I'd slept with since Hanna, she was the only woman who'd wiped the last thoughts of Hanna out of the back of my mind. Since our early morning groping session, Nix has been sleeping in my guestroom and dodging any and all physical contact with me, and though that's a far cry from a relationship, it does more for me than any date I've been on since Hanna and I broke it off.

"What can I do for you?" I ask Hanna.

"I don't know exactly." She gives a tentative smile and drops her gaze to her lap. "You deserve to be happy, you know. I hope my friendship with Nix doesn't make this weird for you. I hope that's not why you two aren't . . ."

"Aren't what?"

She shrugs. "I don't know. More?"

I release a puff of air. "Hanna, and I mean no offense when I say this, but what's happening between me and Nix isn't about you. Not at all."

She flinches. "Okay then."

Sighing, I drag a hand over my face. "I'm sorry. I'm not trying to be a dick."

She shakes her head. "You're not. That was completely self-absorbed, and *I'm* sorry."

I nod and lean back in my chair. "It was a reasonable question. I'm sorry I snapped at you."

"You didn't." When she smiles, I catch myself

bracing for that rip-your-guts-out feeling, but it doesn't come.

"You're happy," I say softly.

"I'm sleep-deprived and run ragged. Morning sickness is a bitch this time around, and our twins are into everything, and my stepson is going through a phase where he thinks he doesn't need to listen to me." She shrugs. "But yeah. Life is good. I'm happy." Then her smile fades and her big brown eyes go sad. "What about you?"

"I'm working on it," I say. "The upside of all this stuff with Nix is that it distracts me from missing Claire."

"I guess I don't understand. If *I'm* not the problem . . ."

I lift my hands, palms up.

"So are you two . . .?" She doesn't have to finish for me to hear the question in her words.

"I don't know." I fold my hands behind my head and stare at the ceiling. "It's like she's using one hand to keep me close and the other to push me away. She won't date me, but then she crawls into my bed."

Hanna's eyes go wide. "You're sleeping together?"

"Not like that." I've said too much. I turn my chair and look out the window.

"You're sleeping together *platonically*? Like brother and sister?"

I turn back to Hanna, and I'm sure she can see the truth in my eyes, but I say the words anyway. "There is nothing brotherly about the way I feel about Nix being in my bed."

Hanna leans back in her chair. "Wow. Okay then."

"Why do I always want the girl who doesn't want me, Hanna? That seems pretty fucked up to me."

"Hmm . . . are you *sure* Nix doesn't want you?"

A smile tugs at my lips. "Sometimes she lets me kiss her." Maybe Hanna's a weird choice, but I've been so stuck in my own head where Nix is concerned, and it's nice to have someone to talk to. "I know she's attracted to me. Hell, the way she looks at me when she thinks I'm not paying attention makes that much clear. But being attracted to someone isn't the same as wanting to be with them, and she's definitely made up her mind about not wanting to be with me."

"I'm not so sure about that," Hanna says, biting back a grin.

I study the symbol on my computer screen. "Do you know much about her past?"

The humor falls from Hanna's face. "You know, I really don't. She doesn't talk about it, not like the rest of us. She's private."

That's an understatement. "She's fighting some demons. Maybe I need to give her some space."

Hanna nods. "Or maybe you fight them right alongside her."

CHAPTER FIFTEEN

Nix

I'M SITTING AT A TABLE with a handsome man, an expensive meal, and a damn fine glass of wine.

Truth be told, I expected Cade would cancel. I mean, I'm just starting to wrap my brain around Max's interest in me, and it's weird to think that two ridiculously handsome men want to take me out.

"Thanks for agreeing to come out with me tonight," Cade says, his dark eyes studying me.

I shift awkwardly in my seat and take a fortifying sip of my wine. "I have a confession to make."

Cade arches a brow. "A confession? Should I be prepared to Mirandize you?"

I feel the blood drain from my face and my stomach

pitch into a free fall before I realize he's joking. Man, am I screwed up. "No, not that kind of confession."

"Oh, good. Because it's kind of a killjoy when I have to arrest my dates."

Laughing, I shake my head. "No, I wanted to tell you that I'm not looking for a relationship. I just don't want you hurt if you're thinking this date might be the start of something serious."

He leans back in his chair. "I'm pretty sure that's my line."

"Sorry." I take another gulp of wine and my cheeks heat. "No one shared the script with me."

"Is that what's going on with you and Hallowell? He wants something serious, and you don't?"

"Nothing is going on with me and Max. We're friends." *Friends who sometimes share a bed. And sometimes kiss. And sometimes more.* Oh hell, I don't know whom I'm trying to convince anymore.

Cade leans forward and rests his elbows on the edge of the table. The way he studies me is almost unnerving. "Can I ask you a question?"

"Sure."

"If you're not interested in a relationship, why did you agree to come out with me? You don't strike me as the kind of girl looking for the random hookup."

"I'm not!" *Except that time with Max.*

"You wanted to send a message to Hallowell, and I was as good a way to do that as any?"

I grimace. Spelled out like that, it sounds terrible. "It's not just that."

"But that's part of it."

I shift my gaze to the other side of the restaurant. There aren't many ritzy restaurants in New Hope, but Lenore's certainly qualifies. Crisp white linen tablecloths, servers who pull out your chair, and a wine selection to die for.

The place reminds me of a former life. Kent used to treat me to dinners like this one. He loved to feed me, loved to talk about wine and teach me how to distinguish one from another. He also loved fancy craft beer and ridiculously expensive cigars.

For two years, I lived that life. Then he found out about my past.

That's why I'm afraid to let anything happen with Max. I know how much it hurts to make a life with someone and have it taken away. And yet I'm still sleeping there, allowing our connection to strengthen when I know nothing good can come of it. When Cade asked me out, a big part of me *was* interested in sending Max the message that I wasn't available. Now I'm not sure that's a message I want to send.

"I also agreed because I need your help, but I don't want my friends to know." *I don't want* Max *to know.* "I think I'm being stalked."

Cade straightens next to me, and I see it in his eyes the moment he stops being my date and becomes *Officer Watts.* "Tell me."

I take another long swallow from my wine. It's a crisp red that reminds me of Kent and makes my heart ache. "I don't know for sure," I say. "But I've had this feeling, and then the fire . . ."

Cade puts his hand over mine. It's warm and nice,

but it's not like the electric storm that Max's touch ignites. "How long have you had this 'feeling'?"

"A few months."

"Nix—"

"I thought it was in my head, that I was being paranoid."

"If your gut warns you you're being followed, then you need to listen. Tell me about when it started."

"A few months ago, I came home and was standing in my foyer when I thought I saw a reflection, but I turned around and he wasn't there. I looked all over the house, and no one else was there. And after that, when I'd walk alone at night or be alone in my house, I'd get this weird feeling."

"Why didn't you call the police?"

"Because I thought I was just imagining it." I shake my head. There's more behind my reluctance to get help. I'm trying to protect this life from my old one, and asking for help is as good as asking for someone to dig into my past—to bring the nightmare of it into this life. "Then I started getting these weird phone calls where I could hear someone breathing and it sounded like there was fire crackling in the background."

"Fire? Jesus, Nix. Did you get a number?"

I shake my head and set my cell phone on the table in front of him. "The number was always blocked. I don't know if they were using the same line they used for these texts or a different one."

Cade scans the brief exchange then lifts his eyes to mine. "Who the fuck is it, Nix? He talks like he knows you."

"I don't know who it is. I just know I'm afraid, and I think that's what he wants."

"But you think you know," he says. "That's why we're here. You think you know who's been following you, calling you, who lit that fire in your front yard and sent you these text messages." When I don't answer, he stares at me, his eyes hard. "I want to help you, but that's going to be a fuck of a lot easier if you tell me everything you've got, everything your *gut* has been telling you from the beginning. Who did you see in the mirror that day?"

"Patrick McCane." In the name, I hear the click of the chains, shackling me to my past. "He was my boyfriend when I was sixteen."

"What can you tell me about Patrick?" Cade asks.

"He was my first boyfriend. We were together less than a year but it was intense, and he was . . ." I take another sip of wine but stop myself before I drain the glass. I need my wits about me. "He didn't want to let me go."

"When was the last time he was in touch with you?"

"When I was in medical school. He sent me an email asking if I'd meet up with him. He wanted to talk to me."

"And what did you say?"

I shake my head. That email came at such a shitty time in my life, it didn't upset me half as much as it should have. "I didn't reply. I didn't want to talk to him."

"Do you still have that email message?"

"I don't even have the email address anymore."

"Tell me about your relationship with Patrick," he says.

I stare blankly. I decided I could get help without exposing everything, but maybe I was lying to myself.

"Did he hurt you, Nix?"

I rest my fingers over the scar on my ribs and nod. "I believed he loved me. Even at the end." I know how this sounds—like I'm a clichéd domestic violence victim recounting her lover's abuse. But it's true. Patrick loved me and he wanted to save me—up until the moment he accepted he couldn't have me. Then he snapped. He stopped trying to save me and tried to kill me.

"What's changed?" Cade asks. "Do you have any idea why he might be after you now?"

Because I'm happy, and he wants to punish me for that. But I won't open that can of worms, so I only say, "My birthday is coming." I make myself meet Cade's steady gaze. "I don't understand why this year might be different than the others, but it's only a few weeks away."

"Why is your birthday significant?"

"I left Patrick on my seventeenth birthday."

Cade squeezes my hand. "I'll help."

* * *

"Just drop me here," I say as Cade pulls in front of my house. "You don't have to get out."

He shakes his head. "Whatever your reasons for going on this date with me, it was still a date." He climbs out of the car and comes around to open my door before I've pushed it open. "And I fucking walk my dates to the door."

I swallow. I could go into my house and pretend that is where I'll sleep, but I fed Marmalade beforehand, and I don't have the energy to face those demons tonight. "Well, okay, but I'm staying at Max's."

He arches a brow. "At Max's? Is that so?"

"I told you I was afraid. And he offered."

"You could stay with me. I'm offering."

I roll my eyes. "I like this arrangement," I say. "I can check on my cat as often as I need to, and I get to stay close to home." *And close to Max.* Which I love, whether I should or not.

Cade's lips curl until his grin is what could only be described as shit eating. "Well then, I'll walk to you Hallowell's door."

"It's right there," I say, heading toward the door. "Not necessary."

Cade matches me stride for stride. "Maybe not, but if you're interested in using me to send him the message to back off, let's take advantage of this moment."

I come to a dead stop in the middle of the lawn. "You make it sound like Max is my creepy stalker. He's not something bad I'm trying to shake off. I just don't want him tangled up in my mess."

"And yet you're sleeping at his house." He cocks his head. "Can I ask you a question?"

"I guess."

"If it weren't for this 'mess,' as you call it, would you have been out with Max tonight instead of me?"

"What-ifs are nothing but a masochistic waste of energy." I head for the door and say a silent prayer that Max will be out with the guys.

"Hey, Cade," Max calls as he steps out onto his front porch. "What are you doing here?"

Couldn't be so lucky.

Cade grins at me then looks to Max. "Nix and I had dinner at Lenore's. I was just walking her to the door."

The smile falls from Max's face and he stiffens. *Shit.*

Cade climbs the porch steps with me then squeezes my hand. "I guess I won't push my luck and ask for a kiss," he says.

It's all I can do to keep my eyes off Max. "Good plan."

"I'll call you," Cade says. He winks, then jogs down the steps and back to his car.

Avoiding Max's eyes, I make a beeline for the door and go straight to the spare room.

"Nix," he calls behind me, the door thumping as he throws it closed.

"Yeah?" I gather my pajamas. It's late, and I have early rounds at the hospital. I'm going to take a shower, climb in bed, and pray for a couple of hours of uninterrupted shuteye. But when I turn toward the hall, Max is filling the doorway.

"You went on a date with Cade?"

I shrug. "He took me to dinner. It was no big deal."

"And he's going to call you?"

Another shrug. "He's a nice guy, but it's not anything serious. I'm not interested in serious." I duck under his arm and into the hallway, but before I even make it a step in the direction of the bathroom, Max has me in his arms, his mouth coming down on mine.

The kiss starts angry but softens as quickly as it began, and because I'm helpless against this man, I soften too, opening under him and reveling in the feel of him invading my mouth. Every sweep of his tongue sends another thousand nerve endings sizzling, and his touch is so electric it's a wonder I don't combust under it.

When he pulls away, his eyes aren't warm like they usually are when he's been kissing me. They're hot, burning with the dangerous cocktail of arousal and frustration. "You come alive when I touch you, but turn away every time I try to step closer. You sleep in my bed but shut down every time I ask about your past. You've never let me take you out, but fucking Cade gets to date you?"

I spin on my heel and start toward the guest bathroom, but Max grabs my wrist and stops me. It's not the strength of his grip that keeps me from moving forward—I could escape it. And it's not the anger in his question that has me wanting to run—I don't fear him. I stand trapped between the will of my heart and the warning in my brain. I steady my gaze on the dark hardwood floor. "What do you *want* from me?"

"What I *want*?" He steps closer, and when I look up his eyes are blazing. "I want to know why you're scared to let me close. I want to know what this could be if we gave it a chance. I want to know what you hide under your shirt and what keeps you awake when everyone else is sleeping. I want to know who hurt you and why you let *him* have your heart but you keep pushing me away."

But those are all the things I don't ever want you to know. "I wouldn't know where to start," I whisper.

"Start with Kent. What happened with him?"

I turn to face him and lift my chin. "He's the man I was supposed to marry, and when he learned the answer to all those questions you're asking now, he left me."

"Then he's a fool."

"You don't know where I come from."

"Try me."

I should. I should cut open my guts and spill them at his feet. Then he could send me away, and I wouldn't have to wait for that inevitable heartbreak anymore. But I'm a coward, so I drop my gaze to where his fingers hold my wrist and say, "Let me go."

Thirteen years ago . . .

"One, two, three, four, five, six, seven, eight. Onetwothreefourfivesixseveneight. Onetwothreefourfivesixseveneight. Onetwothreefourfivesixseveneight." I'm huddled in the corner of my bedroom, my calendar on my lap wet with tears. My hands haven't stopped shaking since I started counting. My vision blurs but I count again. "One, two, three, four, five, six, seven, eight. Please no. *Please.*"

Dropping the calendar to the floor, I wrap my arms around my legs and rock myself slowly, the number of weeks since my last period like a sick chant inside my head.

Onetwothreefourfivesixseveneight.
Onetwothreefourfivesixseveneight.
Onetwothreefourfivesixseveneight.

CHAPTER SIXTEEN

Nix

"CHAMPAGNE AND MASSAGE LESSONS." Liz hoists her glass of bubbly into the air with a grin. "Here's to the most brilliant business idea you've had all year, Cally."

We're all gathered at William Bailey's art gallery, where Cally just held a women-only class on the art of sensual massage. The idea was to teach them what to do and how to do it so they could go home and surprise their husbands, boyfriends, girlfriends, or what have you, and everyone seemed to love it.

William was happy to allow the women to use his gallery, which makes sense, since Cally's massage studio is located directly above it. Hanna provided the snacks from her bakery, and of course all the other Thompson sisters and I came to support her. I may have picked up a few ideas too.

Cally grins into her own glass of champagne and shakes her head. "I'm not sure how brilliant it is to teach women how to massage their lovers. This town isn't that big, and if I'm a decent teacher I'm at risk of losing clients."

William grunts. He only joined us once the event was over and has been dutifully putting away folding chairs and tables while the girls gab. "No offense to your lesson plan, Cal, but *sensual* massages rarely result in the *therapeutic* benefits of a visit with you."

Krystal giggles. "Truth. These ladies will spend ten minutes rubbing on their honeys and be ready for a different kind of action."

"There's nothing wrong with *that*," Maggie says. "Cally's doing a public service."

"Hey," Will says, "I'm not knocking it. I'm just saying Cally's client list isn't in any danger from nights like these. And anyway, she has a gift." He presses a kiss to her forehead and grins.

Damn. They're cute together. More than cute. Amazing. Perfect. Beautiful.

When I moved to New Hope, I didn't believe love like theirs was real. I thought it was a myth perpetuated by millions of people desperate to believe. Like kids who believe in Santa, despite all the evidence to the contrary.

But then I met all of these wonderful and unlikely couples with their wonderful and unlikely happy endings in this town where wonderful and unlikely things seem to happen every day.

I'm jerked from my thoughts when Liz blurts, "Sam wants to have a baby," and we all turn to gape at her.

"But you aren't even married yet," Hanna says.

"You had the twins before you were engaged to Nate," Liz says, "and you're the one who's already knocked up again."

Hanna throws up her hands. "You don't have to get defensive. I have no room to talk in terms of how things *should* be done. It's hard, Lizzy."

Cally shrugs. "She's right. It is hard. Not marriage, not really. That's the easy part. But trying to make time for that marriage when you're juggling midnight feedings and doctor appointments and your own career. You focus so much on the babies you forget that you also have a marriage that needs tending."

Lizzy's eyes go big. "Are you guys okay?"

Hanna and Cally look at each other and laugh.

"We're fine," Hanna says. "This is just real life and it's awesome in all its imperfection, but we want for you to enjoy yourselves as long as possible without kids."

"So we can live vicariously," Cally says, giggling.

"I'd like to see Sam with a baby," Will says. "Nothing more humbling than having a six-month-old who's in total control of you."

I busy myself by filling the sink to hand-wash the champagne glasses, and think *wonderful and unlikely.*

No matter how much I like Max, I can't count on the wonderful and unlikely. I don't just have imperfections.

I have secrets and scars. Ugly ones. And I can't even imagine a life where my biggest worry is whether to get pregnant on my wedding night or a year later.

The girls are emptying the bottle of champagne when Liz clears her throat. She looks to me, then Hanna, who looks to me and back to Liz.

Krystal snorts. "Just ask her."

"Ask me what?"

"We were wondering . . ." Hanna begins.

"If you're going to use your new skills on Max," Liz finishes.

Will coughs on his beer and holds up a hand. "I think that's my cue to exit this conversation."

He steps away, but Cally wraps her fingers around his wrist and yanks him back. "Don't you dare run away now, William Bailey. You're Max's best friend. We need your input."

Will arches a brow and it disappears under his mop of messy curls. "On massaging Max?"

Cally smacks him in the chest with the back of her hand. "On whether or not Nix should *seduce* him. You talk to him. What does he say about her?"

He cuts his eyes to me, and then looks back to his wife. "You girls do realize that guys don't sit around and share their feelings and fantasies with each other, right?"

"Sure they do," Liz says. "Just like girls get together and have pillow fights in our nighties. Now spill."

"No," I interrupt. "Please don't spill."

"Just tell us what you *do* know," Cally says, releasing his arm.

"No," I say at the same time as all the other girls shout, "Yes!"

Will groans and rubs the back of his neck. "Fine." He turns to me. "He's my best friend. I've known him all my life. He likes you, Nix, and he's been so focused on his daughter the last couple of years, I think he's forgotten what it's like to do anything completely for himself."

"See?" Liz screeches. "He *needs* your sweet lovin'."

Will shakes his head and drags a hand through his hair. "I knew I should have gotten out of here early."

Hanna narrows her eyes and studies me. "What's holding you back?"

"I have—" Ugh. There are too many eyes on me to have this conversation. "Baggage."

Cally and Will exchange a look, and she laughs. "I know a thing or two about baggage."

"I know." I smile politely. "Everyone has problems, right?"

Cally shakes her head. "Listen to me. You are not your past. You are bigger than your past and you are better than your past. Let it be part of who you've become, but don't you dare let it define you."

"Do you know what he's doing right now?" I ask. "He's building a tree house for his daughter."

"The asshole," Will mutters.

I scowl at him. "I'm saying he's the kind of guy who builds a tree house for his daughter."

Hanna props her hands on her hips. "So?"

"He's the kind of guy who asks how my day was and really *listens* when I answer."

"Sounds just awful," Will mutters. "Surely you could do better."

The girls laugh, but I shake my head. They're not understanding. "He's the kind of guy who holds me when I'm sad. The kind who makes me feel safe." I squeeze my eyes shut. "So safe I could let my guard down without even realizing it."

"Nix," Liz says softly, and her arms come around me. "Sweetie. What are you trying to protect yourself from?"

"Maybe I'm trying to protect *him*. Maybe *he's* the one who deserves better."

"Fucking women," Will mutters, and Cally smacks him in the middle of his chest. "What?"

"Don't be a misogynist," Cally says.

"I just think all this trying-to-protect-the-guy-from-herself stuff is ridiculous. He's a grown man and he's going to make his own decisions. If you respect him, you'll respect *that*."

Liz nods. "In other words, say, 'Fuck it. Life's too short!' and leave the baggage at the curb long enough to screw him silly."

Will lifts both hands, palms facing us. "I'm out."

Nix

I found it. I found the most beautiful thing.

PLAYING WITH FIRE

When I was dating Kent, we traveled as often as we could. We stole time wherever possible. A long weekend in Paris, spring vacation in Rome, and Christmas in Chile.

During those trips, I would take pictures of the most beautiful spot or thing I saw in each place. I tried to avoid the obvious, like the Eiffel Tower or the Sistine Chapel. Instead, I opted for the beauty in the living part of the city.

I took a picture of a restaurant chair where I'd seen a three-year-old girl with her arms slung around the neck of her elderly grandmother in Rome.

In Paris, I took one of an alleyway where we'd seen a couple making out. It had been raining and everyone was hustling to get out of the streets, but those two didn't even seem to notice. Her head was tilted to the side and his mouth was on her neck. I watched them from under the awning of a patisserie while the rain showered them until their clothes were saturated. I told Kent I wanted to get a picture of that spot before the sun dried the rain from the streets. He was obliging but a little awkward about it. Then I realized he thought *I* wanted to make out there. But I didn't want to duplicate their experience. I just wanted a photo of the spot. A memory of a beautiful moment.

Now, my fingers itch for my camera because Max is in his backyard, building a tree house for Claire. The beauty isn't just in the man's body—though he's working shirtless, and God knows I'm not complaining about the way his muscles bunch and strain as he positions the wood and nails it into place—but in everything this moment says about him. Just. Beautiful.

"Need another beer, man?" someone calls behind me, making me jump. "Oh, hey, Nix."

Sam comes out of the garage with a bottle of beer in each hand. "Is that for me?" I ask.

He hands one to me and grins. "Why not? Max can get his own beer."

I take a long pull and shift my gaze to Max's bare back as he nails more boards into place.

"Looks good, doesn't it?" Sam says.

"Mm-hmm."

For the first time, Max looks over at us and notices I'm here. He grins, and I melt. Because *damn.*

Sam clears his throat. "Um, no offense to my buddy over there, but you do know I'm referring to the *tree house*, right?"

"Mm-hmm."

Another throat clear. "I think I'll get out of here." He lifts a hand to Max. "See you tomorrow."

Max waves to his friend. "Thanks for your help, Sam."

"No problem," Sam says. "Call me any time you need help getting it finished."

As soon as Sam leaves, Cade appears in the doorway to the garage. He's also shirtless, and I can't help but do a mental comparison of the men.

Cade is *smoking.* I mean, hard body, narrow hips, nice smile, and bedroom eyes to seal the deal. But he doesn't make my tummy do that free-fall, flip-flop thing that Max does.

He runs his eyes over me from hairline to sandals.

"Any more problems since we last talked?" he asks, his voice low.

"Nothing. Did you find him?"

"There was an issue with tracking him down." He shifts his eyes to where Max is working then back to me, ensuring his words will remain private. "The Patrick McCane you described doesn't exist."

"What's that supposed to mean? Are you saying the fire in my yard started itself? That the phone calls didn't really happen?" I sound defensive. Panicked. All I can do is stand here and try to breathe.

"That's not what I'm saying," Cade says. "I'm saying there's no public record of a male aged twenty-nine to thirty-two with that name. But that doesn't mean there isn't someone trying to intimidate you." He lifts his palms. "Maybe he was operating under a false identity."

"Operating? He was an eighteen-year-old kid, not some grown man hustling me."

Cade sighs. "Or, it's possible, since it was so long ago, that you misremembered his name."

I shake my head. That name is burned on my brain. I didn't misremember anything.

"Is there anything else you can tell me, Nix?" Cade asks. "Where did he go to school? Who were his parents?"

"He was . . . homeschooled." More or less.

"You said he was around eighteen when you started dating. Was he registered for college somewhere? Who were his best friends?"

More questions I don't want to answer. Because the

truth is this: I may have found the courage to ask for help finding Patrick, but I don't have the courage to take it to the next step by opening the doors to my past.

"You know what? Let's drop it. Nothing has happened all week. Whoever was trying to freak me out has clearly gotten bored with their mission."

"Nix—"

I shake my head. "I'm sorry I bothered you about this, Cade, but please let it go. Half of it was probably paranoia anyway."

"What is it that you don't want anyone knowing? Why are you holding back?"

"Why do you assume I am?"

"I think we're done here," Max says, his voice hard and closer than before.

I look over Cade's bare shoulder and see Max standing on the patio behind him, his arms folded across his chest, irritation all over his face.

Cade doesn't step back right away. Instead, he drops his gaze to my mouth and holds it there for a long beat. "You have to decide if you really want help," he finally says, his voice so soft I'm sure Max can't hear. "I can't help if you're hiding details I could use to find this guy."

I don't bother replying, because Max is on his way over to me.

"I'll show myself out," Cade says, giving Max one of those chin-lift things they must teach in Hot Guy School. "Nix, call me if you want to talk more." Then he's gone, and Max is looking at me with narrowed eyes.

"Are you two going out again?"

I shrug and force a smile. "We're just friends."

He scowls. "Like *you and I* are just friends?"

I bite back my smile. He's jealous, and I am a very shallow girl for enjoying that fact. I ignore his question. "You look hot." My gaze dips to his bare chest and flat stomach, all coated in a thin sheen of perspiration.

Max smirks. "You're pretty hot yourself. Have a good time tonight?" He takes the beer from my hand and downs half of it.

My eyes are glued to his throat as he swallows. Can this man make everything into an obscenely sexy gesture? "Mm-hmm."

"How was your class? Sam said Cally was giving massage lessons?"

My cheeks heat, and I ball my fists to keep myself from pressing my hands against them. "I was just helping."

Max skims his gaze down the front of me then slowly lifts his eyes back to my face. I can't help but compare the experience to Cade doing the same thing moments ago. I felt almost nothing when Cade looked at me like that, but when Max does it, it sends my skin tingling.

My mind spins with thoughts of getting my hands on him, rubbing down the tight muscles between his shoulder blades, then opening my hands to work the tension from his lats and farther down to his waist and lower back. He'd let me pull his pants from his hips and knead his glutes. Then he'd roll over and I—

"Want to see it?" he asks.

My eyes snap back up to his face as I realize I've been staring at his crotch. "See what?"

His lips quirk and he nods toward the yard. "The tree house?"

"Oh. I thought . . ." I shake my head. No need to share what I was thinking. "Yes, I'd love to."

He sets the beer on the patio table. As he leads the way to the tree house ladder, I stay a few steps behind, shamelessly drinking him in.

He reaches the top of the ladder, turns, and offers a hand to help me up. When our hands touch, his eyes lock on mine and electricity crackles in the air. Today they built a platform and framed out the walls, a door, and a couple of windows. There's enough room up here for Claire and a few of her little friends to play with dolls or pretend they're the Swiss Family Robinson.

I do a slow spin to take it all in. "She's a lucky kid."

"I like working with my hands, and I don't get to do much of that running the gym. Who knew owning a health club would require me to put so many hours behind a desk?" He shrugs. "Anyway, it's been fun, and she's worth it. Coolest kid ever."

"You miss her."

"So much my chest aches." He takes a breath, studies the half-built structure, then says, "Wait here a minute?"

I obey, watching as he climbs down. I have nowhere better to be, and going inside will just bring up all that who-sleeps-where awkwardness we've been dancing around for the better part of the week. Maybe it's safe to sleep in my own house. Like I told Cade, nothing new has happened since the night he walked me home from Asher's bonfire. That's a relief, but I'm reluctant to leave.

Max returns with two beers and a basket. He hands me a bottle and pulls a blanket from the basket to spread on the tree house floor. "Watch the sunset with me?"

CHAPTER SEVENTEEN

Nix

I COULD DECLINE and head into the house, but I don't want to. I want these quiet moments with Max while I can have them. I don't know what's going to happen, and I'm not sure what to hope for. So I nod and lower myself to the blanket. Max takes the spot beside me, and we sip our drinks in silence.

When I'm alone with him, the air tightens with tension—the kind you feel when there's something within your grasp that you aren't allowed to have but want so much it's hard to breathe. I wonder if it's like that for him, even a little bit.

I look over at him and catch him rubbing the back of

his shoulder. I put down my beer. "Let me."

He doesn't say anything, just drops his hand and lowers his head as I lift to my knees and move to sit behind him. I've never been a touchy person. Maybe that comes from being raised by a woman who was too busy being a prisoner in her own mind to cuddle with her children, or maybe my time with Patrick fucked me up for life. Kent wasn't touchy either, consistently preferring smiles to kisses, and conversation to cuddles. The sex was rare, and I suspected a bit more like a chore for him than a pleasure he sought, so we just didn't do it often.

Never in my life has physical affection come easily to me, and yet when I'm with Max my hands itch to touch him, to stroke and hold.

"Damn, that feels good," he says when I dig my thumbs into the knot at the base of his neck. He rolls his head to the side, giving me better access to the spot.

His eyes are closed, his face soft, and I bite back the urge to follow my fingers on his neck with my mouth. He's been working all afternoon, and I want to taste the salt on his skin. He's the kind of guy who builds a tree house for his kid—seems to give all of himself for everyone else, and I want him to be on the receiving end of that kindness for once.

Say, "Fuck it. Life's too short."

"Do you want to lie down?" My voice sounds almost husky, colored by my own arousal and embarrassment. Max has made it clear how he feels about me, but still—even if it's irrational—I can't help but worry he might change his mind and reject me at any moment.

He turns his head, and his eyes meet mine for a breath before he lowers to his stomach on the blanket.

I straddle his hips and start at his neck again.

My hands slide lower, kneading the muscle and rubbing out the tension. I hold my breath against the arousal tightening between my thighs. He's motionless while I massage him, his breathing and the knots in his muscles my only clues as to where he needs more attention.

When I reach the base of his spine, I slide lower so I'm straddling his thighs more than his hips, and slip my fingertips beneath the band of his athletic shorts to find the muscles there.

A curse bursts from his lips on an exhale, and he flips onto his back. I don't have time to think before he's pulling me down on top of him. His mouth connects with mine, and his hands tunnel into my hair.

This is the danger in touching. A few minutes of my hands on his skin, and now I want him too much to stop a kiss I would have denied him fifteen minutes ago. I open for him, let his tongue rub against mine. When he rolls again, this time he takes me with him. Now I'm the one with my back to the ground, and he's on top of me.

I moan at the delicious weight of him and draw up my knees so he can settle between my thighs. The thick length of his erection presses into my aching center, and I arch my back at the pleasure. He groans against my mouth, then cups my breast through my shirt as he kisses his way to my neck and down.

I cling to him, hold him close, and curl my nails into

his shoulder blades. I need more. I need him closer. He circles his hips. Even with our clothes between us, the friction of that motion brings me to the edge.

He cups my breast and his thumb grazes across my nipple through my shirt. His mouth nips at my ear. "I dream about having you under me like this."

I bite my lip, cutting off the moan that wants to escape.

He finds my nipple between his thumb and index finger and pinches. Pleasure bolts through me and gathers in an achy mass between my thighs. He treats the other nipple to the same torture and my back arches off the ground. "Do you think about this, Doc?"

"Yes." *All the time.*

"Good." He nips at my ear, then kisses the spot his teeth abused. "And after you've been thinking about it, what do you do?"

He shifts to the side, and I instantly miss his weight, but then his hand slides from my breast, down my body, and between my legs. His touch feathers over the seam in my jeans, promising everything I want but giving only the slightest hint of it.

"Tell me you think of me while you touch yourself," he whispers, continuing with the teasing sweep of his fingers.

"I do." I should be appalled by my admission. Instead, I don't feel an ounce of embarrassment. Only the urge to scream. To whimper. To *beg* him to touch me.

"What am I doing in your fantasies?"

I lift my hips, asking with my body what I can't ask

with words. "Please."

He groans right against my ear, and the sound vibrates against my neck. "You never have to beg with me. Just tell me, and I'll give you everything you want." This time, he adds a little pressure between my legs and scrapes the denim with his knuckles. "What am I doing in your fantasies? How am I touching you?"

I force my eyes open and he's propped on an elbow, looking down at me with those intense blue eyes that do me in on my strongest days. And I whisper, "In my favorite fantasy, you're not touching me at all."

Max

Ten seconds ago, Nix was rocking into my hand and making sounds that turned me on so much, I worried I might embarrass myself. Now she's telling me I don't touch her in her fantasy. Not exactly where I hoped that conversation was headed.

When she nudges my shoulder, I'm preparing to have her push me away again, but she doesn't. She's urging me onto my back.

"May I?" she whispers. Straddling my hips, she scrapes her gaze down my body. "Would you let me?" Pressing her lips to the hollow between my pecs, she scoots herself down my body and pulls my shorts from my hips, and I'm thankful as fuck for the privacy provided by other trees in my yard because, judging from the direction she's headed, I won't have a prayer to find the strength to stop her.

When she lifts her gaze to meet mine, her eyes are hot and tortured. "I want to put my mouth on you."

Oh, hell. I'm not just turned on by the words; something in my chest tightens with the way she says them, as if she's preparing for me to cut her off at any minute. *As if I'd fucking stop her.*

Steadying her gaze on my erection, she wraps her hand around me and strokes—once, twice—then lowers her mouth and licks the head. My hips jerk off the floor.

"Is that okay?" she whispers. God, she's so timid. If I didn't know better, I'd think she were a virgin.

"It's *all* good," I manage, because I can tell she needs to hear it. "Any time your mouth or hands are on me, it's good."

She licks her lips and then I watch as she lowers them over me—slowly, carefully.

"Aw, fuck, baby," I growl. "That's good."

Her movements are slow and exploratory and driving me fucking insane. I gather every ounce of my control to keep still. She's not new to sex, but I know instinctively that she's new to *this,* and the last thing she needs is my cock at the back of her throat.

The hand squeezing my shaft releases and drops lower to cup my balls. *Fuck.* I don't want to come like this. *I'm dying to come like this.*

My hands go to her hair, and her moan of approval sends vibrations through me, and if that isn't enough, she lifts her eyes, watching me watching her.

My lips part, and I fight for my hold on that last thread of control.

She explores me with her tongue, tracing the length of me from root to tip before following that same path with her finger. Every time she wraps her hand around the base of my cock and slides her mouth over me again, her movements are surer. She tightens her grip, takes me deeper, and sucks me harder. It's the most fucking delicious torture I've experienced in my whole life. And the way she moans? As if doing this is getting her off? So fucking hot. And she has no idea.

When I don't trust myself to hold back any longer, I tug gently on her hair and guide her on top of me. She straddles my hips again, and my damp cock presses against her panties.

Her eyes flash with worry. "Was it okay? I thought you'd want to . . ."

"It was amazing."

"Then why . . .?"

Oh, hell. "Because I want inside you, Nix. I want to get this condom I've been carrying around in my wallet like some pathetically randy teenager, and I want you to straddle my hips, just like you're doing now. But I want to be buried deep inside you and have you ride me until you come." My fingers grip her hips as she circles them. Her eyes float shut and she rocks—so fucking wet and beautiful. We could both get off like this—her wet panties rubbing her clit and my cock—but I'm greedy and need more. I need deeper and harder. And when I come, I want her wrapped around my cock.

"But what would happen after that?" she whispers.

She's fighting this. That rational mind of hers is trying to talk her out of it, but her hips are still moving in the rhythm of sex. "After?" I manage. And it's hard to talk when I'm this close to coming—when I see how close *she* is to coming. She wants to know what will happen to our friendship, to know where this thing between us is going. But I don't know the answers any better than she does, so I give her what I do know. "After, I take you inside and to my shower. And when I've touched and teased you so much your legs won't hold you up anymore, I take you to my bed." I drop my gaze to her lips. "And this time I want to do a hell of a lot more than sleep when you're in my arms."

I can't stand the torture anymore. I need to know if her face is as beautiful when she comes as I remember. I slide my hand between our bodies and stroke her clit through her panties. Fuck, she's wet, and at the first contact of my thumb, she arches her back.

"Oh, God," she whimpers. She starts to lift up, but I clamp my hand down on her hip.

"Don't run from it. Do you need more?" I ask, stroking her again. "Can you get off like this for me?"

"I . . . *Max* . . . I . . ." Her lips part and I stroke again, then again, and then her body shudders and she collapses onto my chest.

I was wrong. When she comes, she's even more beautiful than I remember.

CHAPTER EIGHTEEN

Max

Nɪx sɪɢʜs ᴀɢᴀɪɴsᴛ ᴍʏ ᴄʜᴇsᴛ as I comb my fingers through her hair. "I had no idea."

"About what?" I ask.

She traces some invisible pattern on my chest. "I didn't know how sexy *talking* could be." She pushes herself up with one arm and looks down at me. "How do you know what to say?"

I chuckle. I can't help it. "Everything I said was the truth. But I'm glad talking turns you on. Nice to know what I can use in situations where I can't touch you."

She tugs her bottom lip between her teeth, and my cock aches. I don't want this night to be over. Not yet.

"We missed the sunset." The dusk has slipped into twilight since we first climbed up here, and the stars are starting to shine.

She frowns. "I'm sorry."

"There will be more sunsets." I graze her bottom lip with my thumb, remembering how that mouth looked wrapped around me. "I hope a lot more."

That's when I lose her. Her eyes go wide and panicked, as if she just realized she was in the presence of a known sex offender, and she scrambles off me.

I press my palms to my eyes, and take a deep breath. "What just happened?"

"I'm sorry." She sits up and draws her knees to her chest. "I'm so sorry, Max."

That just pisses me off. "I'm not some asshole you can't talk to." Only, I sound like a complete asshole. I sigh. "I don't understand what's going on in your head. I *want* to understand what you're afraid of, and I hope you'll explain it, but you don't owe me an apology."

"I really do."

I sit up too, but I make sure to leave room between us. I've learned that when Nix withdraws, she needs space. Crowding her doesn't help.

The panic has drained from her face, and she's starting to look like herself again.

I drag a hand through my hair and try to decide whether or not to ask. A week ago, I would have said it was none of my business, but I don't believe that anymore. I'd begun to believe we didn't have any future together, but then our lives began to merge, to overlap. I've tried to be patient, but it's past time I knew more. "Were you raped, Nix?"

Her eyes widen. "What?"

I flinch. "Is it just me, or is it all men? When I touch you, it's amazing and you're right there with me, but sometimes, it's like I do something that throws a switch and you panic. Did someone hurt you? Force himself on you? Did Kent—"

"No. Kent didn't rape me or force me to do things. Nothing like that." She pushes to her feet and wipes her hands on her jean shorts. "I'm just a little screwed up."

I sigh as I stand beside her. "We're all a little screwed up."

"I've been hurt before. I don't know if I have it in me to go through it again."

"Hey. Why are you so convinced I'm going to hurt you?" I cup her face in my palms and let my fingers slide into her hair. She puts up such a strong facade that I'm always shocked at how fragile she feels when I hold her. "Look at me. Tell me."

She opens her eyes and leans her face into my hand. "Because I've never been with a man who didn't."

That admission slams me hard in the chest, and all I can do is wrap her in my arms and hold her close. "I've been hurt before too."

"You don't get it. I was *engaged,* Max. I was in love with Kent. Maybe what he and I had wasn't as passionate as what I feel when I'm with you, but I loved him and he loved me. He promised to give me forever and then he broke my heart and walked away."

"Yeah, I wouldn't know anything about what *that's* like." I feel my jaw harden and force it to relax. "I get that it's scary because we both know nothing's guaranteed. But I do know that this—this thing between you and me, whatever it is—it's *good*, Nix. Hearing your laugh is the best damn part of my day. It smooths out my rough edges and stitches together the shit I thought was broken in me forever. When you're in my arms, I forget there was a time I wasn't whole. And I like to think it does the same for you, because when you *do* let me kiss you and you're not thinking about whatever it is that makes you panic like that, you don't respond like a woman who's afraid of being hurt. You blossom in my arms. Can you look at me and tell me that happens with every man who touches you?"

Her lips part, and the hand on my chest fists my shirt and pulls me closer, and she leans into me. "Only you," she whispers. "I'm only like this with you." She pulls back and looks me in the eye. "I like you, Max, but I'm scared. And not just for myself."

I like you. That admission makes me want to pound my chest, but I just hold her close and press a kiss to the top of her head, and when she relaxes, so do I. "I'm scared too. I know better than to promise neither of us will end up hurt, but I decided a long time ago you're worth that risk to me. You have to decide if it's worth the risk to you."

She squeezes her eyes shut. "If we're going to try this, I need to move slowly."

"We don't have to do anything you don't want to do."

"I don't mean physically," she says. "It's not as simple as that. I'm saying I need to slow this down emotionally. It's not easy for me to open up to people."

"Then I will astound you with my patience."

She swallows so hard that I hear it. "It's not going to be easy for me. Any of this. Can you promise me that if I need to end this, you'll let me go? No questions asked?"

"I don't want you to be my prisoner." I trace her bottom lip with my thumb. "I want you to be my girl."

Nix

Instead of a sexy shower and a trip to Max's bed, he made me dinner. Honestly, after my little freak-out in the tree house, this is exactly what I need—no-pressure intimate moments with Max. Before we came inside, I made a decision. I'm going to tell Max about Patrick.

He grilled a couple of steaks and some veggies and threw some potatoes in the oven. The only problem with this romantic setup and perfectly delicious meal is that after twelve hundred second guesses where my plan is concerned, my stomach pretty much hates me.

I attempt a small bite of my steak before leaning back in my seat. "You can cook."

Max grins. "Yes, well, when you're trying to raise a princess and get a struggling business off the ground, money for takeout isn't exactly in the budget."

"Do you still cook a lot?" I ask. "Now that money

isn't an issue?"

He nods. "Claire and I have dinner together every night. My mom did that for us. No matter how shitty my dad was being, I had that stability. A hot meal with Mom every night. It's not that Claire has anything bad in her life like my dad was for me, but those memories of simple meals at the dinner table stuck with me. I wanted to give that to her."

My heart squeezes, like it does every time he talks about his daughter.

"Tell me what you're thinking," Max says.

I drop my gaze to my barely touched steak. "I don't think you'd like it."

"I don't *have to* like everything you're thinking, Doc. That's the beauty of free will and all that. Remember, I'm not interested in a prisoner."

"Okay." I take a breath. "I was thinking that, as much as I'd like to indulge in an affair with you, I'm not sure it should extend beyond when Claire gets home."

He props his forearms on the table and rubs his forehead before shaking his head. "Well, I guess you called that one."

"Don't like it, do you?"

He holds up a hand. "Only because I thought we had this conversation outside an hour ago."

"That was about me falling for you. *This* is about you protecting your daughter."

Any humor left in his face falls away, just as I knew it would. "What are you talking about?"

My stomach churns unhappily. "You ask me what

I'm so afraid of, and the question isn't what but *who*. I went to dinner with Cade because I wanted his help tracking down the man I thought might be stalking me." Max tenses, and I say, "His name is Patrick McCane." I hold his gaze as I speak. "I haven't seen him in thirteen years. Cade was trying to track him down because I thought he might be behind some of the stuff that was happening."

"Stuff? What's happened other than the fire in your yard?"

"Weird phone calls, feeling like I'm being followed and once . . . I thought I saw him in my house." I lower my voice. "That's why I'm afraid to sleep there."

"You told Cade about this and not me?" His voice is a deadly whisper, and hurt shows in his eyes.

"I didn't want you to know anything about my past; it's the reason Kent left me."

"It's okay," he says. "I'm not Kent. I don't scare off so easily." When I don't speak, he says, "Start from the beginning."

The beginning. Jesus. I don't know if I can.

Max squeezes my hand. I take a deep breath and start at the *very* beginning.

"There was a fire the night I was born. My mom inhaled a bunch of smoke and they weren't sure she was going to make it, but she did. And they did an emergency C-section, and I made it too."

"And that's why she named you Phoenix?"

I nod. "She lived in a commune when she got pregnant with me. It was strict. People had a hard time getting out."

"So, like a cult?" Max asks.

I flinch. "One person's cult is another person's community. People on the news talk about cults like there's a clear-cut definition—this is a cult and that isn't—but we all live in the confines of communities. Some are just more culturally acceptable than others." Fear of what Max must think of me knots my throat, but instead of looking at me with disgust, his eyes are full of patience and compassion.

"Okay," he says. "So she was living in a *commune.*"

"It wasn't very big. A few houses and a church. Someone torched the church while everyone was inside."

"Jesus."

"She named me Phoenix, and I imagine at first she was grateful that I'd risen from the ashes of that old life." I shift my eyes to the wall. I can't look Max in the eye while I tell him the truth about my family. My mother used to accuse me of being ashamed of who I am and where I came from. She was right.

"She didn't talk about the old commune much. But when she did, it was almost as if it was a living thing to her—a spouse she'd wanted to escape and then regretted losing." I take a deep breath, and the words seem to tumble from my lips. "Mom tried, but she couldn't handle living on the outside, and little by little she began to convince herself that I brought that fire into her world. I took away her family."

Max's jaw hardens, and his nostrils flare. "Her *family?*" he asks. "What about you?"

"My mother is a paranoid schizophrenic, Max. For

whatever reason, the commune made her feel safe . . . or at least gave her a place to direct her paranoia. Us versus them was comforting to her, and on the outside she couldn't have that. There was no 'us,' only 'them' everywhere she turned."

"Was she officially diagnosed? Did she ever get help?"

I trace the scars on my ribcage through my shirt. "Some social workers tried, and she was medicated on and off for a few years, but she got pregnant with my little sister and had to stop taking the meds. Honestly, in retrospect, she was never what professionals would call *stable*. She probably should have been institutionalized. But she was the only mother I'd ever known, and she did have good days."

His fingertips brush across my shoulder. I love how patient he's being. When I tried to tell Kent about this, his questions were rapid-fire, as if he could be protected from my family's illness if only he had the information fast enough. He didn't mean to be cruel. He was just so far out of his element.

The thought of Kent sends a sharp pain through my stomach, and I squeeze my eyes shut. Max isn't Kent. I need to trust that he's stronger than Kent was and that he can handle this. When I open my eyes, Max is waiting, his lips pressed together.

"It was okay, though," I say. "I learned her triggers early on and sheltered her as much as I could from anything I thought might set her off. She worked from home writing articles for some evangelist's website, and I went to school, took care of my little sister, and made sure no one ever met my mom who didn't have to."

"That must have been hard," he says.

"I wish I could say it wasn't that bad, but the truth is it was rough. When I was sixteen years old, I met Patrick. He was eighteen and charming and *smart*. I fell for him before I ever learned that he had ties to a commune much like the one my mom had once lived in."

"Shit," Max whispers.

"Everything happened so fast. One minute, I was dating this guy, having my *first kiss* long after all the other girls I knew, and the next Mom, Amy, and I were moving into a commune, and I was being told I had to dress a certain way and act a certain way." I tug my bottom lip between my teeth. "At first, it was nice. I'd been carrying the brunt of the adult responsibilities at home for so long, it was nice to feel like everything wasn't on my shoulders." I exhale slowly. "And, of course, there was Patrick."

"You were in love with him."

I nod. "The crazy hard, irrational love unique to young people. He could talk philosophy and he read voraciously. If someone had asked my sixteen-year-old self about my dream guy before I met Patrick, he's pretty much what I would have described."

"Only he was tied to this cult."

"He'd been raised in Camelot," I explain, still squirming at the word "cult." "His father was the commune leader—he'd established the place when Patrick was a toddler. Patrick's mother had the dubious

210

honor of being Vicar Jeremiah's first wife."

"*First* wife? So were they Mormons or something?"

I laugh, an ugly, hollow sound. "Or something. Camelot wasn't that simple to pin down. In some ways, they were very fundamentalist—women were to serve, children seen not heard, male-centered leadership within the community and the individual households. But then they believed in things like runes and Tarot cards and solstice celebrations. It was an amalgamation of all the pieces of religions that appealed to Vicar Jeremiah. He had many wives. The other men—the few there were—could only take one wife."

"Where did he find his wives?" Max asks. "Was it a large commune?"

"Not very big at all. When I was there, the vicar probably had fewer than a hundred disciples living in Camelot. Some of them seemed to have been with him forever, and others were like my mom—like-minded single mothers who, from what I could gather, were desperate for help in a world that seemed stacked against them. Jeremiah welcomed them into the fold and taught them and their children. Just like he took in my family." I take a breath and lift my eyes to Max, who kisses my knuckles. The sweetness of the gesture nearly destroys me. When I told Kent the story of my time in Camelot, he was disgusted that I would try to defend it. It's easy to criticize that world when the outside has always been good to you, but as grateful as I am to have escaped, I recognized then and now that it offered the stability my family needed.

"So it was good at first," Max says, "if

unconventional. But something happened?"

I nod and feel tears fill my throat. It's not grief that's bringing it on. It's Max's compassion. With every word of my story, he takes a tiny piece of its weight, as if a mighty dam has held my tears back for thirteen years and he's deconstructing it one pebble at a time.

"I wasn't raised there," I say. "Maybe I'd read too much or seen too much, or maybe my mind has always been too analytical to fit into a community like that. I don't know. But as nice as it was, I had a bad feeling from the moment Jeremiah asked us to move, and it grew with every day I spent there. There were a few other girls my age, and none of them wanted to go to college or have a life outside of Camelot. In fact, it seemed like the only aspiration they had was to become one of the wives of the next vicar. One of Patrick's wives."

"Your boyfriend was going to be the next leader?"

I nod. "He was the Chosen One."

"But you knew that wasn't the life you wanted. You wanted to go to college."

"True." I'm not ready to explain just yet that my reasons for leaving were so much more complicated than my dreams of higher education. "I didn't belong there. I belonged on the outside. And when things got bad and I told Patrick I wanted to leave, he told me the only way I could leave their world was to rise from the ash again. Destroying that world was the only way to escape it. Just like my mom had escaped her old commune in the fire."

"What was that supposed to mean?"

"He said I'd have to destroy Camelot if I wanted a life outside." Tension squeezes the back of my neck in a tight fist, and I try to rub it away. "The symbol you saw burning outside my house is the rune of protection, but it's also the rune for people who challenge old tradition. Patrick would tell me again and again that it was a reminder."

"Of what?"

I squeeze my eyes shut. "A reminder that it's best not to start a battle, but if you do, you'd better finish it." I bite my lip hard and taste blood. "I haven't seen him in thirteen years—haven't even heard from him aside from the email he sent me when I was in medical school. Nobody at the commune knows where he is. He disappeared the night I escaped."

He studies me for a beat, his brow creased. "Was that what you were afraid to tell me?"

I shake my head. "There's more. But I can't . . . give me time."

The struggle plays out on his face. He wants to ask me questions but doesn't want to push. "You asked Cade to help you. What has he found?"

I shrug. "Nothing. He says there's no public record of anyone with that name and description."

"What the fuck good is he, then?" Max leans back in his chair and stares at the ceiling.

"You aren't totally freaked?"

"Do I look calm? I'm ready to buy that fucking stallion and ride it to kick Patrick's ass, and I don't even like horses."

That makes me laugh. "The only problems with that

plan, of course, are that I don't even know it's him and we don't know where he is."

"Minor details," he mutters.

"You aren't freaked about where I come from?"

Standing, he comes around the table and pulls me out of my seat. "I don't scare off that easily." He presses a kiss to my forehead.

"I needed to tell you about Patrick. You have a daughter to think of, and as long as Patrick is after me, my presence in your life is dangerous."

"What does that mean for you and me?"

"It means what happens next is up to you."

He shakes his head slowly and traces the edge of my jaw. "No, Doc. What happens next is up to *you*. We take this at your pace, remember?"

I wish I could hide my heart and lock it up tight. When I look into his eyes, I feel as if I'm stumbling, losing my footing on a ledge over unknown heights, and it's only a matter of time before I fall.

Thirteen years ago . . .

"Phoenix," Vicar Jeremiah says. "Thank you for joining us today."

I bow my head, avoiding eye contact, as I know I'm expected to. "Of course." I know why they called me here.

"Are you aware of the punishment for premarital sex in this community, Phoenix?" Vicar Jeremiah asks.

My gaze flicks to Patrick, who's recently taken the seat beside his father in the meetings of the elders. It's been four months since Patrick and I went to the honeymoon cottage. He stares right through me, and even though I knew he wouldn't be able to speak up for me, even though we talked about this and I begged him not to take responsibility, I feel my heart crack a little under the weight of what's coming.

"I *have* sinned, Your Grace." I swallow. This is the only way. Blatant lies to protect Patrick. I'll be punished either way, so why bring him down with me? "I'm an imperfect and sinful creature, and that's why I need your guidance. But premarital sex isn't among my sins."

Vicar Jeremiah lifts his chin, leveling me with the intensity of his gaze. "Then how do you explain the child growing in your womb?"

"She's lying," Elder Jeffery says. "Another sin. Tell us who the father is."

I shake my head frantically and squeeze my eyes shut so I can't look at Patrick. "There's no father."

"Would you take us for fools?" Elder Wallace says.

The room bursts into noise as the elders voice their distrust of me. Then Vicar Jeremiah holds up a hand to silence them. "We will pray on this, Phoenix. I ask that you do the same."

CHAPTER NINETEEN

Nix

"I NEED A HOT BATH and a foot massage," Krystal says.

Next to her, Hanna tilts her head from side to side, then rubs the back of her neck. "I'd be getting both of those things right now if I weren't here with you ladies. In fact, Nate said that if I get home before he falls asleep—"

"No!" Krystal covers Hanna's mouth with her hand. "No more. I can stand zero more details about your perfect husband today. I have an itch I haven't been able to scratch since I moved back to this godforsaken town, and hearing about my sisters' perfect sex lives is *not* helping."

Liz giggles. "The guy at the mall offered to take you home and cook you dinner. Maybe you should have let him *scratch your itch*."

Krystal narrows her eyes. "I'm not going to go home with an eighteen-year-old college kid. Dear God, how desperate do you think I am?"

Liz and Hanna exchange a look but apparently know better than to answer that question.

Instead of a traditional bachelorette party, the girls spent all day shopping in Indianapolis. I begged off the shopping—since twelve hours of fashion-oriented socializing fails to appeal to me on so many levels—but promised I'd meet them for drinks at Brady's after.

"Oh!" Hanna squeaks, pulling one of her bags off the floor and plopping it on the table in front of me. "We got you something."

The bag says *Pillow Talk*, and it's so pretty my throat goes tight. I have friends who surprise me with gifts in pretty bags. *This* is my life now. *This* and Max tucking me into bed every night, no matter what crazy hour I get home, and kissing me good night in ways that put ideas in my head and make me want to cut the bitch who told him to take things slow.

"You didn't have to do that," I say.

"Oh, yes we did," Liz says. "You're living with Max but you're not sleeping with Max."

Uh-oh.

"And that would be okay," Hanna chimes in, "but when you look at Max, your face says that you really wish you were sleeping with him."

A gift to help me sleep with Max. This does not

sound good. But, hell, they could have bought me a toad and I'd still be touched to get a present.

I part the white tissue paper to peek inside. "Lingerie?"

"*Great* lingerie," Krystal says. "The best. It's from this boutique north of Indy. Their selection is to *die* for."

Liz nods. "The best."

"I'm not much of a lingerie girl," I admit.

"That's what you think, but you need to try this stuff. It's amazing. You'll never want to sleep in anything else."

I put the bag by my purse and smile at my friends. It's kind of adorable that they think teaching me seduction could be as simple as giving me the right sleepwear.

"Thank you," I say. "I can't wait to try it. Tell me what you bought for yourselves."

I sip my drink while the girls regale me with tales of bargains and pushy salespeople and the cute but way-too-young guy at the shoe store who had a thing for Krystal.

As they talk and laugh, I keep thinking of Cally's words to me: *"You are not your past. You are bigger than your past and you are better than your past. Let it be part of who you've become, but don't you dare let it define you."*

Maybe she's right. Maybe I'm running from ghosts when what I really need to do is appreciate the life I have. I haven't felt like I was being followed for over a week, and haven't gotten any more creepy text messages.

My phone buzzes halfway through Krystal's description of the shoes she loved but didn't buy, because she was afraid it would give the too-young guy the wrong message.

Max: Should I expect you tonight?

Those words send a shimmy through my belly.

Nix: Don't wait up. I'll see you in the morning.

When I slide my phone back into my purse, the girls are staring at me. "What?"

"Was that Max?" Liz asks.

I give what I *hope* is a mysterious smile.

"Should we let you go?" Krystal asks, her brows wriggling suggestively.

"Umm," I say, then sigh. "Yeah, if you wouldn't mind?"

"Have fun!" the girls chorus as I leave.

"Let loose," Krystal advises.

"Use the gift," Lizzy adds.

Nix

I roll over in bed and stare at the beam of moonlight

coming in the window.

When I arrived at Max's tonight, he was already in his room. He was probably in bed flipping through the latest thriller spy novel, but I didn't want to disrupt him, so I came to bed.

The house is quiet but my mind is chaotic with noise.

I roll to my other side, giving the window my back, and stare at the nightlight that appeared in my room sometime last week. Max found out I'm afraid of the dark and bought me a nightlight. He found out I was afraid of falling for him, and he's giving me time.

Damn.

He has so much to offer, and I don't just want to accept it. I want to gobble it up like a starved woman offered a six-course meal.

My eyes float closed and my mind conjures images from the last time I was in his bed. The feel of his arm wrapped around me. His breath against my neck. But hot on the heels of those images are older memories— ones from an old life where women aren't supposed to feel the things Max makes me feel, where I was sneered at for wanting things that are only supposed to matter to men. Where all my physical contact was a dirty secret.

This time, I roll onto my stomach and scream into my pillow. I want Max, but more than that, I want the past out of my head. Everything has been good. For whatever reason, whoever was sending the texts, making the calls, they stopped. But not before they scared me away from living my own life.

I want . . . to seize. To take charge of my life and my

happiness rather than handing it over to someone who may or may not be after me.

Suddenly, the choice seems so simple, and I hop out of bed. I'm halfway to the door when I stop and look down at myself. I'm wearing shorts and a scrappy old gray T-shirt that I wore to the gym until the neck ripped. Because nothing says "seduction" like pit stains.

If I wanted to prove Max was right about me being a tomboy, wearing this to his bed would be the way to do it.

"Fuck." I grab the gift bag from the girls and rush into the bathroom, my stomach twisting with nerves.

A quick look in the mirror shows my ponytail is askew—flat on one side and falling out on the other. The puffy sleep-deprivation bags under my eyes would make me look demented if my smeared mascara weren't already beating it to the punch.

I grab a clean washcloth from the cabinet and run the water hot. Then I scrub my face clean and pull the gift from its bag.

I have to give them credit. It's no frilly thing that would make me feel ridiculous. I could imagine Hanna or Liz wearing lacy lingerie and rocking it, but I'd just feel like I was trying too hard. I wouldn't say there's any lingerie that I would call "my style," but if there were, this would be it. It's a whisper-soft blue-gray cotton—so thin it could just as well be spun from clouds.

I strip out of my clothes and decide my legs could use a shave. The first time I slept with Max, I didn't exactly prepare. This time, I want to be ready.

I climb into the shower, wash my hair, scrub my skin, and take special care with the razor. After, I moisturize my legs and arms, but when I'm applying my facial cream, I decide I need a little makeup—not too much, just enough to feel pretty if he turns on a light—so I swipe on lip gloss and mascara, then I dry my hair, putting a dab of that special goo in it first so it turns to waves instead of frizz.

By the time I'm through the whole routine, the clock in the hall says it's nearly two a.m.

His bedroom door is cracked, and my stomach hitches as I approach it.

I know he wants me as badly as I want him. But still, I'm new to seduction, and my hands shake as I nudge the door open and step into his room.

It's dark, but I can make out his silhouette on the bed. Pulling back the covers, I crawl in beside him before I can talk myself out of it.

It's not until I rest my head in the crook of Max's shoulder that it occurs to me that he might be sleeping.

"Max?"

His chest rises and falls with soft, steady breaths under my hand. He's not just sleeping, he's dead to the world.

I don't know much about seduction, but I think it generally helps when the seducee is awake. I turn, intending to climb out of bed and head back to my room, but Max follows me. He grumbles something in his sleep and slings a heavy arm around my waist, bringing his scent with him.

When I had his place to myself earlier this week, I

caught myself smelling everything—his deodorant, his laundry detergent, his soap, and his aftershave—but none of those make up his smell. It's some potent combination of all those things. It's *him*.

And since I don't want to wake him, and since my muscles are all still relaxed from my shower and my eyes are starting to close of their own volition, I decide it won't hurt to take a few minutes to stay right here.

CHAPTER TWENTY

Max

SHE'S BEAUTIFUL WHEN SHE SLEEPS, but somehow more so when it's in my bed, her dark hair on my pillow, her long fingers wrapped around my wrist.

I'm not sure when she came in here. Hell, when I climbed in bed last night, I didn't think I'd ever fall asleep. I was so fucking hard and completely unwilling to settle for my hand when I wanted her. Then I woke up to the alarm on my phone and found her in my arms, her back to my front, her fingers wrapped around my forearm, as if she was scared I might try to escape. Absurd. There's nowhere else I'd rather be.

I managed to silence my alarm with my free hand

and go back to holding her before she woke up.

I've never met anyone who sleeps as little as Nix does, and since she started staying here, I learned just how real her insomnia is. Aside from the nights we've slept together, she spends more of the night out of her bed than in it. If being in my bed is going to help her get more than the three hours she usually runs on, I figure it's my duty to make that happen.

I lower my head back to the pillow and inhale the scent of her shampoo. She moans softly, then rolls in my arms to face me, which, incidentally, gives me a fabulous view of her cleavage.

Then she jerks awake and her eyes widen in horror. "*Oh my God.* I'm so sorry."

Linking my arms behind her back, I hold her tight before she can scramble away. "Sorry about what?"

"I fell asleep in your bed." Her eyes drop to my chest. She likes my body and does a shitty job trying to hide the fact. Not that I mind.

"That's not a problem."

"I . . . um . . . didn't have your permission."

A grin tugs at my lips. "I think I made it pretty clear that you're welcome in my bed anytime you please."

"Yeah, but I . . ." She searches for an explanation then relaxes. "What seemed like a good idea last night seems foolish this morning."

"Which part was foolish? Climbing into bed with me? Or not waking me up to enjoy having you in my arms? Because I can promise you only one of those two things could possibly be construed as foolish."

Then, because she's here in my bed and in my arms

and because she has a damn fine mouth, I kiss her. She doesn't stiffen when my lips touch hers anymore. She's ready for it, and she kisses me back.

Nix isn't one of those dainty kissers. This woman kisses with her whole body. She presses against me and slides a hand over my bare torso and up my back. Rolling on top of her is as natural as slipping my tongue into her mouth. In seconds, a kiss I intended to be a gentle, unassuming "good morning" becomes something much more intense.

She parts her thighs and bends her knees at each side of my hips so my cock is nestled against her heat, nothing but our underwear between us. Her moans fill my ears and her hips shift in tiny circles.

"God, that's sweet." I drag my mouth from her lips to her neck. "I love when you rub against me."

When I latch on to her neck and suck, she moans under me. I shouldn't mark her. It's lame and juvenile, but I'm overcome by the instinct to suck harder and let that bastard Cade know she's mine in the most primitive way I can. I resist. Barely.

Instead, I pull away the sheets and trail my lips lower, following her neck to skim kisses over her collarbone, then the dip in the hollow of her neck and back up. Her nightgown is bunched at her hips, and I slide my hand beneath it, sweeping the pad of my thumb against her hipbone.

I proceed with the single-minded purpose of making her tremble with need. When my hand nears the hem of her nightgown, she stiffens, then seems to force herself to relax.

"It's okay," she whispers. Teeth sinking into her lower lip, she locks her eyes on mine and nods.

I don't know what to expect, but I do know that going up a woman's shirt has never in my life felt as erotic as getting my hand under Nix's. Inching the slip up her body reveals three thick intertwined circles of scar tissue across her ribs—as if someone carved a partial Olympic Games symbol in her skin again and again.

I swallow hard. Someone did this to her.

"Not very pretty, is it?" she whispers, heartbreak on her face.

My mind swims with questions, but every one of them can wait. I skim over the scars with my fingertips, then my lips, wishing I could kiss away any pain she ever felt there. Slowly, I move my way up. I cup her breast and flick my tongue across her nipple before drawing it into my mouth.

I can't take away the pain from her past, but I can make her forget it—even if just momentarily—with pleasure. And that's what I intend to do.

I want the whole morning just to explore her breasts and then the afternoon between her legs. Her nipples are sensitive, and I let her moans guide me, completely absorbed by the rhythm of her body rocking under mine.

"Please," she whispers. "More."

I lift my head. Pleasure washes over her face. And more. *Need.* "Let me make love to you, Nix."

Her eyes open wide at my words, but I hold her gaze. *Fucking* is great and all, but we've done that. This

227

morning I want to make love to her, to show her just how special and beautiful she is, scars and all.

She answers with a nod.

Then the *goddamn-motherfucking doorbell* rings.

Yeah, not gonna happen. Not when I have Nix in my arms. My knuckles brush the underside of her breast, and she moans. Her wet heat penetrates my briefs, and blood surges to my cock.

The doorbell rings again, only this time, pounding follows it.

I lift my head. "Jesus."

Nix giggles and pushes up on her elbows. Her cheeks are flushed and her teeth sink into her bottom lip. "You should probably go get it."

"I'm not sure I should. If it's not a goddamned emergency, I might turn homicidal."

She shimmies out from under me and hops off the bed, the slip sliding down to cover her as she moves. "It might be one of the girls wanting to grab coffee or something." She spins in a half-circle, looking around the room. "Do you have a robe I can borrow?"

As pissed as I was about the person at the door, I'm grinning now because I just realized what she's wearing. When she was in my arms I didn't notice— because, let's face it, I'm a guy, and I couldn't give two shits about clothes. Typically, that is. But these are not typical clothes.

The doorbell rings again, and I follow her out of bed and press a hard kiss to her lips. "*You* stay here. I'll get rid of whoever it is and then I'll be back."

"Okay," she whispers.

I drag my gaze down the length of her—*damn*—and force myself to leave so I can answer the door.

Fucking Cade is standing on the other side. "Morning," he says. "Reason you don't answer your phone?"

"Because I have fucking voicemail?" I fell asleep with it in my room last night, just in case Nix called and needed a ride home. It probably died while I was sleeping.

"I need to talk to Nix, but she's not answering her phone either."

"It's not a good time."

He folds his arms across his chest, universal man-language for *I'm not fucking going anywhere.*

I pull the door open wider and point to the couch in the living room. "Fine. Have a seat. We'll be with you in a minute." I turn on my heel and go back to my bedroom before he can respond.

When I get there, Nix is shoving her arms into my old terrycloth robe. "Who was it?"

"Cade. But he can wait a goddamned minute." I shut the door and lean against it.

She cocks a brow at me. "Why are you looking at me like that?"

"Because earlier I didn't realize what you were wearing in my bed."

She tugs her bottom lip between her teeth. "Oh."

"This, sweetheart, is the face of a man who just realized the chick he's hot for didn't just climb into his bed for the company."

She looks down at herself and then back to me,

before closing the robe and tying it tight around her waist.

"You're not going to try to tell me that you usually sleep in stuff like that, are you?"

She lifts her chin. "You called me a tomboy."

I stalk toward her and put my hands on the closet door on either side of her head, pinning her in. "I did. And for the record, you're the sexiest tomboy I've known. The only one I've ever had the privilege to have in my bed." I snake my hand between our bodies and tug the knot she just tied until it loosens and exposes her slip again. I'm too close to see much, but I'm not about to back away. I cup her breast in my hand and graze my thumb over her pebbled nipple.

"Max," she says on a ragged exhale. "Cade's waiting."

"He sure is." I shift my hand to the other breast, giving that nipple the same treatment and loving the way her lips part as I do it. "Let him wait. It serves him right for asking you out when I made it *damn* clear you were mine."

"Yours? You claimed me when we weren't even dating? Isn't that a little caveman?"

The corner of my mouth ticks up in a grin. "You like it."

Now it's her turn to smile. "Maybe a little."

"You know what the sexiest thing is about this slip?"

She shakes her head, her eyes locked on mine.

"The sexiest thing about any item of clothing a woman can wear. They're just clothes. Clothes do nothing for me. But you wore it for *me,* and *that* is a turn-on." I groan and drop my head to her ear. "I want to make sure you know that you're just as sexy to me in a T-shirt as lingerie. In fact, you could wear a paper bag to bed if it meant I got to take it off you."

"I like when you say things like that."

"You have no idea how badly I want to make Cade wait." I kiss the sensitive spot just beneath her ear and she shivers.

"What would you do?" she whispers. "If we made him wait?"

Without hesitating, I tug up a fistful of the slip and slide my hand between her legs. Her breath catches and she's so damn wet that I'm hard all over again. "I'd wrap your legs around me," I say, sliding my fingers beneath the saturated cotton of her panties. "And I'd take you against this wall." I enter her with one finger, and she gasps. When I add a second, she bites back a cry and grabs a fistful of my hair. "Maybe I'd kiss you the whole time my dick was inside you to keep you quiet." She squeezes tight around my fingers, and I find her clit with my thumb. "Or maybe I wouldn't. Maybe I'd want him to hear you scream my name as I made you come."

She comes apart then, her sex convulsing around my fingers, her body quivering in my arms. She's beautiful, but when she comes, those walls she works so hard to keep fall away. I want to take her to my bed and watch her get off over and over. I want to spend my day tearing down those walls until she can't ever shut me out again. And *fuck* I want to feel her tight pussy squeeze my cock as she comes.

But we have to go talk to Cade. Fucking Cade.

"I can't believe we just did that," she whispers. Her cheeks are flushed and she keeps tugging her bottom lip between her teeth.

Reluctantly, I remove my hand from between her legs. "I kind of enjoyed it myself."

"I've never been with anyone who makes me feel like you do."

"Glad to hear it. For the record, the only reason we're leaving this room is because Cade might know something important about this guy who's been harassing you, and I want to keep you safe." I rub the hem of her slip between my fingers. "Now let's go get this over with so we can come back in here and finish what you started when you slipped that on and climbed into bed with me."

Nix

Max drops his hand from my breast and steps away from me, and it's way too early for dramatics, but his body no longer being pressed against mine kind of feels like a tragedy.

"Cade's waiting," he murmurs, "but he'd be fine waiting a little longer if you wanted to get dressed first."

Right. I have to go talk to a police officer now. A

police officer who was waiting on the other side of this wall while Max gave me an orgasm.

My brain is more in gear to get naked in bed, but we're going to get back to that when Cade leaves. I'm sure I can put all thoughts of what Max's going to do to me aside and carry on an important conversation. *Right.*

"I'll meet you out there," I mutter. I rush to my things in the guest bedroom and pull on jean shorts, a bra, and a shirt. And, okay, yeah, maybe it's my prettiest bra and my shortest jean shorts, but Max just whispered really sweet and sexy things in my ear, and I don't want him to forget his promise.

When I reach the living room, the guys are holding mugs and sitting on opposite sides of the coffee table. The earlier heat in Max's eyes has gone cold and his jaw is hard, so instead of taking the seat next to him on the couch, I sit in the chair between them.

Cade's eyes immediately drop to my Daisy Dukes. Or, more accurately, to the flesh said Dukes do little to cover.

Max passes me a mug of steaming hot coffee.

"Thank you." I tear my eyes off Max and look to Cade. "What's going on?"

Cade hands me a short stack of glossy photos. "This is Patrick Henry, thirty-two-year-old technical writer living in Lafayette. Is this the guy you're afraid of, Nix?"

The picture on the top of the pile sends a harsh chill through me—the kind that wants to freeze me down to my bones and paralyze my limbs and my heart. That's Patrick. The picture is in profile and he's a little older, but he's still as striking as he was when I fell in love with him—the hard angles of his face, the intense eyes.

"Nix?" Cade says.

I nod and struggle to find my breath so I can speak. "That's him."

Cade leans forward, resting his elbows on his knees. Again, he shifts his gaze to Max and then back to me. "Are you aware that this man has ties to a religious extremist group operating a short drive from here?"

"Camelot," I say, nodding.

"Max told me that nothing more has happened since the texts you got the night I walked you home."

"That's right. Maybe he lost interest. Or . . . ." I shake my head. "I don't know."

Cade takes a breath. "Patrick is at Methodist Hospital in Indianapolis. He's in the ICU in critical condition."

My head snaps up. "So it wasn't him."

"More likely," Cade says cautiously, "it *was* him, and the incidents have stopped because someone broke into his house a few days later and worked him over real good. He probably would have died if the neighbor hadn't had a key. He stopped by to borrow the paper, and when he saw Patrick beaten and bloody on the floor, he called an ambulance."

"Oh my God," I whisper.

"Thanks to Patrick's ties to Camelot, I convinced the judge to give me a warrant. He probably wouldn't have otherwise, given how minor the incidents have been, but he did."

"And?" Max says, his jaw ticking.

"We're sending officers today to search his apartment for the burner cell phone you were getting texts from."

"Who do you think assaulted him?" I ask.

"We don't know. According to the police report, the place was ransacked, and it appears a lot was stolen, so it may have been a home robbery gone wrong."

A chill rushes over me.

Cade takes a breath. "The hospital has instructions to call me if his condition changes. The second he wakes up, you'll know. In the meantime, we can draw up a restraining order, a no-contact order, the works."

"Do they think he'll wake up?"

"He's in bad shape. We just don't know," Cade says, but the truth flashes across his face. Patrick is going to die.

I slowly flip through the pictures in my lap until I find one of Patrick head-on—showing both his beautiful side and the opposite, fire-ravaged side of his face. Next to me, Max draws in a sharp breath, and I know he sees it.

I cut my eyes to him and wish I had telepathy so I could tell him what I'm too much of a coward to speak. *I did that. Would you still want me in your bed if you knew?*

"He can't hurt me anymore," I whisper. I wish the thought of him dying gave me comfort, but my emotions are a quagmire I'm not sure how to navigate.

Once, Patrick was the man I loved. Once, he was the man I believed I would do anything to protect. That all changed in a single night, and if he dies, I will mourn

PLAYING WITH FIRE

for the boy I loved.

CHAPTER
TWENTY-ONE

Max

THIS ISN'T OVER. I can see it on Nix's face. She's still afraid of something. Maybe I'm not the only one who thinks something is off about all this. What Cade said makes sense—it probably was Patrick stalking her, just as she suspected, and it's stopped because he's unconscious in the hospital. But a random burglary gone wrong just seems too convenient.

"Well," Nix says after we show Cade out, "I didn't expect that."

I step forward and wrap her in my arms. "Do you need anything? Or want to talk about it?"

She shakes her head. "I need to stop by the hospital

for a few hours today for my rounds, and I guess . . . I guess I can stay at my own house now."

That's a fist in the gut, but what did I expect? That she'd move in with me? I'm not sure *I'm* ready for that. But I hear myself whisper, "Stay. Until we know for sure he was the one. And then after that . . ." I swallow hard. "Claire won't be home for another week. I'd like to spend that week sleeping with you in my arms."

She leans into my chest and sighs. "Careful, Maximilian Hallowell. You keep saying those things and I'm going to fall for you whether I want to or not."

I grin. "Oh, she's discovered my evil plan." I resist the urge to kiss her. After the news Cade delivered, I'm avoiding anything that might give her the idea I intend to pick up where we left off this morning. "Go out with me tonight. Let me take you to dinner and hold your hand."

"Like you're my boyfriend or something?" she asks.

I wouldn't know how to describe the tangle of emotions those words cause in my chest. "Yeah. Like I'm the guy who spoils you and takes you home and kisses you whenever he wants. And like you're the girl in my *life* and not just my dreams. Not just my bed."

She bites her lip. "That sounds really nice."

"Okay. So it's a date. I'll spend the whole day looking forward to it."

"Me too." Her eyes drop to my mouth. "I'm going to go feed my cat now."

"You do that."

Her tongue darts out to wet her lips, and she nods then heads out the door. And my balls may be so blue they're setting new records, but I'm smiling like a fool. Because the girl I've been crushing on for months just agreed to be my girlfriend.

Damn straight.

Nix

When I get back to Max's, he's in the shower. I stand in his bedroom for a solid minute, staring at the bathroom door and imagining his hard body under the spray. I should go to the hospital. I should *definitely* wait until tonight to see him naked. Do the whole wine-and-dine thing first.

Fuck it. Life's too short.

I strip out of my clothes and head into the bathroom, only to stop in my tracks at the image that greets me.

Max is in the shower, head bowed under the spray, hand wrapped around his cock as he strokes himself. My throat goes dry and my pulse kicks up.

He's beautiful, and the sight of him working his hand up and down his shaft in long, even strokes is about the most erotic thing I've ever seen.

I could let him finish. I almost want to. I'd like to see his face as he brings himself to orgasm, would love to know just how he uses his hand when he touches himself. But I'm too greedy, and two weeks of foreplay is more than I can handle. So I open the glass door and step into the shower.

He stills when he sees me. His nostrils flare and his eyes go dark, but he doesn't take his hand from his cock. Turning sideways, I step under the spray behind him and press my breasts against his back. Any nerves I had about doing this fizzle away under the weight of my need.

I lather my hands with soap and let them roam his back and along his sides. When I slide my soapy hand over his, he exhales heavily.

"Show me how you like it." I fumble as I stroke him, my grip awkward over his.

Turning to face me, he removes his hand and guides my fingers to wrap around his length. He cups my face in his hands and kisses me breathless as I stroke him. He's so thick and hard. I could drop to my knees and take him into my mouth, suck him, the water washing over us until he's coming onto my tongue.

His hands roam down my neck and to my breasts, where he toys with my nipples. "Have you ever made love in the shower, Doc?"

I shake my head, tiny shivers of anticipation racing through me.

"Don't move."

I blink at his back as he leaves the shower, but seconds later, he returns, rolling a condom down the length of his erection. I draw in a ragged breath. I'm not sure what I'm supposed to do.

He comes straight for me, backing me against the cold tile as his mouth crashes down on mine. I don't have time to panic about not knowing the proper techniques for shower sex.

"Link your hands behind my neck," he demands against my mouth.

I do as instructed, and he hooks his hands behind my knees and guides my legs to wrap around his waist. He holds me there, propped between his body and the tile wall, and he slowly enters me.

"I've fantasized about this since the first time," he whispers, his voice husky against my ear. "I've thought about how you'd look under the spray, imagined these fucking perfect legs wrapped around me as I fucked you." With those words, he begins to move.

All I can do is hold on as he drives into me, his hips thrusting and circling, and his dick pressing deep against my cervix. When he frees a hand to find my clit with his thumb, I bite his shoulder to hold back my scream.

"Let me hear you," he demands. "I want to hear you scream when I make you come."

"I can't," I whisper. "I'm not . . ." He adds more pressure to my clit and I bite back a moan.

He scrapes his teeth against my neck. "You don't ever have to hold back with me." He sucks my earlobe between his teeth and I cry out. "That's what I want to hear. Let go."

Something snaps inside me, lowering a wall I hadn't even realized I'd been holding between us. I kiss him. Hard. Bite his lip. Drive my fingers into his hair and pull as I rock my hips against his and moan into his mouth.

He returns every crazy, desperate touch with his

own. Our pace turns frantic. I lead his head to my breast, unashamed to show him where I want his mouth. He groans his approval before drawing my nipple between his teeth and sucking hard.

His dick swells inside me. "I'm so close," he whispers. "Come with me. I want to feel you come around my cock."

The words shatter me, and I fly over the edge. My orgasm whips through my whole body, leaving me quivering and shaking. I open my eyes in time to watch his hit. His fingers dig into my hip and his thrusts grow jerky. When he throws his head back and comes inside me, I know I've never seen anything as beautiful as the pleasure on his face.

Max

"I've never been much for playing hooky," Nix says, "but you sure do know how to make it fun."

We're in bed, the sheets twisted around us, her wet hair sprawled across the pillow. After we cleaned up in the shower, I led her here, parted her legs, and tasted her until she was moaning and begging for more. When I was inside her the second time today, I went slower. We kissed and touched and took our time. After, she looked at me with that wonder in her eyes, and I bit my tongue so I wouldn't tell her the words so anxious to fall from my lips.

I have fallen in love with Phoenix Reid, and I'm afraid if she finds out she'll run.

"Nix . . ." The words sit on my tongue, not heavy but light and airy. I press my lips together so they can't escape. *I'm in love with you.* But the memory of releasing that truth and finding it unrequited is still too fresh. I might be over Hanna, but that doesn't mean I'm ready to hand out my heart without being cautious.

I'll tell her. Soon.

"Tell me about the scars."

"They're from Camelot," she says softly, her fingers tracing each of the three circles. "When we moved in, Vicar Jeremiah baptized us and marked us so God would know who to save at the second coming."

"God wouldn't know otherwise? I thought He was omniscient?"

She smiles. "Yeah, me too, but that was the reasoning. Even at sixteen, it was so obvious to me that it was just another way for Patrick's father to exert control over his 'flock.'"

I kiss my fingers and touch them to the scars. "How did he do it? I thought it was from a knife at first, but the circles are too perfect."

"Branding iron. Like we were cattle. Patrick held me down and praised me after because I didn't scream." She shakes her head, but her eyes have gotten a far-off glaze. "My sister's still there, you know."

"Why? Can't she live with you?"

She rolls to her side and puts her hand on my face, her eyes sad. "She's there because that's where she wants to be. I've tried to convince her to leave—repeatedly—but she won't. She's drunk on the proverbial Kool-Aid."

"Maybe someday she'll change her mind."

"I hope so."

I want to ask her why she looks so sad, but what a fucking stupid question when we're talking about her sister living in a cult. Of course she's sad. "What about your mom?" I ask. "Is she still happy there too? Does she miss you?"

"She hates me." She drops her gaze to my chest and shrugs as if it doesn't matter. "She likes to say, 'The Devil's fire runs through Phoenix's veins.' She blames me for . . ." Her eyes flick to mine then back down. "Everything that went wrong."

I pull her into my arms and kiss her forehead. I need her to know that I'm her safe place, but also that I know there's more to her story than she's telling. "I have all these questions," I whisper, "but I won't let myself ask them until you're ready."

"Max?"

"Yeah?"

"It's not that I don't want to tell you more. I do."

"We'll take this slow, remember? We can talk about it whenever you're ready, but no pressure."

"The stuff I haven't told you is the stuff that made Kent decide he couldn't be with me. We were engaged, had our picture in the paper, and were planning one of those big-ass weddings. The kind that costs so much you could use the money to feed the people in a small country for a year. Then one day he told me he couldn't marry me, and he wouldn't talk about why. But the way he looked at me . . . it was like he'd woken up and realized he was engaged to a monster."

I can't hold her any closer, but I would if I could. Grief radiates off her when she speaks about Kent. I want to soak it up and free her from the weight of it.

"Later, my sister told me that Kent had tracked down my mom. He knew we were estranged and he thought it would be a great surprise if he could get her to show for the wedding. But instead of agreeing to that, she told him about the night I escaped. And I guess he panicked."

The night I escaped. That's where her story is. Her secrets. Her shame. But I don't let myself ask about it. "I'm sorry, baby," I whisper. I lace my fingers through hers.

"He left the country after that. Just picked up and moved to South America. In the span of three days, I went from engaged and planning a wedding to a man I loved deeply to reading a note from my fiancé saying that he'd left the country, and that he didn't want me in his life. A *note.* He couldn't even tell me to my face."

"You told me his mom had died, but what about the rest of his family? What did they think of him running away?"

She shakes her head. "He didn't have any. I was the only one he had and the only one he was leaving."

I bring her hand to my mouth and kiss each knuckle. "I'm not Kent."

"Do you believe a person can do a bad thing and still be good?"

Those words make my chest ache. All of this does, but those words more than the rest. "Yes, Nix." I hold her hand to my lips. "And I believe good people sometimes do bad things because they don't have a choice."

I stroke her hair and wait for the tears I expect to come next, but they don't. I hold her for a long time, and when I draw back to look at her face, she's fallen asleep.

When my phone buzzes on the bedside table, she doesn't stir.

"Hello?" I answer softly.

"We found the phone," Cade says. "As well as kerosene, the keys to Nix's house, and pictures of her. Lots of pictures. Max, Patrick Henry has been stalking Nix for *years*."

CHAPTER
TWENTY-TWO

Nix

"I KEEP THINKING ABOUT those twinges of worry that all the girls in the movies get before they get married," Lizzy says. "Cold feet or horror that they'll never know another man's sweet lovin'—*something.*"

"Yeah?" Maggie asks. "And what's the verdict? You feeling that?"

"Not even a twinge," Lizzy says.

I smile. "*That's* because he's the one, Liz. You found your match."

"She might not be the only one," Hanna singsongs at me, and my cheeks blaze.

"Look at us," Liz says, raising her martini glass.

"Keeping you out when you have *Max* to go home to."

Hanna giggles. "Lizzy, you don't have to look so damn proud of yourself."

"I am proud," she says. She points to me. "Proud of this girl for finally letting nature take its course."

I roll my eyes. "You make our relationship sound like a bowel movement."

Krystal snorts. "Doctors are so gross. You need to tell us about Max's mad skills so you can convince yourself it's real."

She's not wrong. Though I haven't given details—they *wish*—I may have mentioned how pleasantly exhausted I am. It's been four days since Cade told me Patrick was in the hospital. I've been staying at Max's house and sleeping in Max's bed and generally falling harder and faster than I've ever fallen in my life.

And it's okay to fall because I know Max won't hurt me.

Even as I'm enjoying our time together, I know things are about to change. This weekend is bound to fly by with Lizzy's wedding, and then Meredith and Claire are scheduled to fly home on Monday. Once Claire's home, I need to sleep at my own house. Putting myself in Claire's life before I know what's going to become of Max and me isn't fair to her. Which means I have four more nights.

"I do think I'll get going." I stand and look around the bar, scanning the crowd for potential dates for Krystal.

"Don't bother," she says, reading my mind. "There's nobody."

Sighing, I shrug. "Can't hurt to keep our eyes open."

After saying my goodbyes, I go out to my car, and find Amy sitting in the passenger seat, toying with my radio. I don't bother wondering how she got inside a locked vehicle, though I do wish she'd use those skills for good instead of evil.

I slide into my seat and start the car before I speak. "You could have come inside to get me."

Her eyes go big. "In a bar? *Phoenix . . .*" She shakes her head and drops her gaze back to the radio, pushing buttons even though the car's off and it doesn't do any good. "I wish you could see what your life has become."

I take a deep breath and exhale slowly. "I don't want to have this conversation again." Crap. But I don't want to alienate her either. "How are you? Are you okay? Do you need anything?"

"I do." She bites her lip and her eyes water. "I need my sister. I'm scared."

My blood chills. "Tell me what you're afraid of."

"I'm afraid that I'm going to live my eternal life without my sister."

For fuck's sake. "Seriously?"

She folds her arms and scrunches her mouth into a sullen pout. "You might not care about your soul, but I do. God will reward you if you do what's right."

"I'm not interested in any rewards that come from living under Vicar Jeremiah."

She shakes her head. "Haven't you suffered enough punishment for your sins?"

"What punishment?"

"If you hadn't left, God wouldn't have taken your baby from you."

The words are a heavy fist to my gut. "Amy . . ."

"Please move back to Camelot. We need you. Things are . . . tense."

"What do you mean?"

"There are a few elders who think . . ." She looks out her window and worries her bottom lip between her teeth. "They think Vicar Jeremiah should step down. Give his position to someone else. You saved us the night you left. Your return would be good for morale."

"I did what anyone would do, but I'm not going back, Amy. Never."

She reaches across the console and squeezes my arm. "But you don't have to worry about Patrick anymore. Come *home*." My key halfway to the ignition, I freeze. She obviously mistakes this for consideration, because she adds, "If you come now, you could be all settled by your birthday."

I didn't tell her about Patrick, so why does she know? "Why do you say I don't have to worry about Patrick anymore?"

"We took care of him," she says. She cocks her head. "Don't you remember telling me that you thought he was after you? He set that fire in your yard, Phoenix. He's not a good man."

My heart slams painfully against my ribcage. "What do you mean you *took care of him*?"

"I know you and Mom have your issues, but the rest of us just want what's best for you. If you come home, we can protect you all the time. God is good."

Putting my hands over my mouth, I draw in a ragged breath. The girl who just told me she was too holy to set foot in a bar is admitting to playing a part in nearly beating a man to death.

"Don't look at me like that," she says. She tugs her bottom lip between her teeth. "I couldn't let him hurt you again."

I ignore that explanation. I *did* want to be protected from Patrick, but not like that. "You shouldn't have hurt him."

"I have nightmares about that night," she says, "about him trying to finish what he started when he set that fire."

I swallow hard. "So do I." Nightmares of the fire climbing the walls of the chapel, the way it hissed and snapped in every direction, the smoke filling my lungs.

"He can't hurt you now," Amy says softly.

I shake my head. I don't want her trying to comfort me. "Are you headed back?"

Amy shakes her head. "No, I'm meeting some other girls in Avon. We need to do a supply run tonight."

Supply run, a.k.a. breaking and entering.

"What do you need? I'll give you money."

She rolls her eyes. "Stop judging, Nix."

PLAYING WITH FIRE

Thirteen years ago . . .

I'm crying. I can't stop crying.

The elders have decided that they believe my virgin pregnancy story, and I'm to marry Vicar Jeremiah on my seventeenth birthday.

And I can't stop crying because I know what I need to do. I have to run away. I have to leave my sister and my mom behind in this place and escape Camelot once and for all. I have to leave Patrick behind. And I will or I'll die trying.

But I'm afraid that "die trying" isn't just an expression. I could have escaped easily before, but since they found out about my pregnancy, they've had me guarded by an elder at all times.

"Phoenix."

I look up to see Patrick coming into my cabin. Grief etches his beautiful features, and when he squats beside me, my hands lift to try to smooth it away.

"I heard," he says. "What are we going to do?"

"What kind of sick man wants to marry his son's girlfriend?"

Something flashes in his eyes and he shakes it away. "You've always been special to him."

I don't ask why. I don't care. "I won't marry him. I have to run away, Patrick."

"It's not that easy. He's already decided you're his. The elders have decided."

"You want me to marry your *father*? Have him touch me like you do?"

"No." His eyes blaze with torment. "But you need to

know what you're up against. You can leave Camelot, but as long as it stands, you can't escape it."

"What's the difference? I don't understand."

He opens my hand and places a rune into my palm. Thurisaz, the rune of protection. He folds my fingers over it. "Do you know this one?"

I nod. "Protection. Fertility."

He draws in a long, ragged breath. "Yes, but it's more. It's also about having wisdom in combat."

"I'm not fighting anyone."

"If you plan to escape, you've already begun. It's best not to start a battle, my Phoenix, but if you do, you'd better finish it."

CHAPTER
TWENTY-THREE

Max

Nix is spooked. I don't know why or about what, but as she changes into a sleep shirt, worry creases her delicate features.

She sits on the edge of my bed, and I close my book and put it to the side before pulling her into my arms. She comes easily, resting her head against my chest as if this is exactly where she wants to be.

Four more nights.

I'm a man divided. Half of me is wishing the days away as I wait for Claire's return. The other wants time to stand still. Nix has made it clear that our sleepovers end when my daughter returns, but I can't get a read on what that means for our relationship outside of our sleeping arrangements. Not that I've asked. She has enough on her mind without me piling on my insecurities, and I promised we'd do this at her pace.

She closes her eyes and sighs.

"Do you want to talk about what's bothering you?" I ask, brushing the hair out of her face.

"I'm that easy to read, huh?"

"Only sometimes."

"I saw my sister Amy tonight. She was waiting in my car when I left the girls at the bar."

I stiffen. I can't help it. Even with the little I know about her old life, I don't like the idea of anyone from the commune contacting her. "What did she want?"

"She wants me to come back to Camelot. She's visited several times in the last few weeks, and she's been pushing for me to return, but tonight was the first time she admitted that things aren't going well there."

"Did she explain why?"

She shakes her head. "Not really. I guess there are some rumbles about a change in leadership, or maybe Camelot disbanding altogether. It's her home, and that scares her."

I stroke her hair and try to wrap my mind around what she must be feeling, but the truth is I have no context for what Nix is going through. I can't imagine having someone I love living in a cult I despise. "Maybe it will fall apart and you'll get your sister back."

She swallows hard. "She's not as sweet and innocent as she looks."

"I wouldn't know," I remind her. "I haven't met her."

"Patrick is dying and it's her fault."

"Why do you think that?"

"She first came around a couple days after the fire," she says. "I told her about it and that I thought Patrick might be after me, and she 'took care of it.' Those were her words to me tonight. She said she *took care of him* like he was a bag of dirty trash she took to the curb. She had him nearly killed."

My body chills, and for a moment I want to push Nix away and climb out of bed. She's warned me before that her connections make her dangerous, that I should think of Claire. This is the first time it's really sunk in. Patrick isn't the only threat out there.

But any instinct to pull away leaves me in a flash, and I hold her tighter. Claire is in Paris. She's safe. And I'll find a way to make sure she's just as safe when she comes home.

"She wanted to protect me," Nix whispers. "She sent men in to hurt him and believes with every fiber of her being that she did the right thing." She nuzzles her face against my chest and wraps her arms around me.

"Do you believe Patrick would hurt you, Nix?"

"Yes."

"And your sister believes that too?" I ask, and she nods against my chest. "Your sister's not the only one who'd be willing to go to extreme lengths to protect you. You asked me if I thought you could do a terrible thing and still be a good person, and I do. Your sister did a terrible thing, but that doesn't make her a terrible person."

She draws back and meets my gaze. I don't understand the series of emotions flicking across her features, but I can see that whatever she's feeling right now is laced with the kind of torment that eats at your soul. I would do anything to free her from that.

"Please don't tell Cade what I just told you. If the police went poking around Camelot for information about Patrick's assault, Amy would never trust me again, and if I'm ever going to get her out of there, I need her trust."

My chest aches for her—she's horrified and appalled by her sister's actions in one breath and planning to save her in the next. "I can keep your secrets." I bring her hand to my lips and press a kiss to the middle of her open palm. "As many of them as you need me to."

When I release her hand, she kisses me, softly, slowly, nipping at my lips before pulling away. "I'm going to miss this after Claire gets home," she whispers.

The ache in my chest spreads, fanning into my gut and making it clench painfully. I can't handle the idea of losing this woman, and I yet I know better than to believe she's given herself to me. She's the one holding back and I'm the fool rushing in.

I ignore the siren in my brain warning me that I've been here before and been burned. Fuck caution. Love isn't love if it isn't worth facing the fire.

"Even if you aren't sleeping here when she gets home," I say, telling myself that my caution is for her, not me, "nothing else between us needs to change."

Her hands slip from my neck and down to my chest, where her fingers map every ridge of every muscle. "Can we leave tomorrow's problems for tomorrow?" Sliding down the bed, she dips her head and skims her lips across my abdomen. "Tonight, I just want to focus on you and me in this bed together."

She presses her hot open mouth against the sensitive skin beneath my navel. I roll to my back and she strips my shorts off my hips. She straddles me, a knee on either side of my waist.

I press a hand against each of her bare thighs. "Beautiful," I murmur, sliding my hands up and under her T-shirt and around to her ass. I groan. "It seems you're nude under this shirt."

Her lips quirk into a grin. "Am I?" She rolls her hips, pressing her hot sex against my aching cock. "How convenient."

I squeeze my eyes shut. She feels good. "Christ." *Too good.* "Do you want me to put on a condom?"

Her grin falls away and her hips stop their torturous teasing. "I'm on the pill," she says, "and I have a clean bill of health."

Oh hell do I want this. "Me too." I shake my head. "Not the pill, but the clean part." She rocks against me so the tip of my cock presses against her opening. "Fuck, Nix. I want you. I want to feel you."

She shifts her hips and slides down my cock, taking me deep. "I want you too."

God this feels good. She's so fucking wet and tight, and watching her like this is amazing, but I want a view of her naked body as she rides me. "Take off your shirt."

She stills and shakes her head. "My scars. You don't need to look at those while we—"

"You're beautiful, Phoenix." I take her shirt, lift it over her head, and throw it to the floor. My hands on her torso, my gaze locked on hers, I move slowly underneath her, and she joins me, instinctively meeting each thrust. "And when I say I want you, I mean *all of you*." I graze my thumb over the symbol branded onto her stomach. "That includes your scars."

* * *

Nix

"Cade is here," Max says from the other side of the bathroom door. "We'll be in the living room when you're done with your shower."

"Okay," I call over the spray. "Give me a couple minutes."

He probably has new information on Patrick. My fears seem kind of silly now. I mean, all it really amounted to was a couple of creepy phone calls and that fire in my yard. If he'd really wanted to hurt me, he could have. But still, I want all the information I can get. I wonder if his condition has changed. I wonder if he knows my sister played a role in nearly killing him.

I turn off the shower and finger-comb my hair, telling myself to stop thinking about it. It's Lizzy and

Sam's wedding day, and I intend to put all this mess behind me for the night. I'm going to put on a pretty dress that shows off my legs, watch my friend get married, drink a little too much, and dance with my boyfriend.

I grab my towel and step out of the shower, and a scream lodges in my throat. Not twenty minutes ago Max had me under him in bed and every inch of me was warm and tingly. I wouldn't have thought it was possible for all that heat to dissipate so quickly, but when I see the bathroom mirror, my whole body goes cold.

There in the steam is Patrick's rune for me. Thurisaz. Here inside Max's house.

I shake as I force myself to pull on shorts and a T-shirt. When I go into the living room, the men are staring at each other, their faces grim.

"Patrick's out, isn't he?"

Cade sighs. "Patrick left the hospital AMA last night."

"AMA?" Max asks.

"Against medical advice," Cade explains. "Or in this case, against all common sense. The nurses checked on him around ten, and when they were back forty-five minutes later, he was gone."

I shift my gaze to Max, who's glaring holes into the coffee table. "He was here." I point toward the bedroom and my hand shakes. "That rune showed in the steam on Max's mirror. Patrick was here." I lift my hand to my mouth, then Max is there, wrapping me in his arms, murmuring in my ear while Cade is rushing to the bathroom. "What does he want from me? I just don't understand."

"If he was here, he's gone," Cade says when he returns. Max releases me and Cade levels me with his gaze. "Tell me why he would come after you when he's knocking on death's door. Tell me something I can use to get eyes on this guy. If you feel like you're in danger, I want to pick him up as soon as we can, but right now I don't have enough to get any manpower on this."

"Why now?" I whisper. "My birthday? I've had so many birthdays since I left. I don't know. After all this time." I realize I'm rambling and incoherent, and press my lips together.

"Then try just *why*?"

Why. "Revenge."

"For what?"

"For the night I escaped Camelot." I lift my eyes to meet Max's. I've come this far. I might as well go deeper. I may not want to tell my story, but I need to. Have to. Max deserves to know the kind of danger I've put him in. The danger I brought into his home. "Revenge for the night I tried to burn him alive."

CHAPTER TWENTY-FOUR

Max

My stomach knots painfully, and I want to personally track down Patrick McCane or Patrick Henry or whatever the hell his name is and tear him apart. Not just because he came into my *home,* but because Nix is so terrified right now, her fear is a palpable thing.

She watches me from under her lashes as if I might turn on her at any moment, but I know this woman and I know without her explaining that anything she did to Patrick she did in self-defense.

"It's okay," I whisper, and Cade says, "Tell us what happened."

Nix takes a seat and steadies her gaze on her hands in her lap. "A few months after I moved to Camelot, I decided to run away. I had to. I was pregnant."

Pregnant. That word is just another in a long line of kicks to my gut. I don't just want to hold her while she tells her story; I want to crawl into it and back in time so I can protect her. A young, pregnant Nix trapped with a group of fanatics.

"It was Patrick's," she says, "but I couldn't tell anyone that. Regardless of how I felt about Camelot, it was Patrick's home. He was to be the next vicar, and I didn't want him to lose that and worse—be exiled because of me."

I sit on the couch near her but far enough away to give her the space I instinctively know she needs. "What did you do?"

"I lied. I said I was still a virgin to protect Patrick. And maybe they knew I was lying or maybe they're all fucking crazy, but they said they believed me and that a pregnant virgin was clearly a gift for Vicar Jeremiah. They were going to make me his eleventh wife on my seventeenth birthday."

Cade's looking at Nix, his face grim.

"But you were a child," I say.

She attempts a smile. "That's what I kept telling them, but my fate was sealed. I made a plan to run away, and Patrick? At first I thought Patrick was on board. He didn't want me to leave, but he couldn't stomach me as his father's bride either. He gave me his Thurisaz rune and told me that if I was going to start the battle, I'd better finish it."

"That's the symbol that keeps popping up?" Cade asks.

I nod. "The night before I was supposed to marry Jeremiah, I was going to escape while the men were in the sweat lodge preparing the groom for his day. They'd been guarding me closely since the discovery of my pregnancy, and I wasn't sure what they'd do if they caught me trying to leave. They decided his bride needed to spend the night in the church, soaked in holy water so I would be cleansed before the ceremony. They tied me to the altar, wet in my white gown like some virgin sacrifice. Patrick was ordered to watch me while the elders took his father to the sweat lodge."

She draws in a breath, and I can tell she's not here with us anymore. She's there. Trapped in the memory and the horror of her old life.

"What happened?" I ask.

"Patrick left. I thought he was checking to make sure the coast was clear. I thought he was going to help me escape. But when he came back, I could hear the fire crackling outside. I could smell the kerosene and feel the fire's heat as it ate its way into the building. I think he was on some sort of drug. Maybe he'd taken something so he could get through what he'd decided he had to do. I don't know. But for whatever reason, instead of freeing me from my restraints so I could leave Camelot, he decided to burn the church while I sat tied up inside."

She stares into space for a long time, then shakes her head. "Sorry."

"Take your time," Cade says.

"He sat down next to me at the altar. Eventually, I gave up on reasoning with him and asked him to untie me so I could hold his hand. He gave me one free hand. Smoke filled the church, and we could hardly breathe. He lost consciousness first, and I used my free hand to untie my other."

The memory is dragging her through a mental hell, and I can't sit here and watch anymore as she endures it alone. I scoot over so I can pull her into my arms. She lets me, resting her cheek against my chest.

"I left him in there," she whispers. "I was afraid he would kill me if I tried to save him, and I left him there to burn."

"But he didn't." I stroke her back. "You did what you had to do, Nix. It was self-defense."

"He was unconscious. I could have dragged him out of the church. I could have saved him and then run, but instead I trapped him. There was always something a little *off* about Patrick, and I knew that, so maybe I wasn't as surprised as I should have been when he set the fire. And because of that, it was instinct that made me leave him there. I was so afraid he'd never let me go."

"Where did you go?"

"I got out to the road and flagged a car down. I called the fire department and had the guy take me to the hospital. I was having contractions, but I was only four and a half months along."

"Did they come for you?" Cade asks.

"No, and I didn't go back for my family. I called my mom later and learned they never found Patrick's remains in the church, so I assumed he escaped. I was grateful."

"And the baby?" I ask.

She pulls back and meets my eyes, and the loss there breaks my heart.

Nix

Max wraps his arms around me and presses a kiss to my forehead. "Are you doing okay?"

I force myself to breathe. Nothing is great, and yet everything is better than I'd anticipated. Cade left a few hours ago. He's working with a friend of his at the Indianapolis PD to find Patrick. I got a lecture about how his job would be easier if I'd have reported everything thirteen years ago, but they're going to put an APB out for Patrick. According to the hospital, he should be very weak and easier to track. At least in theory.

And Max . . . Max isn't running away from me. Even after learning about what I did.

"I'm okay." I nod. "That's the first time I told it to anyone outside of Camelot."

His arms tighten around me. "Are you up for tonight? I'm sure she'd understand if you just wanted to hole up for a while."

For a minute, I'm not sure what he means, but then I

remember. *Lizzy's wedding.*

I go to the living room and sink onto the couch. "I can't go." I take a deep breath. This is the way it has to be. "I don't know what he'll do next," I whisper. And as terrified as I am, there's also a sense of relief in the feeling that we've begun racing to the inevitable conclusion. After thirteen years, I'm ready for this to be over. One way or another.

Max sinks next to me on the couch. "I'll stay with you. Can you take time off work? We could get the hell out of Dodge. Go to Indianapolis or Chicago for the weekend. Longer if you want." He grins. "I'm sure Claire wouldn't mind a few more nights in Paris."

He's trying to make light so I won't feel guilty, but it's not working. "No," I say. "You're going to Sam and Lizzy's wedding. You're a groomsman, and they'll want you there. I just need to stay away." And pray like hell Patrick won't hurt any of my friends to punish me.

"I understand," Max says, "but I don't want you to be alone."

"If he wanted to hurt me, he would have done so already."

He shakes his head and takes a breath. "I want you to stay with Cade. Not the whole night, but while I'm at the wedding and until I can get away from the reception."

"Cade?" I ask. "Seriously? What happened to all that irrational jealousy you were harboring toward him?"

"Oh, it's still there." He smiles softly, slips a hand into my hair, and lowers his mouth to mine, kissing me long and soft and sweet. "I'm more concerned about your safety than I am about him stealing you away from me." He touches his forehead to mine.

I lift my hand to his face and stroke the stubbled edge of his jaw. "Why haven't you pushed me out of your life yet?"

"Why would I do that?"

"Because I've brought you nothing but trouble."

He cups my face in both of his hands and draws back to look me in the eye. "You bring me a whole hell of a lot more than trouble, Doc."

"Like what?"

"I could kick Kent's ass for leaving you. He made you believe you aren't worthy when the reality is . . ." Something flashes in his blue eyes, then he's trailing kisses along the edge of my jaw, the side of my neck, and up to my ear, where he whispers, "You're the most amazing woman I've ever met. You're beautiful." He kisses the tip of my nose. "Strong." The side of my mouth. "Resilient." The other side. "And I'm not going anywhere."

Then he slants his mouth over mine, and I'm dizzy with wonder, lust, and something I'm too scared to name.

Maybe I should try to convince him to keep his distance from me, but for the first time in my life, all the objections from my mind aren't loud enough to be heard over the delirious pounding of my heart.

CHAPTER TWENTY-FIVE

Max

"Stop looking at me like that," Nix says, straightening my tie. "I'm going to be *fine*."

Sam is one of my two best friends in the world, but I have no desire to go to his wedding tonight.

"I know you are," I grumble. "But I'd have more fun here in bed with you."

That makes her smile. *Mission accomplished.*

Sure, Cade can protect her, and I'm not worried about him trying to steal her out from under me anymore, but the idea of walking away—even for a day—leaves a bad feeling in my gut. How could that idiot Kent have his ring on her finger and then leave her forever when he learned what she did to protect herself? It just doesn't make sense to me.

Three taps at the front door have Nix and I turning in that direction, but Cade pokes his head in before I can reach it.

"Come on in," I call. He's early. He wasn't supposed to pick up Nix for another twenty minutes.

"We got him," he says, his lips stretching out into a grin. "A couple of officers caught him collapsed outside Nix's house and took him in. He's in the hospital under armed watch."

Nix stills next to me, and I take her hand and squeeze—my best effort to remind her she's not doing this alone.

"That's great news," I say when she remains silent.

"What's he saying?" she asks.

Cade shrugs. "He hasn't admitted to anything yet, but that's typical. We'll work on him and he'll crack."

Incrementally, she relaxes beside me. "You have him," she says, as if trying to process the information. "He can't get to me."

Cade nods, a self-satisfied smirk in place. "We got him."

She throws herself into my arms, and I hold her while she takes in shuddering breath after shuddering breath.

"It's going to be okay," I whisper, stroking her hair. "He can't hurt you anymore."

"So I guess this means you can go to your wedding," Cade says.

"Shit. I need to find something to wear!" She bites

back a smile then rushes off toward the bathroom.

"Is that normal?" Cade asks as the door down the hall clicks closed. "I just picked up the man who's been stalking her and threatening her for the last three months, and she didn't shed a tear."

I shake my head. "As far as I can tell, she doesn't cry. At all." I *have* noticed. It's almost as if Nix doesn't believe she's entitled to her own grief. "I guess all this is nothing compared to what she went through as a kid."

"Maybe," Cade says. "Listen, I didn't want to say anything to Nix. She deserves to have a good time tonight, but the truth is, I don't know how long we're going to be able to hold this guy. His recent crimes are minimal, but I'll dig up whatever I can, see if we can bust him for something else."

"What about what happened before? Arson? Attempted murder? Those are hardly minimal."

"There's no statute of limitations on murder, but attempted murder is a Class B felony. The statute of limitations on that is five years."

"He murdered their child when he set that church on fire."

"We could dig up the hospital record for the child, but we'd have to prove causation, which means proving he set the fire." Cade gives me a grim nod and pats me on the shoulder. "I'll work with the prosecutor and do everything I can."

"Thank you."

"I'll be around tonight. Call me if you need anything. I don't want her alone. Not yet."

"You think Patrick might be innocent?"

"Unlikely," he says, "but in my line of work, I've learned never to take anything for granted."

"I'll make sure she stays with the girls when I can't be with her today," I say. "Good thing you're the one who has to question Patrick and not me. I don't think I could talk to him without using my fists."

"Resisting the urge to use your fists on well-deserving candidates is kind of a job requirement."

"He fucked her up so badly," I mutter.

Cade studies me, and the silence stretches so long between us that it grows thin and uncomfortable.

"What?" I finally say.

Cade smirks. "I'm trying to figure out if you even know . . ."

"That I'm in love with her?"

His smirk turns to a grin and he nods. "Yeah, I guess you do. Have you told her?"

I'm shit at hiding my emotions. "No."

"A woman who's been through as much as she has?" Cade shrugs. "Pretty sure she's gonna need to hear it. A lot."

I arch a brow. "Thinking of a second career as the new Oprah?"

Cade grimaces. "Fuck off. I'm trying to help."

"Yeah. I know. And I'm trying not to scare her away."

CHAPTER
TWENTY-SIX

Max

"CAN WE GET EVERYONE out here for the Humpty Dance?" the DJ asks.

Girls rush to the dance floor, giggling and dragging their friends with them.

The bride grabs Nix's hand, and Nix shakes her head, laughing. Liz, of course, wins that battle, and I'm treated to the sight of all the women attempting that ridiculous nineties dance move.

I haven't seen her this relaxed in months. They have Patrick, and she's safe. And she has me, and nothing I've learned about her past has scared me away. And for now, she doesn't need to know that they might not be able to hold Patrick for long.

I catch her eye, and she grins and lifts her palms to the ceiling, then limps to the side along with the song's direction.

Even while she's acting like a goof, she's sexy as hell. She's wearing a dark blue number that hugs her tight curves and shows her long legs. After Cade left, she sauntered out of the bathroom in her underwear, holding the dress and asking me if I thought it would be okay. I almost dragged her into the bedroom right then and there, but Sam would have kicked my ass if I missed pictures. Would've been worth it, though.

By the time the song ends, the girls are laughing more than dancing.

"How about we slow it down," the DJ says, transitioning to a slow, jazzy number.

Nix and I meet at the edge of the dance floor.

"Come on," I say, wrapping my arms around her. "Dance with me."

She shakes her head and smiles. "As I just so expertly demonstrated, I have zero dance skills."

"You can stand on my feet, then." I lead her onto the dance floor and loop her arms behind my neck.

She sighs and melts into me, her head against my chest, her fingers finding their way into my hair. "Thank you," she whispers.

"For what?"

She lifts her head and studies me, and the hand in my hair drifts around to touch my cheek. "For sticking by me. For believing in me and understanding the terrible decisions I've made."

"Not all guys are like your ex-fiancé."

"Sure," she says, "but I don't think *any* guys are like you."

I hold her close, dip my head, and press my lips to hers.

Nix

A dream. That's the only way I can describe tonight. A dream wrapped in happiness for two of my best friends who just vowed to love each other forever. And Max. He holds me as if I'm something precious, and I'm starting to believe that maybe, to him, I am.

The dance ends, and though I'm reluctant to leave his arms, I'm too vulnerable in them.

"Want a drink?" he asks.

I nod. "Red wine?"

He heads to the bar, and I head to our table, one of those long, soft sighs building in my chest.

My phone flashes up at me with an alert, and I unlock the screen to see a series of missed text messages from a number I haven't seen before.

Unknown Number: Are you done playing games yet?

A chill ricochets through me and my fingers fly across the screen before I even think about what I'm doing.

Nix: Patrick?

Unknown Number: Oh no. Patrick is with the police now, thanks to your friends. That's fine by me since he desecrated our graveyard last night. But God will take care of him.

Nix: Who is this?

Unknown Number: Your other half. I asked God to show me who was true, and he led me to the fire. You rose from it and then again. Now come home. God made you for me.

I stare at my phone, my stomach churning and my hands shaking.

Unknown Number: It's time to sever ties. Either you do it or I will. I could rip Max from your life as easily as I did Kent.

Nix: You can't control me. I can go to the police.

Unknown Number: I will yank Mr. Hallowell from your life as easily as I did your fiancé. Only involve people you're willing to sacrifice to the fire, sweet Phoenix.

When I look up, my heart is pounding hard, each

beat like a fist to my sternum. Max is standing in front of me with my wine and all I can see is a man I would die to protect.

* * *

Max

"I want to tell you something," I say, setting the wine on the table in front of Nix. "I spent my entire time in line at the bar working up the courage, but I want you to know."

She blinks at me. "What?"

I take a long drink and then a deep breath. I'm pretty sure I'm already making a mess of this, so I put my glass on the table and take her hands. "I'm in love with you."

"What?"

"You don't have to say anything. It's not like that." I swallow hard. "You're amazing. I've been walking around trying to pretend my life is complete, but it's more like I have this jagged edge that's been sawing into me since Hanna left. You don't just soften that edge; you eliminate it. We fit. And the hurt is gone when I hold you."

Her lips part. "Max . . ."

"I'm in love with you. You've had enough shit in your life lately that I thought you might like to hear something good." I attempt a smile, but it's shaky. I

277

expected a little more reaction from her, and she looks stunned.

"I can't do this," she whispers.

The floor might as well have just been snatched from beneath my feet. "What?"

She flinches and turns away. "You and me. I can't do this. You're sweet and I really like you, but this . . . I can't. I shouldn't have ever let it go this far. We have to end this."

"What just happened?" I look to the dance floor and back to her. "What changed since we left that dance floor?"

"Nothing changed, Max. You are wonderful, and I've never met anyone like you. But I don't think that you and I want the same things at all."

"We don't know that yet. We haven't even . . ." *Fuck.* I can't do this. I feel like I'm groveling, and I swore I'd never let myself get in this position again. "Are you breaking up with me?"

"Yes. I'm sorry."

I step closer, but she shakes her head and presses a palm to my chest, as if to remind me to keep my distance. "Look at me and tell me you don't feel *anything* for me."

"You know I do. But can you look at me and tell me you'd be happy with this relationship never going anywhere. You need a woman who will be your *family*. I can't be that woman."

"Yes you can. You're just scared."

"You promised," she whispers. "You promised me that if I needed to end this, you'd let me go." She shrugs, as if this is just another meaningless conversation we'll both forget tomorrow. "I'm sorry, Max. I never meant to hurt you."

Those words ring so familiar that it's all I can do to stay upright as I stumble back. "Right." I fist my hands to keep myself from grabbing her shoulders and kissing her until she remembers how good we are together. But who the fuck cares if she likes my kisses? What does it matter if I turn her on? Or that she thinks I'm a *nice guy*. Being *nice* never got me fucking anywhere.

She looks around, tugging her lower lip between her teeth. "I think I should go now."

"I'll take you home."

She shakes her head. "I don't think that's a good idea. This is hard enough."

"Can we have all the groomsmen to the back for some more pictures?" the DJ asks through the speakers.

"This isn't about us. I don't want you to be alone."

"Patrick is in custody, right?"

Fuck. I can't do this. I can't stay here all night, smile for the camera, and pretend the woman I love didn't just rip my heart out and stomp on it. But insisting on being with her when she wants me gone would be so much harder. "I'll text Cade. He can take you home."

She nods, and I open the messages on my phone to ask Cade if he can pick her up. Ten minutes later, he sends me a text letting me know he's waiting outside.

I do as I promised. I let her go. I stand there, the party raging on behind me as I nurse my drink and try to figure out how the hell I managed to once again lose my heart to a woman who doesn't want it.

PLAYING WITH FIRE

* * *

Nix

"Why your place?" Cade asks as he pulls up in front of my house. "I thought you were staying at Hallowell's."

I shrug. "I think it'd be better if I stayed in my own bed tonight." I climb out of the car and he follows me.

"Why?"

"We broke up." I try to keep the words even, but betraying my heart is too painful and my breath hitches on *up*.

"You broke up? Why?"

"We just want different things." *He wants to be with me, and I want to protect him.*

"You're not sleeping here alone," Cade says.

I shake my head. "Sure I am. You got the bad guy, right?" I'm not sure how I'm managing this conversation without letting my voice shake, but I am somehow, and instead of waiting for Cade to agree, I head straight to the house, unlock the door, and disable the alarm.

I flick on the lights, walk into my kitchen, and feel like I've stepped out of a nightmare and into one much worse.

I don't realize I'm screaming until Cade is wrapping his arms around me, my back to his front. I can't stop staring at the scene waiting for me on my kitchen island.

"Breathe," he whispers in my ear. I obey, and he slowly turns me in his arms to face him. He's tall, and when he tightens his arms around me, my cheek rests against his chest, right between his pecs. "Breathe," he repeats. Then he must see it, because his whole body stiffens and he curses softly.

I squeeze my eyes shut, but the image is burned onto my eyelids.

He desecrated our graveyard last night.

"Fuck," Cade breathes. He's already ushering me back out the front door. He closes up the house and lowers me to sit on my porch swing. I'm shaking. Not just a little. I'm *quaking* with whole-body tremors that I can't stop.

I squeeze my eyes shut tighter, as if that might banish the image from my head, but it doesn't work.

Cade is on the phone, shooting clipped commands that I don't bother to process.

He ends the call and sits next to me on the swing, wrapping his arm around my shoulders. Sweet. He's a sweet guy. Not as sweet as Max, but . . .

Oh, God. *Max.*

I will yank Mr. Hallowell from your life as easily as I did your fiancé. Only involve people you're willing to sacrifice to the fire, sweet Phoenix.

Cade strokes my hair and tucks me into him protectively. I wish he wouldn't. I bring evil and horror and deserve none of this kindness. But my mouth won't form the words to ask him to stop.

"She's in shock," Cade says to someone.

I force my eyes open and see a tall uniformed officer on my porch.

"I'm Officer Wrigley," he says, offering his hand.

I blink at him before realizing I'm supposed to shake his hand.

"Are you okay?" the officer asks.

I nod, then shake my head. "Tell me it's not real."

A second officer emerges from my house, a grimace on his face. Where did he come from?

"Call Hallowell." Cade tosses his phone to the other officer. "He'll want to be here."

Wrigley grunts. "Got it."

Desperate to escape this nightmare, I squeeze my eyes shut, only to open them again.

I don't think I'll ever again be able to close my eyes without seeing Kent's partially decomposed body sprawled on my kitchen island.

CHAPTER TWENTY-SEVEN

Max

I LEAVE THE RECEPTION and rush to Nix's house as fast as I can.

Cade greets me on her front porch. Behind him, Nix is on the swing, curled into a protective ball, her face tucked into her knees. It fractures something inside of me to see her like this—drained, terrified. Defeated.

My strong, brave, amazing Nix is curled up like a child who knows the boogie monster is real and doesn't believe there's anything she can do to defeat him.

"Baby," I murmur. I sink to my haunches in front of the swing and tuck her hair behind her ear.

When she lifts her head, the misery in her eyes

chunks off a piece of my heart. No tears. Still not one fucking tear. Any other woman would have flooded the city. But the misery is there.

She opens her mouth to speak and starts shaking violently.

I sit beside her on the swing and pull her onto my lap and wrap my arms around her. "I'm here," I whisper into her hair. "Breathe, baby. I'm here." I rub her back with slow circles, and when I feel the violent tremor of her muscles beneath my hand, I know she's having a panic attack.

She clings to my chest and I exhale a sigh of relief. It would have killed me if she'd asked me to let her go when she's like this. I would have if that was what she needed, but it would have been the hardest damn thing. But since she's good with me holding her, I continue rubbing her back, whispering into her hair, and reminding her to breathe until her chest rises and falls evenly and her trembling has subsided.

Nix's head is against my chest, her eyes closed, her fists clenched and curled into her body. Her shoulders loosen and her hands relax.

That's when I see it. The edge of a picture is peeking out from her fingertips.

I slip it from her hand, and the image staring back at me causes my stomach to hitch. It's an engagement photo. One of those poses where the woman's hand is positioned just so on the man's shoulder so the whole world can see the rock on her finger. The man's in a khaki sports jacket. He's a big guy, built like a linebacker, but with a smile that counterbalances any intimidation that might come from his size. And he's looking at Nix as if she made him believe in miracles. And she's looking at him like . . .

"He was an amazing guy," she whispers.

I'm so enthralled by the picture that I'm surprised to hear her speak.

"I want to get her out of here," Cade says. "Okay if I have an officer take her to your place?"

Nodding, I hand him my keys. "What happened?"

He turns to Nix. "We'll meet you over there. Wrigley will be by your side the whole time."

Nix dutifully uncurls and extricates herself from my arms before standing. I miss having her there, but I'd rather take her home and hold her in my bed. I just want to keep her close and remind myself that she's safe.

Before she leaves, I press a kiss to the top of Nix's head, and she closes her eyes and quakes under me.

Cade inclines his chin toward the house. When we step inside, two more officers mill about, taking pictures and doing whatever those guys do. This is New Hope, not New York City, so there's not exactly a crime scene investigation unit to send out.

I'm not sure what I expect, but the sight that greets me in the kitchen doesn't just turn my stomach. It chills my blood.

There's a dead body on Nix's kitchen island—not a fresh kill, but a rotting corpse. As if it's been pulled from the grave but hasn't decomposed enough to keep me from identifying him.

That's the guy from the picture.

"This was her fiancé?" Cade asks. "The coroner is

guessing this guy was killed six years ago. Single shot to the back of the head and then buried, which is why he's not decomposed beyond all recognition."

"He left her a note and told her he couldn't marry her and that he was moving to South America." A sharp chill jackknifes down my spine. "He didn't write that note, did he?"

"I would guess not."

"Patrick's work?" I ask.

Cade shrugs. "That's our best guess. He must have planted it here before we picked him up this afternoon."

I turn toward the door. Nix keeps her doors locked and has an alarm system in place. "He had keys to her house somehow, right? But you confiscated those. How did he get in this time?"

"The locks don't appear to have been tampered with. Maybe he had another key stashed somewhere."

"What about the alarm?"

He shakes his head. "Your guess is as good as mine. We called the alarm company and they said it disabled about thirty minutes before we picked him up. Maybe she came over for something and forgot to re-enable the alarm. Or maybe the guy is just that fucking good."

"That's a lot of maybes." Fuck. I don't like this. "What's this supposed to be? A confession?"

Cade looks at me as if I'm a fool. "It's a threat."

That doesn't sit right with me. If Patrick has the skills to come and go in my house or hers, he could have abducted her, hurt her or worse, any time he wanted. "But what does he want?"

"He wants Nix," he says slowly. "That's the only

thing he's spoken to the officers—a demand to speak with Nix."

Nix

The whole night passes in a blur. At some point, Max arrived in his living room, and I knew he had to have seen what was in my kitchen because his face was sheet white. Cade asked me questions. Did I recognize the body? When was the last time I saw the deceased? Did Kent have any enemies? Now he and Max are talking on the front porch.

"I promise you, we're taking this very seriously," Cade says. Max says something I can't make out, and Cade replies, "I agree. Get her to stay here tonight. We'll see what we can find out. We're talking to the neighbors to find out if anyone saw anything."

Max murmurs something else.

The front door squeaks as it opens and Max comes inside to sit on the couch next to me. His fingers skim the photo in my hand. I'd forgotten I was holding it. I took it out of my purse after I saw his body. I wanted to believe it was someone else. Anyone else. I needed to see his face again.

For years, I couldn't think of Kent without the kind of bitterness that comes with being betrayed by someone you trust more than anyone else in the world, but now that bitterness has evaporated under the hot lights of the truth and guilt has filled its space.

Max removes the picture from my grip and squeezes my hand. That simple gesture makes my throat go thick.

"Kent was murdered."

"Nix," he whispers. "That wasn't your fault."

I lift my eyes to meet his gaze and slowly withdraw my hand from his. "But it was."

"Patrick is a *madman*," he says. "You cannot take responsibility for his crimes."

But it wasn't Patrick. Patrick was only trying to warn me. All these rune signs were a warning from Patrick about Camelot, and I completely missed his message. But what about the night at the church? What about that fire?

"Kent was murdered," I repeat. I bite my lip hard. I should have known. Why didn't I ever question that note? It was his handwriting, but you hear about people being forced to write letters all the time. Yet I believed every word.

Was it just too easy to believe that I'm that despicable?

"Let's get you to bed," Max says.

I shake my head. "No. Not here. I'll get a hotel room."

"That's fucking ridiculous *and* foolish."

Oh God, I can't do this. My heart is breaking and I need to protect Max, but it hurts so much. "They have Patrick. I'll be fine." I stand up and head toward the guest bedroom to grab my bag. It's best that Max wakes up tomorrow morning and I'm no longer a part of his life. I curse the optimism that made me believe I might escape any of this—Patrick, Camelot, or the flames that never left my nightmares.

"There's still too much we don't know." Max follows me. "You're not staying alone in some hotel room."

"Fine. I'll find somewhere else."

"What happened?" he asks softly. "What aren't you telling us?"

"Nothing, Max. I've just had a long fucking night. I don't need the added awkwardness of sleeping in the same house as my ex."

"Don't." He steps forward, invading my space, and dips his head until I'm forced to look him in the eye. "Break up with me, fine, but don't fucking lie to me about what's going on here. There's more to this situation than unrequited love. You don't want to be with me, fine. But I'm going to protect you. Whatever it takes."

"Then let me go and stay away from me."

"Anything but that."

"I'll stay with Cade." I don't mean to, but I look at his face as I say it, and the hurt in his eyes bowls me over. I want to puke. "Would you call him while I pack, please?" My voice cracks on the *please*, but he doesn't seem to notice.

He pulls his phone from his pocket, turns on his heel, and leaves the room.

I close my eyes and hold my hand to my aching heart. I am so in love with this man, and I will hurt him

over and over again if that's what it takes to protect him
and his little girl.

CHAPTER
TWENTY-EIGHT

Max

CADE'S TAILLIGHTS FADE into the distance and I feel empty. After heading back into the house, I collapse on the couch and stare at the ceiling. I know in my gut that Nix is hiding something, but I can't help if she won't tell me what.

Drawing in a deep breath, I decide what I need to do.

It's after two a.m., which means it's after eight a.m. in Paris. I pick up the phone and dial Meredith's number.

"Allo?"

"Meredith?"

"Hi, you! Oh my God, what time is it there?"

I sink into the couch and close my eyes. "After two, Sunday morning."

"Why on Earth are you still awake? Are you rediscovering your bachelor ways and closing down the bars?"

"Not exactly. How's Claire?"

"She's great. She's picking up some French—oh my God, you should hear it. Abso-freaking-lutely adorable."

My chest aches. "I miss her so much."

She sighs. "Now you know how I feel *all the time*. Though I'll be honest, I have no idea how you do this. I hired a nanny to help while she's here, and Claire *still* wears me out."

"She's good at that." I swallow hard. "Listen, I need a favor."

She must hear the intensity in my voice, because hers goes soft. "Anything, Max."

"Is there any way you can delay your trip home by a few days? I can't explain now, but I don't want Claire here until I work some things out."

"Is everything okay?"

No. I take a breath. "It will be. I just . . . need to find a stallion."

"What?"

"Nothing. So, what do you think?"

"That's not a problem. Seriously, I have a friend arriving in the city next week who's dying to meet Mademoiselle Claire, so it'll be great."

"Thank you, Meredith."

"You've sacrificed more for me than anyone else

would. I owe you way more than a little favor." She pauses a beat. "Can I ask a question?"

"Sure."

"Is this about a girl?"

"Her name's Phoenix. I think you've met her before."

"Doctor? Kind of uptight? I mean, I'm sure she's not *really*, but kind of comes off that way?"

That's Meredith. Can't have a conversation about another woman without sticking her foot in her mouth. "She's in trouble."

"Then she's lucky she has you. Shining armor has always suited you, Max."

Laughter puffs from my lips, but it sounds hollow. "That's what I hear. Good night, Mer."

"*Bonne nuit.*"

I end the call and grab my laptop. I haven't done research since I was in college, but I think I still remember a thing or two.

Nix

Sleeping at Cade's was . . . weird. I expected a bachelor pad and found he has a really nice two-bedroom apartment in one of the complexes downtown that overlooks the river. Pretty swanky for a cop.

When I climb out of bed only a few hours after

getting into it, I find him in the kitchen making coffee.

"I hope you didn't get up on my account," I say. "Especially since I invited myself over here."

"I can't ever sleep past five. Old military habits die hard."

"You were in the military?"

"For a few years after high school."

"And you worked as a homicide detective in LA?"

"Did some personal security stuff after that too," he says. He pours two mugs of coffee and hands one to me. "Cream's in the fridge if you want it. Anything else from my résumé you're curious about?"

"You're kind of an enigma to me, Officer Watts. All this adventure and you ended up here."

He cocks a brow. "I'm the enigma? You just dumped the guy you love and spent the night in *my* guest bedroom."

"I never said I loved him."

He grunts. "You didn't need to. Care to explain what you're doing here?"

I drop my gaze to my coffee, not wanting to meet his. "I need to figure some things out."

"Clearly."

Max

I spent a couple hours online last night digging

through Google search results and finding nothing, so as soon as the doors open at noon, I head into the public library.

"Max," the girl behind the circulation desk calls. "Where's Claire?"

I smile politely. "She's still with her mom in Paris."

"Stocking up on books for when she returns?" the girl asks.

I shake my head and approach the desk. "Actually, I'm trying to find old newspaper articles about a church fire that happened thirty years ago."

"Oh, sure. I can help. Where was it?"

I grimace. "Yeah, that's the hard part. I don't really know. But I know it was in Indiana—" I *think*, but I'm not sure. But that's as good a place to start as any. "And I know it happened thirty years ago tomorrow."

"Hmm. Okay, let's see what we can find."

I follow her to the computers in the reference area. "I searched online last night, but none of the newspapers' websites went back far enough."

"No, they usually don't. Nothing was digitized back then. But don't worry. You came to the right place." She shows me how to log on to their servers so I can view newspaper articles from three decades ago. "I'll leave you to it."

Forty-five minutes later, I've found what I'm looking for.

Judge Declares Insufficient Evidence in Church Arson Case Against Jeremiah Henry

PLAYING WITH FIRE

✳ ✳ ✳

Nix

I smile at the armed guard outside Patrick Henry's room and wave a chart.

"Two doctors in as many hours?" the guard asks in disgust. "My mother didn't get such good care when she was dying. Guess it pays to be a criminal in the country."

I duck my head and push into the room, murmuring, "Sorry to hear about your mother."

When I sit down next to the hospital bed by Patrick, I feel as if I've entered the Twilight Zone. I spent years fearing this reunion, and now I've made it happen.

"Phoenix," he whispers, rolling his head to the side to look at me.

"I'm so sorry." I swallow hard. It's hard to sit here and face what I did to him. "I'm sorry about what I did thirteen years ago. I shouldn't have left you there."

"What you shouldn't have done was call the fire department. I told you you'd have to burn Camelot to the ground to escape it."

"And that's why you set the fire? I thought you were trying to kill me."

He smiles slowly, but the smile is twisted on the scarred side of his face. "No. A phoenix will always rise from the ash. You'd done it before. I knew you could do it again. And you escaped, didn't you? But then you called the fire department and saved the whole damn place."

I shake my head. "You've been trying to warn me. The fire in my yard and the text messages—I thought you were threatening me, but you were warning me."

He nods vaguely.

"What about the phone calls?" I ask.

He rolls his head to the side and attempts a frown, though clearly even that requires more strength than he has. Death isn't knocking on Patrick's door—it's sitting right in the room with us, holding his hand. "I never called you."

So Patrick sent the early texts, but it had to have been Jeremiah who was calling me. That makes my stomach churn. "They think *you* murdered Kent," I tell him.

He shrugs. "I'm dead the second they release me anyway. My father will have his men finish the job they started."

"What am I supposed to do?"

"I've been trying to warn you. I wanted you to finish the battle." His voice is weak, and I have to strain to hear him. "But you ignored my messages, and then you told *them* I was around, and I couldn't get to you anymore."

"Why does he want me now?" I whisper.

Patrick's eyes cut to me before floating closed again. "He's always wanted you, Phoenix. From the day you were born. That's why he sent me to woo you. He'd been waiting, and when you turned sixteen, he had me find you. The only problem was, I fell in love with the girl my father intended to claim as his own." His lips twist but his eyes stay closed. "You should have seen how angry he was when he found out your were pregnant. He knew it was mine, but he couldn't tell anyone that. If the elders knew the truth, by *his* rules, you'd have to be exiled. He couldn't have that. He's been obsessed with you your whole life."

"Why didn't you just find me and explain all this?"

"I swore to God that if you escaped the fire, I would stay out of your life. I was trying to keep that promise but still warn you," he says. His irrational logic doesn't faze me. I spent most of last night thinking like Patrick to unravel the puzzle of what's been happening the last few months. "Until Kent was murdered, I was like you. I believed he'd let you go. But when your fiancé disappeared, I knew what had happened, and I knew he had plans for you. So I started watching you closely. I wanted to protect you, but I knew he'd kill me for interfering, so I had to be careful."

"Why now?"

"Because they're turning on him. Slowly, but it's happening. There's unrest in Camelot. And just like he did when there was unrest in Gaia, he's going to burn it down and ask God to save the faithful. But you and I both know he doesn't care about the faithful. He only cares about himself. And you, Phoenix."

"What's Gaia?"

"Your mom's first commune. That was Dad's fire too. He'd been exiled, and when they wouldn't let him return, he burned it down. You survived the first time and you survived my fire, and now he thinks he needs you. You can leave Camelot, but as long as it stands, you can't escape it. Let it burn, Phoenix. Don't make the mistake you did last time."

He's as crazy as his father if he believes I'm going to let Jeremiah burn my mother and sister, but I'm afraid if I send the police I'm sentencing them to burn too.

My phone buzzes with a new text message. It's from the same number that sent last night's messages.

We're ready to light the candles. If you promise not to bring any uninvited guests to our party, I promise to spare these from the fire. Will you come home?

With the message is a picture of my mother and my sister tied to opposite sides of the altar, their hands bound behind their backs, duct tape covering their mouths.

"I have to go to him." When I look up from my phone, Patrick's gaze is steady on me.

"Happy birthday, sweet Phoenix," he whispers, then he closes his eyes. "Finish the battle."

CHAPTER
TWENTY-NINE

Max

CADE OPENS THE DOOR to his apartment after I pound on it the third time. "You know, I have neighbors who are trying to sleep."

"Where's Nix?"

"I told you when you texted that she's doing rounds at the hospital. Why?"

"She's not at the hospital. I was just there. They said she left hours ago." I look at my watch. "And her birthday is in three hours." I've wasted the last hour driving around town looking for her and trying to get her to return my calls. I should have come to Cade's from the start.

"What's going on?" he asks softly.

"Patrick put that body in Nix's kitchen yesterday."

He drags a hand through his hair. "We know he did. His fingerprints were all over the place."

"But I don't think he killed her fiancé."

"I'm not sure Nix believes he did either, but she's not talking. Do you have any idea who?"

"Jeremiah Henry. Patrick's father. The man Nix was supposed to marry the day she left Camelot. He burned down a church with people locked in it the night Nix was born. Her mom was in there but escaped, and Nix survived. And I don't believe it's a coincidence that she ended up meeting his son and moving to his commune sixteen years later."

"What's he going to do?"

"I don't know, but I don't even know where Camelot is."

"I do," Cade says.

I nod. "Then we start there. We need to make sure Nix is safe. Her birthday is significant."

Cade's cell and mine chime one after the other with text messages. We read them at the same time and then look at each other.

"What's that supposed to mean?" he asks.

I shake my head. "Don't worry about it. Let's go."

PLAYING WITH FIRE

Nix

I can't believe the church is still standing—dilapidated and broken, its remains stand like a charred skeleton resurrected in the moonlight. Jeremiah could have had it torn down and a new one built, but I bet he imagined this night and counted on me coming back.

When I escaped Camelot thirteen years ago, I didn't think I would ever return.

I knew what I was leaving behind—my mother, my sister, and Patrick. Patrick, whom I'd loved enough to follow here. Patrick, who had held me down while they burned Camelot's symbol into my skin. Patrick, who was perfectly happy to die by my side and who held my hand while the rafters caught fire and until his lungs filled with smoke.

When I step into the church, my breath catches as the smell of kerosene hits my nose. The place has already been saturated. I spot the first flames—a row of candles in the three Camelot circles around the altar. My steps slow. I can practically feel the smoke in my lungs and the ropes biting into my wrists.

"Phee Phee!"

"Amy?" I rush to the front, frantic, and like in one of my nonsensical dreams that mix memory and fear, Amy is tied to the left side of the altar, ropes crisscrossing her chest, panic in her eyes. On the right side is my mother, anger and defiance blazing in her eyes.

That's right, Mama. Don't let them take the fight from you.

I immediately drop to my knees to untie them.

"Are you sure you want to do that?"

Jeremiah's voice—strong and sure. And the stuff of nightmares. He looms over me, as if he manifested from thin air. There's a knife in his hand and evil in his eyes. My hands freeze. How did I never guess he was my true enemy?

"Hurry," Amy says. "He's crazy. He has everyone locked in the basement."

I swallow hard. "You said if I came you'd let them go."

Jeremiah studies me, his eyes cold and calculating. "I did. If you give yourself to me."

"Just let them go."

"You can't have her!" my mother screams.

"Hush." Jeremiah leans over—slowly, calmly—and when I realize what he's doing, I yank away and scramble backward. He catches my wrist and holds up a thick zip tie. "Who stays, Phoenix? You or your family?"

I stop trying to escape his grasp. "Let them go."

His lips curve into a demented smile. "Then follow me."

"Not until you release them."

With a few swishes of his blade, he cuts through the ropes holding Mom and Amy to the altar, and then he's against me, pushing me to the life-size crucifix behind the altar and using the zip tie to bind my hands to the cross over my head.

"You can't stay here, Phee Phee," Amy whispers as she rises to her feet. "He's evil. He killed your fiancé."

Jeremiah smooths a lock of my hair behind my ear,

and I shudder. "Kent," he says with a soft sigh. "I told him what would happen if he didn't leave you, but he called my bluff." He cocks my head and studies me. "He really did love you, but he couldn't understand that you weren't his to take."

I squeeze my eyes shut, trying to block out his words so I can *think*.

"I'm glad you finally made it home," Jeremiah says, still touching my face. "Just in time for your birthday celebration. God will reward you for returning to me." He steps away. He moves with the calm assurance of a man who already knows he's going to win the battle. He turns to Mom and Amy, who stand staring at me. "Tell your friends to leave or I'll throw them in the basement with the others."

"Leave, Amy." I swallow hard. "Get out of here."

Jeremiah tips over the first candle and the flame races in a circle around the church, forming a ring of flame that begins and ends only feet from the crucifix.

Amy shakes her head, her eyes panicked, and I lock my eyes on hers. "Get Mom out of here. It's going to be okay." Tears stream down her cheeks, and I hope I'm not lying.

For the first time in thirteen years, I put my hope into a prayer. *Please, God. Please.*

"She's my reward," Jeremiah says, wrapping a hand around my neck. "God's will be done."

And just like that, fire sirens blare. Mom rushes at Jeremiah and tackles him to the ground as Max busts through the church doors, Cade at his side.

"The basement!" I shout. "They're trapped in there!"

Jeremiah's knife is at my mother's throat, and blood trickles onto the blade. "Don't hurt her!" I yank at my bound wrists, pulling, kicking, twisting, desperate to find freedom.

Cade rushes to the basement door, slides the wooden bar off, and pulls it open, and people rush out of the basement and toward the exit. The screams and cries fill the church as the fire engulfs it and smoke presses down on us.

"The children," Amy says. She rushes to the basement door and helps Cade guide the panicked mob out the front door.

Max jumps over a burning church pew, racing toward me and the fire that creeps closer and closer to my legs. I can't get my eyes off Mom. She pushes Jeremiah over, and his knife skids across the floor. Max sweeps it up and saws at the tie binding my wrists.

Jeremiah grabs a fistful of Mom's hair and yanks her off and shoves her into the fire.

"No!" I scream, yanking one more time at the ties. I lunge forward, covering Mom's body with my own as I roll us from the flames. Jeremiah hurdles himself toward us, but Max tackles him mid-leap.

"You will be punished for thwarting God's will!" Jeremiah crows.

Max twists his hand behind his back. "I'll show you God's will, motherfucker."

CHAPTER
THIRTY

Max

"Daddy!" Claire screeches as she runs through the front door and into my arms. "I missed you!"

I scoop her up off the floor and swing her through the air. It's been less than a month and I swear she's grown a ton. "I missed you too, Pumpkin," I say into her hair. My throat is too full of emotion. She's a piece of me, and having her home makes the whole world right itself. I can handle anything—any heartbreak, any psycho bad guy—as long as I have my daughter.

"She stayed awake the *whole* flight," Meredith says from the doorway. "She couldn't stop talking about all the things she and Daddy were going to do together when she got home."

Claire wiggles in my arms. "Let me down, Daddy. I wanna visit my dollies. I missed them!"

I reluctantly lower her to the floor and let her go. She bolts down the hallway to her room, leaving her mother behind.

"I have to give you props," Meredith says. "It's not easy single-parenting that ball of fire."

I shrug. "I don't really do it alone. Mom's a big help, and I get breaks when you're around."

She bites her lip and folds her arms. "We had a good time. She's amazing—not that I can take much credit for that."

"You're being too hard on yourself."

Tears fill her eyes and a couple spill over. "Am I? I've spent the last two years putting my career before my own daughter every step of the way."

"Mer, stop beating yourself up. You didn't abandon her." I shake my head and pull her into my arms. "Every day, there are countless men who entrust their children's care with the mother while they pursue their career. They make time to call and visit and are called good fathers. A mom does it, and it's abandonment?"

She sniffs against my chest. "Jesus, you're a nice guy."

"Yeah, that's what they tell me."

"Seriously, you always know the right thing to say." She pulls out of my arms and wipes away her tears. "Screwing up with you is truly my biggest regret, and any woman who doesn't see you for the amazing man you are is as stupid as I was."

"Being a good guy doesn't mean you're any good at relationships." *And saving the girl doesn't mean you get to keep her for yourself.*

"I read about what happened online. That's intense stuff. Is your doctor okay?"

"She will be."

Meredith takes a deep breath. "I have a confession. I'm making the move permanent next time I return to Paris. I love it there and I want to put down roots. I was thinking of asking you to let me move her with me, but after these last few weeks I just can't. She *adores* you, Max."

"The feeling is mutual," I say, but there's a fist clenching my chest at the idea of losing my daughter.

"Once I made my decision to give you full custody, I just knew it was right." She exhales slowly and forces a smile. "Isn't that crazy? How sometimes you just *know*? And frankly, I kind of like being the non-custodial parent. It's all the fun stuff without the daily grind, ya know?"

"I would have fought you for her."

"Yeah. I know. Kind of relieved I don't have to go up against Papa Bear."

"Yoo-hoo!" Claire calls, poking her dark mop of hair out into the hall. "Mommy, come see my new room!"

Meredith grins. "I'm coming, sweetie. Just a minute." When Claire disappears back into her room, Meredith says, "So what's going to happen with you and Phoenix? Is she moving in with you?"

"Isn't there some step between breaking up and

moving in together?"

Her face goes soft. "She broke up with you? I'm sorry, Max."

"Don't be. I rushed things and scared her off, but I'll find a way to fix it if I can."

"Mom-my!" Claire calls again.

"Coming!"

Meredith is halfway to Claire's room when Claire bursts into the hallway shouting, "Tree house! Tree house! Tree house! Mommy! Daddy built me a tree house!" And then she's darting to the back of the house and out into the backyard.

Meredith props her hands on her hips. "You couldn't just settle for being her hero, could you?" she asks, smiling. "You had to build her a flipping *tree house* and elevate your status to *super* hero."

I shrug. "Come on out and see how awesome I am."

We follow Claire to the back, and she's already halfway up the ladder.

"Jesus," Meredith mutters when she sees it. "What'd you do, take that straight out of your own childhood fantasies?"

I grin as Claire hits the top of the ladder and climbs inside. "Pretty much."

"Oh my goodness, Daddy!" Claire calls. "I love it so much!"

"I'm going up." Meredith heads for the ladder, and I follow.

Claire is inside spinning circles, and I have to blink when I see what has her so captivated. The inside of the tree house has been decorated. Swathes of shimmery pink fabric are draped from corner to corner, and tiny battery-operated white lights illuminate the edges of the floor.

"Holy cow," Meredith says. "This is amazing."

"No kidding," I mutter. Then something catches in my throat as I see the wooden signs hanging on either side of the tree house window. One says, "50% Princess – 50% Tomboy – 100% AWESOME" and the other says, "Future Doctor in Training."

"Oh my God, Max, where did you find those signs? They are *so* Claire."

"They are," I whisper, but my chest is too tight to say more. Nix did this. Nix came up here and decorated this tree house for my little girl. If she didn't already have my heart, that would do it.

"Look, Mommy!" Claire opens a rhinestone-encrusted pink chest. "Doctor tools! Just like Doc McStuffins! Thank you, Daddy!"

"They're not from me," I say, my voice gruff. "I built the tree house, but I'm not the one who put this stuff in here."

Claire doesn't care—she's too busy giving herself a pretend injection—but Meredith turns to me and frowns. "Then who did?"

There's not a doubt in my mind. "Nix."

That gets Claire's attention. "Dr. Nix? I love Dr. Nix!"

"Me too, sweetie," I whisper so softly Claire can't hear, but Meredith does, and she reaches over and squeezes my forearm.

"She obviously has feelings for you too, Max. A

woman doesn't do this kind of thing for the daughter of a man she isn't interested in."

Nix

"Everything is good," Amy tells our mother.

"God took care of us," Mom says, nodding. "He brought my Phoenix home to save me, even when I doubted my own daughter."

"It's okay, Mom," I say, but my voice catches and the words come out as a whisper. I draw in a deep breath and look out the pretty picture window that looks out onto the hospital courtyard. My mom had a meltdown the night of the fire and had to be admitted, but luckily I was able to find this residential facility in Indianapolis where they take a progressive approach to conditions like my mom's. She'll never be "cured" of her schizophrenia, but with the proper care, medication, and treatment, she should be able to live her life without being trapped in the prison of her own mind. Maybe someday she can live "outside" without being crippled by fear.

"Where are you staying, Amy?" Mom asks.

Amy squeezes Mom's hand and looks at me. "I moved in with Phoenix for now. The town where Phee Phee lives is beautiful. There's a river and this cute little downtown area with an art gallery and a bakery

PLAYING WITH FIRE

with the most amazing chocolate croissants. I found a
new church already. Phee Phee is going to help me get
a job and my own place eventually."

"You're a good sister," Mom says, and her simple
nod of approval leaves a lump in my throat.

It's been five days, but I still don't think all the
adrenaline has left my system. Jeremiah is in police
custody, and has a laundry list of charges against him—
including Kent's murder and arson—and Cade tells me
he won't see life outside of a jail cell for a very, very
long time.

Patrick passed away in the hospital the night after
the fire. Part of me believes that once his father was
caught, he knew he could rest. And although I'll never
understand why he handled things the way he did, I
know he loved me and was trying to do right by me, in
his own misguided way.

"How's that man?" Mom asks. "The one who saved
us?"

"Max is fine." The lump in my throat grows. I
haven't seen much of Max since the night at the church.
Between getting my mother settled at the mental health
facility, moving Amy into my guest bedroom, and the
many hours I've spent answering questions at the police
station, we haven't had the time to have the heart-to-
heart we really need.

"Phoenix is in love with him," Amy tells Mom. "I
told her she needs to marry him before some other girl
steals him away, but she doesn't listen."

Mom smiles. "She never did."

"His daughter has been away for weeks," I say. "She

312

just got home a few days ago." I shake my head. I don't know why I'm trying to explain myself to these two. "He has more important things to think about right now, but I have plans to see him tonight." Not just Max. A bunch of us are going out for drinks after work, per the request of the new bride, who returned from her honeymoon this morning, heard about what she missed while she was gone, and declared a need for "friend time."

"Nix arranged for a surprise for Max's little girl," Amy says. "So excited about that!"

Mom folds her hands on her lap and studies us as tears well in her eyes. "It's so good to see my girls together again."

"I've missed you both," I say. "I should have come for you years ago."

"Don't put that on yourself," Mom says. A tear rolls down her cheek. "We were stubborn. We didn't see Jeremiah for the man he really is. The devil is tricky like that."

"All that matters," Amy says, "is that we're together now."

Nix

"I guess I still don't know what that text message was supposed to mean," Cade says.

Most of our group has left our table to play pool, and it's only Cade, Max, and I left with our beers and the strange bond of people who survived a crisis together.

"The text Nix sent?" Max looks at me and grins.

"What did it say?" I ask. "I don't even remember what I wrote anymore."

Max props his elbows on the table and leans forward. "I believe it said, *Turn right off Highway 59, just past the old Robinson Park barn. You'll see the church. Bring help. Expect fire. Stallions optional.*"

"Oh, yeah. I remember now." I cut my gaze to Max then turn to Cade. "Max likes to rescue damsels in distress. When I was preparing to walk into that church, I thought I might qualify."

Cade cocks a brow, clearly still not getting our little inside joke, but whatever. I don't bother explaining.

Max swallows. "I'm just glad you asked for our help."

"Yeah, I tried it without last time and it didn't go so well. Patrick told me I needed to destroy Camelot to escape it. He thought with fire, but I figured out a better way."

"Here's to a better way," Cade says, lifting his beer.

"A better way," Max echoes.

We clink our glasses and I drain the rest of my beer, then settle my glass on the table and stand. "I better get out of here. Early rounds."

"I'll walk you out," Max says.

We head out of the bar side by side but not touching, and neither of us speaks until we reach my car, then we both talk at the same time.

"Listen, I—" I start as he says, "Nix, would—"

We laugh—not the easy kind, but the kind with *all* the sexually charged, angsty awkwardness.

"Thank you for what you did for Claire," he says.

I smile. "Did she like it? Amy helped. I'm not so great at the girly stuff, though I am the one who picked out the signs."

"She loves it. And I love it. It's perfect for her."

"You must feel complete again now that she's home."

His eyes go sad and search my face. "Not exactly."

I lift my hand, hesitant but desperate to touch him. I brush my fingers down the stubble along his jaw. "I miss you."

Grabbing my wrist, he turns his face into my hand and kisses the inside of my palm. "Then go out with me. I'll buy you dinner. What? Why are you frowning?"

I tug my lip between my teeth and shrug.

"Doc?"

"I heard you tell Cade that Claire was at your mom's tonight. I was kind of hoping you'd ask me to go *home* with you, but I'd take a date in public too. I guess maybe I need to earn my way back into your bed after lying to your face."

He swallows hard. "Which part was the lie?"

"Don't you know?" I whisper.

"I want you to say it."

"I am so pathetically, desperately, irrevocably in love with you."

"Hmm." He steps closer and dips his head so his lips

hover just above mine. "I don't know. What about *amazingly* and *awesomely*?"

I giggle. "Those are terrible word choices. How about *completely*? You take away my ragged edges too, Max. And I'm so sorry I thought I had to make you believe otherwise."

Then he kisses me, and *damn* can this boy kiss. His hands go into my hair and his mouth slants over mine, and I think I might melt right here in his arms.

"*Complete*," he murmurs against my mouth. "Suddenly that word feels right. I love you."

"I love you too." Tears slide down my cheeks, and they feel foreign and beautiful. "*Awesomely and amazingly.*"

"That's more like it." Then, as he kisses me again, his arms snake around my body and his hands grab my ass.

I hear someone shout at us to get a room, and I'm pretty sure it's Krystal, but I don't care enough to check.

EPILOGUE

Cade
Two moths later . . .

I'VE NEVER BEEN a big fan of Halloween. Too much bad shit goes down when people have an excuse to pretend to be someone else for a night. But here I am. Playing the wallflower at a fucking costume party because two of my best friends begged me to come.

I watch Nix and Max from across the room and tell myself the twisting in my gut isn't from envy. But hell. Who am I kidding? They're so high on love I practically get a contact buzz just standing in the same room. They're dressed as Wonder Woman and Superman and can't keep their hands off each other— not so different from the times they're dressed in normal clothes.

They're perfect. No. That's not it. They're not perfect. In fact, they're both kind of screwed up. Which is probably why I find their relationship so compelling. Nix and Max make my baggage look like nothing, and they don't just make it work, they make it look easy. And Max's daughter Claire thinks Nix walks on water.

Max sees me watching them, whispers something to Nix, then crosses through a throng of masked guests to stand by my side.

"Batman?" he asks, and I have to resist the urge to groan. Fucking costume.

"Only comic book character I know," I lie. I'm usually up for a party, but they had to twist my arm to get me to come to this one because the host's only requirement was that everyone come dressed as a comic book character. I relented and figured I couldn't go wrong with Batman, but I'm one of at least three dudes here dressed as Batman. Not exactly the most original idea.

Max folds his arms and studies me. "We were hoping tonight might help get your mind off what's been bothering you."

"Nothing's bothering me," I lie. "But thanks for inviting me." If I didn't know better, I'd think he could read my mind. I haven't told anyone here about Cara. I don't plan to. That shit's behind me for good.

"You and Nix seem pretty serious," I say.

His eyes immediately find her through the crowd. "Every day that I wake up next to her, I think I'm dreaming. She's . . ." He shakes his head, as if he can't find the words. "Did you know she and Claire have campouts in the tree house?"

"I didn't know that, but I'm not surprised. She loves that little girl like she's her own."

Nodding, Max exhales slowly. "I'm taking it slow even though it's killing me. But I'm telling you now I'm going to marry her."

I cock a brow. "Yeah?"

"Yeah."

"Lucky fucking bastard," I mutter.

Max grins. "Don't think I don't know it." He smacks me on the back. "Have fun tonight. I'm off to convince my girl to dance with me again."

No sooner has he left my side than someone's grabbing my wrist and tugging me toward the dance floor. "What the—" I'm confronted with an image from my teenage fantasies. Catwoman.

I swallow hard and pull my gaze up her slowly, from her stiletto boots to her patent leather suit that hugs every curve to her mask.

I've never been much of a comic book guy, but Catwoman? Well, you don't have to be a closet nerd to get behind that.

Before I can figure out who's hiding behind the mask, she loops her whip behind my neck and presses her body against mine.

"Hey there," I murmur.

"Just shut up and make this look believable," she says, then her mouth is on mine.

I only hesitate for a beat—I mean, who the fuck does this—but her lips are soft and her breath is sweet, and I can't help myself. I slide my hand under her jaw and slant my mouth over hers.

She gasps then curls a hand around my bicep and slips her tongue against mine.

For a moment, I'm lost. I'm not in the middle of a party. I'm not some idiot who let a woman steal his heart and make a fool out of him. I'm nothing but a man touching a woman, our bodies pressed together, our mouths searching for something more than anyone should expect from a kiss.

She jerks away. Her breathing is uneven, her cheeks are flushed, and her eyes are clouded with confusion. She lifts my mask off my face. Her eyes go wide.

"Who are you?" I whisper.

Shaking her head, she backs away—slowly at first, and then she's running, racing to the door as quickly as she came.

As quickly as she arrived, she's gone, and I'm left with the taste of her on my lips, my mind swimming with the vulnerability that filled her eyes when she saw my face.

Do I go after her?

A few feet away, Nix and Max are wrapped up in each other's arms, embodying every bit the kind of relationship I want, and I'd bet my badge that Catwoman isn't the one to give it to me.

But hell. It's Halloween. Time to pretend to be someone else for a night.

THE END

Thank you for reading *Playing with Fire,* the first book in the Mended Hearts series. In the next book in the series, *Holding Her Close,* Cade Watts finds himself falling hard and fast for the last woman he ever expected. If you'd like to receive an email when the book is available, please sign up for my newsletter.

PLAYING WITH FIRE PLAYLIST

"I See Fire" by Ed Sheeran

"You Ruin Me" by The Veronicas

"I'm on Fire" by AWOLNATION

"32 Flavors – Live" by Ani DiFranco

"I Know You" by Skylar Grey

"A Girl, a Boy, and a Graveyard" by Jeremy Messersmith

"Down" by Jason Walker

"Believe" by Mumford & Sons

"The One" by Kodaline

"Things We Lost in the Fire" by Bastille

"Snake Eyes" by Mumford & Sons

"Nothing Without Love" by Nate Ruess

ACKNOWLEDGMENTS

I've never written a book that felt "easy." The truth is, it takes a profound number of hours for me to write and revise before I believe a book is ready to go out in the world. Sometimes, as was the case with this book, I'm scheduled to write a book during times when real life demands more of my attention than usual. In these cases, writing time must be found anywhere possible— the wee hours of the morning, the thirty minutes in the doctor's waiting room, or even during dinnertime while the rest of my family is at the table talking about their day. All my books seem to require some of that special "carved out" time, but this book required more than most. I can't express how grateful I am to have a husband who steps up at home so I can *eventually* find my way to the end. Thank you, Brian. You might not write the books, but you truly make them possible.

A huge thanks to my family for all their support. To my kids for making me laugh and giving me a reason to work hard. Jack and Mary, I am so proud to be your mommy. To my sister Kim, for watching the kids and giving my husband and I much-needed date nights, which I inevitably hijack as plotting sessions. Thanks to my mom, who checks on me when I'm putting in too many hours, who reminds me to take care of myself but is always careful not to nag.

PLAYING WITH FIRE

I owe enormous gratitude to my friends. To my critique partner, Adrienne, and my BFF, Annie, we may not see each other as often as we'd like, but you two always lift me up and make me smile. Mira Lynn Kelley, I love your face! Thank you for fangirling me and becoming one of my favorite people. To my friend Toni, who understands the importance of dreaming, Starbucks, and the occasional good cry. And, of course, thanks to my favorite group of friends, Brent, Mendi, Bart, Laura, Justin, Margaret, Lisa, Neil, Angie, Nathan, Stephanie, Chris, and Stef. Books might not be built on silly text messages, beer, and Cards Against Humanity games, but when I'm treated to these things with this group, I'm renewed. Love you guys more than you know.

To everyone who provided me feedback on Nix and Max's story along the way—especially Heather Carver, Dina Littner, and Samantha Leighton—you're all awesome. To Lexi's Midnight Readers, who inspire me daily with their love for all things New Hope.

Thank you to the team that helped me package this book and promote it. Sarah Hansen at Okay Creations designed my beautiful cover. You may have noticed I'm partial to her work, and will keep her on my team as long as she'll let me. Rhonda Helms and Lauren McKellar, thank you for the insightful line edits and for being so understanding of my crazy I-just-moved-and-my-life-is-in-chaos schedule this time around. Thanks to Arran McNicol at Editing720 for proofreading, and my PA, Chris, who does her best to keep me organized, even when we're juggling fifteen tasks at once. A shout-out to all of the bloggers and reviewers who help spread the word about my books. I am humbled by the time you take out of your busy lives for my stories. You're the best.

To my agent, Dan Mandel, and my foreign rights agent, Stefanie Diaz, for getting my books into the hands of readers all over the world. Thank you for being part of my team.

To my NWBs—Sawyer Bennett, Lauren Blakely, Violet Duke, Jessie Evans, Melody Grace, Monica Murphy, and Kendall Ryan—y'all rock my world. I'm inspired by your tireless work and always encouraged by your friendship. Thank you for being a part of this journey.

To all my writer friends on Twitter, Facebook, and my various writer loops—especially to the Fast Draft Club, and the amazing Brenna Aubrey who introduced me to pomodoros—thank you for keeping me company during those fourteen hour work days.

And last but certainly not least, a big thank-you to my fans—the coolest, smartest, best readers in the world. I owe my career to you. You're the reason I get to do this every day and the reason I *want* to. I appreciate each and every one of you. You're the best!

~Lexi

LOVE UNBOUND
BY LEXI RYAN

If you enjoyed *Playing with Fire*, you may also enjoy the other books in Love Unbound, the linked series of books set in New Hope and about the characters readers have come to love.

Splintered Hearts (A Love Unbound Series)
Unbreak Me (Maggie's story)
Stolen Wishes: A Wish I May Prequel Novella (Will and Cally's prequel)
Wish I May (Will and Cally's novel)
Or read them together in the omnibus edition,
Splintered Hearts: The New Hope Trilogy

Here and Now (A Love Unbound Series)
Lost in Me (Hanna's story begins)
Fall to You (Hanna's story continues)
All for This (Hanna's story concludes)
Or read them together in the omnibus edition, *Here and Now: The Complete Series*

Reckless and Real (A Love Unbound Series)
Something Wild (Liz and Sam's story begins)
Something Reckless (Liz and Sam's story continues)
Something Real (Liz and Sam's story concludes)
Or read them together in the omnibus edition, *Reckless and Real: The Complete Series*

Mended Hearts (A Love Unbound Series)
Playing with Fire (Nix's story)
Holding Her Close (Cade's story—Coming Soon!)

OTHER TITLES
BY LEXI RYAN

Hot Contemporary Romance
Text Appeal
Accidental Sex Goddess

Decadence Creek Stories and Novellas
Just One Night
Just the Way You Are

CONTACT

I love hearing from readers, so find me on my Facebook page at facebook.com/lexiryanauthor, follow me on Twitter @writerlexiryan, shoot me an email at writerlexiryan@gmail.com, or find me on my website: www.lexiryan.com.

Made in United States
Orlando, FL
25 September 2023

37269120R00200